That's the way love goes . . .

"What a lot of people don't understand is that it's cultural," Janet continued. "Like a lot of black parents, they say: 'Girl, if you don't stop, you're going to get a beating.' Or a 'whipping.' That's the way they talk, and what they mean is a 'spanking.' Like a lot of black parents, my parents were very strict. I'm happy my parents raised us like that. Nothing was handed to us."

To an impartial observer, it may seem that Janet Jackson is rationalizing, or that she simply doesn't want to admit to any of the apparently tragic circumstances of private life in the Jacksons' home. Perhaps she feels the past has nothing to do with her or the way she is today. But in actuality the past would seem to have everything to do with how she is as an adult. Though Janet probably wasn't abused as much as the rest of the siblings claim to have been, their reaction to that alleged abuse—and the subsequent stress it caused in the family—no doubt affected Janet's upbringing and also shaped the fiercely private and protective woman she is today. . . .

THE STRICTLY UNAUTHORIZED BIOGRAPHY OF

JANET JACKSON

out of the
MADNESS

BY BART ANDREWS

with an introduction by
J. RANDY TARABORRELLI

HarperPaperbacks
A Division of HarperCollins*Publishers*
Produced in association with
ROSE BOOKS

HarperPaperbacks   *A Division of* HarperCollins*Publishers*
10 East 53rd Street, New York, N.Y. 10022

Produced in association with ROSE❦BOOKS
Copyright © 1994 by RoseBooks

Cover photograph © 1990 Kevin Winter/DMI

First printing: April 1994

Printed in the United States of America

HarperPaperbacks and colophon are trademarks of
HarperCollins*Publishers*

❖ 10 9 8 7 6 5 4 3 2 1

ACKNOWLEDGMENTS

Deepest appreciation to Geoff Hannell, Katie Tso, Matthew Martin, and everyone at HarperCollins Publishers who worked on this project, for their confidence and assistance.

J. Randy Taraborrelli, author of the best-selling book *Michael Jackson—The Magic and the Madness,* interviewed Janet Jackson several times from 1977 to 1984, and comments from those interviews have been incorporated in this text. Quotes from Taraborrelli's numerous interviews with Michael Jackson; his brothers (Jackie, Tito, Marlon, Jermaine, and Randy); his sister LaToya; and his parents, Joseph and Katherine, have also been used throughout.

Special thanks to John Niendorff for his invaluable contributions to *Out of the Madness.* Without his tremendous talent, this book would have been a very different work. I thank him so much for his patience and understanding during a challenging time.

Special thanks to David McGough and DMI. Their many excellent photographs have added significantly to the impact of this book. The author is grateful to Mr. McGough and also to Scooter McGough.

Thanks to Matthew Miles Barasch for guidance and wisdom and a positive viewpoint.

Thanks to Marco DeLeon for many years of friendship and trust.

And to Chuck Dransfield, thanks for never-ending understanding.

Special thanks to Steven Ivory for his invaluable insight.

Thank you, also, to all of those who were interviewed for this work, whose recollections were invaluable. Some asked for anonymity, and their requests were respected. Those who gave permission for their names to appear are cited in the appropriate places.

Special thanks to these individuals for their support in tangible and intangible ways: Rev. Marlene Morris, Rev. Roger Aldi, Allan Kramer, Rev. Edward Viljoen, Randall Friesen, Ken Bostic, John Redmann, James Spada, Eddie Carrol, Laurie Feigenbaum, Richard Tyler Jordan, Billy Barnes, David Bruner, George Zeimer, Derek Brown, Lydia Encinas, Wayne Brasler, Gerard Evans, Scott Haefs, Cathy Griffin, Matthew Hamel, Reed Sparling, Curtis Kelley, Liz Smith, Sal and Cathy LaGreca, Tina LaGreca, Karen LaGreca, William Dunn, Rocco and Rose Taraborrelli, and the entire Taraborrelli family. Thanks also to Angelica Leon, and especially to Sven Paardekooper.

For Cathy LaGreca

OUT OF THE MADNESS

The Strictly Unauthorized Biography
of
Janet Jackson

introduction
by J. Randy Taraborrelli

Though it seems almost impossible to imagine today, once upon a time, back in the "Dark Ages"—the seventies and early eighties—the Jacksons were not only accessible to the media, but they actually courted them as well. In fact, it was common practice for the family to host special days for the press at their home in Encino, California, making the siblings available to reporters such as myself on a schedule of alternating shifts. Thus, one could interview Michael at 10:00 A.M. in the kitchen, meet with Janet at 11:00 in the living room, chat with LaToya at 11:30 by the pool, then, after lunch, play a game of basketball with Jackie, Tito, Jermaine, Marlon, and Randy (this usually consisted of the brothers' shooting baskets with the more athletic members of the press while Michael and I stood by keeping score).

Those were the days, my friends.

It all ended in 1981. In September of that year, I was sitting at my desk in the Los Angeles offices of *Soul* magazine, a popular African-American entertainment publication I edited and published in the eighties, when I received a perplexing telephone call from a source inside the Jackson camp. I was told that a young secretary had just accused Katherine Jackson, the family matriarch, of having assaulted her in a hallway of the Motown building on Sunset Boulevard. I found this difficult to believe. Keep in mind, this was ten years before any of us knew just how much dysfunction existed in the Jackson family. Personally, whenever I thought of Katherine Jackson, I pictured a mild-mannered, hospitable woman serving lemonade and graciously ushering members of the press around. The very thought of her beating anyone up was laughable.

In the same conversation with my source, I was told that Katherine had brought her daughter Janet along to the alleged beating. The youngster was only fifteen, and so introverted that one could hardly persuade her to say anything at all during an interview. To conceive of Janet as having been involved in anything so violent took a major stretch of the imagination. I didn't believe a word of the story.

In time, however, proof would come forth that the assault did take place.

A few weeks later, on October 3, 1981, I was scheduled to interview Michael Jackson at the family's Encino home. I had been warned by a CBS executive not to mention the name of the woman who made the charges or even ask about what was referred to by higher-ups as "The Incident." I agreed. At that time, the allegations were so ambiguous there seemed no reason to inject questions about Michael's mother into an interview with him.

I was at home compiling a list of questions for the following day's session when my telephone rang. It was Michael Jackson.

He got to the point immediately, telling me there was "a certain way I want to do this interview." He said he wished to enlist the assistance of his younger sister Janet.

"Janet is going to sit in on our interview," he informed me. "You'll direct your questions to her, then she'll pass them on to me. I'll give her the answers and she'll pass them on to you. It's the only way I'll do the interview. I hope you understand."

"Say what?"

He repeated his plan.

"Michael, I don't get it," I said. "You're giving me an interview, but you're not talking to me? What kind of madness is that?"

"It might seem like madness to you," he insisted. "But there are reasons for the things I do. You just have to try to understand."

"But . . . but . . ." I stuttered.

"If you're willing to do it my way, I'll see you tomorrow. Good-bye."

After he hung up, I sat there for a moment staring at the telephone, as if I had just received a long-distance call from outer space.

The next day, I arrived at the appointed hour to interview a twenty-three-year-old barefoot superstar.

After Michael and I exchanged pleasantries in the

living room, fifteen-year-old Janet walked in, wearing a red leather miniskirt, plaid sweater, and black boots. She stared at me as if we had never met, although I had conducted a number of interviews with her prior to that day.

Michael introduced us, as if for the first time. Ill at ease, Janet fidgeted, looking like she wanted to be anyplace on earth but here with her brother and me. We took our places. The two of them sat on a sofa opposite me.

"You'll do the interview the way you promised, won't you?" Michael implored.

"I didn't promise anything, Michael," I said sternly.

"Then we can't do the interview," he declared, motioning to Janet that the session was over.

The two of them rose.

"Hold on," I insisted. (This was too good to pass up, I thought to myself. Just think of the amazing story I'll have to tell in years to come.) "Let's give it a shot. Let's try." They exchanged looks, came to an almost imperceptible and silent agreement, then sat down again.

"Let's start with the new Jacksons' album, *Triumph*," I began. "How do you feel about it?"

Michael looked over at Janet, who sat there staring at me. I got the hint and redirected my questions.

"Janet, please ask him how he feels about the new album."

Janet turned to her brother. "He wants to know how you feel about the new album."

Michael said, "Oh, tell him I'm very happy with it. Working with my brothers again was an incredible experience. It was magical."

Janet faced me and, as if all of this was normal

behavior, repeated Michael's response. "He told me to tell you that he's very happy with the album and that working with his brothers was an incredible experience for him."

There was a long, uncomfortable pause. Janet shifted nervously in her seat, as if she had forgotten something. She had.

"You forgot the part about its being 'magical,'" Michael scolded.

"Oh, yeah. He said it was magical."

"Magical," I repeated, astounded by what was taking place.

"Yes," she said. "Magical."

The three of us stared at each other for a moment. How do I proceed with this? I wondered to myself. I looked carefully at Michael, as though perhaps he might burst into engaging laughter and announce that this all had been a joke. He didn't. Nor did he appear agitated or distracted, as though his odd behavior was a result of his being under stress. He was perfectly composed, even genial.

Suddenly everything I planned to ask seemed too complicated, but I persisted, raising another question, which Janet repeated to Michael. Michael gave her the answer; she gave it to me. And so it went. On and on.

Abruptly, Janet said to Michael, "Remember when that girl got upset because she heard you had a sex change? She got so upset, she jumped out of a window. I think she died." Michael didn't say a word.

There was a long silence as we looked at each other. Finally I asked another question.

After five more such questions directed at Michael—and five answers transmitted by way of his sister—I decided I'd had enough. When Michael offered to have Janet tell me what happened during a recent visit with Katharine Hepburn, I said I'd rather hear it directly from him. He declined. So I told him we should just end this now.

Janet let out a sigh of relief.

"Okay, if that's how you feel," Michael said, grinning. He stood up, shook my hand, and left. I noticed Janet's barely discernible expression of disbelief as she rolled her eyes and followed her brother out of the room.

What in the world was this all about? I asked myself, still astounded. But a moment later I realized I was getting caught in my own surprise. When I looked at the situation from Michael's point of view, things suddenly made sense: Michael, fearing questions about the allegations brought forth by the young secretary, did not want to face any reporters. But despite his wishes, the press grind continued. (It is amazing to consider that, in 1981, Michael Jackson had to take orders from CBS, his record company. If CBS Records told him to give an interview, he was contractually obliged to do so.) So what does a superstar do when he is compelled by legal agreement to give an interview he doesn't want to give, perhaps to discuss things he doesn't want to discuss? He can create an essentially benign circumstance in which the *interviewer* is moved to call off the exchange. No lies had been told, no one's feelings were hurt, no obligations had been overtly violated, and altogether it had been a pleasant if strange afternoon in sunny Southern California. Michael's ploy, I realized as I canceled the whole idea of the feature article, was pretty smart.

And when I look back on that odd day in Encino, I can't help but remember Janet Jackson in the role of big brother Michael's docile little helper—yes, participating in an amusing scheme to dull the fangs of the press, but still none too happy about the whole exercise.

Well, those "docile little helper" days were destined to become history before long.

Little more than a decade later Janet Jackson has become an international superstar, first with her 1986, career-altering *Control* album, in which she declared hard-earned independence from her family, and then with her 1989 *Janet Jackson's Rhythm Nation 1814,* in which she took the ground-breaking career step of addressing the world's social ills in her music. Together, both albums sold nearly twenty million copies.

Then, in 1991, Janet signed one of the most lucrative record deals in show-business history—a $32-million contract with Virgin Records, eclipsed only by brother Michael's $50-million-plus deal with Sony. The first album released as part of that new deal—1993's *janet.,* in which she brandished her new sensual longings both on the record and on its cover—has already spawned a series of number-one singles and could possibly be her biggest album to date.

But for all of her chic, forever-in-the-moment, rock-star trendiness, Janet also represents something very basic: the good old-fashioned American Dream. Where else but in America could a spoiled, snotty-nosed kid from an affluent family transform herself into a hardworking, one-woman cottage industry and icon-in-training? True, Janet does come from a talented and famous family. But brother Marlon has the same bloodline and, ultimately, the connection hasn't worked for him. Nor, sadly, has it worked for her sister LaToya, who seems with distressing frequency to behave as though she had no common sense at all.

No, the Janet Jackson the world sees today is the result of hard work. To be sure, a combination of ingredients—the same kind that built General Motors or McDonald's—also created Janet Jackson: timing, a considerable amount of good fortune, the fortuitous appearance of appropriate insight and vision, and the state of society itself in the context of contemporary history. Unlike Shirley Temple, Aretha Franklin, or even her brother Michael, Janet was not a "natural." Rather, like Disneyland, Diana Ross, and Tina Turner, Janet is man-made. That is, Janet didn't wake up one morning with an overabundance of innate, fully developed musical talent. Rather, as in the case of Ross and Turner, savvy managers, record producers, choreographers, and an assortment of handlers helped her along the way to develop what she *did* have. And then, when Janet took control, she reinvented the invention and continues to do so with each new project (unlike Ross and Turner, who retread basically what their teachers taught them).

In addition, if she is nothing else, Janet is certainly the world's first cosmopolitan Jackson. She has evolved a style that is a meld of both elegance and accessibility. She knows how to dress, and looks as good (and comfortable) in Armani as she does in Gap. Unlike her brother Michael—a guy who could have an audience with any of the world's most famous designers but who chooses instead to demonstrate, via those predictable pseudo-military costumes, no real regard for style or taste—Janet's next fashion statement can never be predicted.

Musically, Janet—whether unwittingly or not—achieved the remarkable feat of practically creating her own musical genre and then standing just to one side of it to watch it consume her imitators. Thanks in part to the music of producers Jimmy "Jam" Harris and Terry Lewis, Janet was able to harness the exciting essence of rhythm and blues, funk, and dance, yet not let it pigeonhole her. She championed a musical style with her *Control* album and then watched contemporaries such as Jody Watley and Paula Abdul first embrace her sound then fight to avoid being stereotyped by it. Meanwhile, Janet was on to other things, other sounds, other video images.

Some would argue that Janet Jackson has competition in big-voiced newcomers such as hip-hop's Mary J. Blige or in a more formidable opponent such as Mariah Carey, who not only owns a beautiful voice but writes and coproduces her albums and the projects of others. Or perhaps, it could be argued, vocal dynamo Whitney Houston is Janet's greatest rival for the favor of pop audiences. However, Janet has something special, and perhaps this *is* something she was either born with or simply absorbed from her famous family. Hollywood's old-fashioned cigar-chomping agents and publicists called it Star Quality. Others call it charisma. The kids call it a vibe. Whatever it is, Janet's got it. You can't buy it, and unlike sensual designer perfumes, men and women in white coats can't develop and bottle it in a laboratory. Either you have it or you don't. Janet's got it. Whitney, a terrific recording artist but not much of an entertainer, simply ain't got it.

Wisely, Janet has used this charisma to launch one

of the most fascinating and ongoing coming-out parties ever. Her album covers, music videos, and magazine and press photos illustrate the physical metamorphosis. Once the chubby kid, Janet is now clearly a woman, sometimes elegant, sometimes playfully sassy, but always a woman—a strong African-American woman. Camille Paglia, the socio-sexual pop scholar, recently wrote of Janet, "Her unique persona combines bold, brash power with quiet sensitivity and womanly mystery."

Indeed, Janet has made us see the sexy, ravishing creature she wants us to see. Only those who really know Janet—Jan, as her friends call her; "Booty," as her touring dancers call her (in honor of one of the greatest butts in show business)—can see through the smoke and mirrors. Look closely and you'll see that Janet Jackson, like the tomboy she remains at heart, still mostly eschews nail polish. She also has to be the only female sex symbol in the history of show business to acquire that status without showing her legs. (Think about it—when was the last time you saw Janet Jackson in a dress?)

It does seem that Janet has escaped the family curse of having to accept a wretched personal life as a sort of sick penance for tremendous fame and worldwide attention. Unlike her famous siblings Michael and LaToya, Janet enjoys a healthy and, seemingly, happy and well-adjusted personal life, complete with romantic interludes and (gasp!) sexual encounters. Though she is smooth-spoken in public, the private Janet won't hesitate to swear like a truck driver when she gets her feathers ruffled. "It makes me interesting," she has joked. "I let it out when I'm angry. It makes my life run that much smoother."

Not that she hasn't had her personal challenges. "I've suffered more than anyone can ever imagine," she has said. "Because of the way I grew up, people think, 'How can you possibly experience pain?' But they just don't know. They don't understand. I went through a great deal of pain that I really wouldn't wish upon anyone."

Like Michael and to a lesser extent LaToya, Janet is a savvy career strategist. As a businesswoman, she runs her own affairs. She has managers and an assortment of advisers, but at the end of the day, Janet calls the shots. Certainly, Michael—whom she has always looked up to—has set the example for her. As she told writer Angela Holden, "Look, he can do whatever he wants; he owns himself. Nobody owns him. He can do whatever the fuck he wants. . . ."

Unlike Michael and LaToya—both of whom have become more frank in their appraisals of life as Jackson-family members—Janet still clings to the family's traditional PR line, the one to which the rest of her siblings and her parents, Joseph and Katherine, seem hopelessly wedded: "We are very close. Everything you read about our in-fighting is a lie."

Yes, folks, according to Janet Jackson, Michael has only had two nose jobs and no other plastic surgeries, the siblings were *not* abused by their father, and everyone still loves LaToya and is waiting for her to come to her senses and return home where she belongs. Oh, and yes, Janet, there *is* a Santa Claus. . . .

So she's human. But isn't that the point?

Family loyalty, discretion, hype, or whatever it is aside, Janet's biggest triumph is having proven to the world that you *can* be raised in show business, come from a dysfunctional family, be a product of Hollywood (where nothing is what it seems), and *still* come out okay. In that sense, this engaging twenty-seven-year-old legend-in-the-making is not only a celebrity and master media manipulator, but she is also something much more meaningful. She is a person who has lived in an astonishing vortex of sustained international attention and shown that the everyday human virtues of grace, emotional honesty, and stubborn determination can back down the forces that have brought corruption and destruction to so many others. Yes, this woman is a survivor, and worth watching.

chapter ONE

Today you can listen to any one of a dozen different psychologists lecturing on dysfunctional families or read any one of a hundred different books on abused children and you'll learn what folk wisdom has been teaching for a hundred centuries and what most people already know anyway if they stop to think about it: *children, when they grow up, tend to turn out like their parents.*

When the similarity is uncomfortable—painful, fearful, antisocial—it does not mean a person is doomed. It does mean the person is being challenged to wake up, take charge, and not repeat the old self-defeating patterns. That's the way out of the madness: wake up and refuse to play the game anymore. It takes courage, perseverance, patience, but it can be done.

Often, that waking up can be stimulated with a look into the past....

Janet Jackson's father, Joseph Walter Jackson, was the eldest of five children. He was born on July 26, 1929, to Samuel and Chrystal Jackson in Fountain Hill, Arkansas. Samuel, Janet's grandfather, was a stern, demanding, controlling man who insisted that his children not socialize with anyone outside the family home because he simply didn't trust "outsiders."

Apparently, Joseph, his son, emulated that behavior when he raised his own family. "In most cases I can think of, we weren't allowed to visit or stay overnight with other kids," Janet Jackson's eldest sister, Rebbie, remembered in 1992, "because Joseph [all of his children refer to their father as 'Joseph'] didn't have control and didn't know what was going on, how their parents were, how lenient they may have been, or what they allowed the kids to do."

Aloof and unapproachable, Joseph Jackson seldom demonstrated affection for his wife and children. Though he insisted that he loved and cherished them, they often wondered if he had any feelings at all. "He was sensitive but didn't know what to do with his sensitivities," said one family friend. "Joseph took after his own father in so many ways."

"He showed only one emotion, and that was anger," LaToya Jackson would one day say of her father. "That's the only emotion he would show, ever."

*   *   *

When Joseph was a teenager, his parents divorced. He decided to drop out of school after the eleventh grade to become a boxer in the Golden Gloves. Shortly thereafter, he met Katherine Esther Scruse, a charming, gregarious woman, at a neighborhood party.

Katherine—who would be mother to the Jackson family—was born on May 4, 1930, in Barbour County, Alabama, a rural, farming region. She was christened "Kattie B. Scruse," after an aunt on her father's side. Her father, Prince Scruse, was employed by the Seminole Railroad and also worked as a tenant cotton farmer, as had her grandfather and great-grandfather.

When Katherine was eighteen months old, she was stricken with polio, which was known more widely at the time as infantile paralysis. Unfortunately, there was no vaccine in those days, and many children—like Joseph's sister Verna—contracted the disease. Many either died from it or were severely crippled.

In 1934, Prince Scruse moved his family to East Chicago, Indiana, in search of work. He was employed there in the steel mills before finding a job as a Pullman porter with the Illinois Central Railroad.

Prince and his wife, Martha, eventually divorced; their two daughters stayed with Martha in East Chicago. Katherine has said she was so crushed by the divorce that she promised herself she would never subject her own children to such emotional turmoil. She vowed that once she found a husband, she would stay married to him—no matter what. Little did she know how severely that vow would be tested in later years.

Emotionally affected by her polio, Katherine was a bashful youngster who was constantly picked on by schoolmates. Her one joy was music; she and her sister, Hattie, grew up listening to country-western radio programs and singing in the local Baptist choir. "But I had no illusions about getting into the business," Katherine has said. "Times were hard, and who ever heard of a black person getting anywhere by singing country-western back in the 1940s? Ernest Tubb, Hank Snow, Hank Williams, comedienne Minnie Pearl—this was the kind of entertainment my sister and I enjoyed."

Though Katherine was not able to graduate from high school due to her illness, as an adult she took and passed high-school equivalency courses.

Katherine used crutches until she was about sixteen and still walks with a limp. "She is the bravest of all women," Janet Jackson has said. "I think anyone with any kind of physical problem has to work twice as hard in every way. She never let anything get to her. She was always strong, a really proud woman who always acted with dignity."

Katherine says she fell in love with Joseph immediately upon meeting him. Though Joseph went on to marry another woman, that marriage did not last more than a year. After his divorce, he began dating Katherine; they were married on November 5, 1949, in Crown Point, Illinois.

The newlyweds settled in the bleak industrial town of Gary, Indiana, where they would raise their family. Their first child, Maureen (nicknamed Rebbie, and pronounced Reebie), was born on May 29, 1950. Then, on May 4, 1951, Katherine's twenty-first birthday, Sigmund Esco (nicknamed Jackie) was born. The rest would follow quickly: Tariano Adaryl ("Tito") on October 15, 1953; Jermaine LaJuane on December 11, 1954; LaToya Yvonne on May 29, 1956; Marlon David on March 12, 1957; Michael Joseph on August 29, 1958; and Steven Randall on October 29, 1961. Over four more years were to pass before their last child, a girl—Janet Dameta—would be born.

The entire family lived in an all-African-American neighborhood, in a small house at 2300 Jackson Street that Joseph and Katherine purchased in 1950 for $8,500. The two-bedroom home, for which their monthly payment was sixty dollars, had one bathroom, a living room, a kitchen, and a small basement.

"I don't remember much about it," Janet has said. "I was just a baby. But I do recall that it was really cramped."

Katherine and Joseph shared one of the bedrooms, while the boys slept in the other, in a triple bunk bed. The three girls slept on a convertible sofa in the living room.

Times were tough. Joseph worked a four-o'clock-to-midnight shift as a crane operator at Inland Steel in East Chicago for about sixty-five dollars a week. The family had no telephone for the first five years they lived on Jackson Street. Katherine made the children's clothes herself or shopped at the Salvation Army store.

"We all had chores. My parents believed in work values," Jermaine remembers. "Scrubbing the floors, washing the windows, doing light gardening. Tito did the dishes after dinner. I'd dry them. The four oldest—Rebbie, Jackie, Tito, and me—did the ironing, and we weren't allowed out of the house until we finished."

But Joseph Jackson was dissatisfied with his life and wanted more for his family than what they had at 2300 Jackson Street. So he, his brother Luther, and three other men formed a rhythm-and-blues band called the Falcons, which Joseph hoped would become successful and perhaps be the family's ticket out of Gary. The group brought in extra income for the family by performing in small clubs and bars, but never made it any bigger than that.

Joseph's three oldest sons—Jackie, Tito, and Jermaine—were fascinated with their father's music and would sit in on rehearsals at home. As Jackson legend—countless books, the Jacksons' ABC-television mini-series, and dozens of family interviews—has it, when the Falcons disbanded, Joseph stashed his guitar in the bedroom closet, insisting that none of his children touch the instrument. Sometimes, however, Katherine would take it out and play it for the boys; she and her children would sing country songs together, and she tried to teach them harmonies. She has recalled, "Those were the best of times."

Gary was a rough town, and Katherine and Joseph were constantly concerned about their children getting into trouble. Their offspring were not allowed to play games or cavort in the streets like other kids. Both parents enforced a strict curfew.

Katherine has recalled that the need for caution was not unfounded. "Tito was coming home for lunch from school one day, and a boy put a gun to his head and demanded a dime. Can you believe that? *A dime.* My husband took Tito back to school in the car, and the principal opened a desk drawer and showed it to my husband. It was full of guns and weapons. The principal explained that the police periodically came to the school, checked the lockers, and gathered up those weapons."

From the beginning, Joseph was a strict father who would not hesitate to strike his children if he felt they deserved to be punished. What inclined him to take that approach to discipline? Maybe the answer was simply that he was accustomed to it. "I got whippings all the time," Joseph would remember in 1992. "The teachers at school whipped me. Then I'd come home and tell my parents I got a whipping at school, and they'd whip me, too. So I got a lot of whippings."

Joseph now says he doesn't remember any discipline he himself administered as having been particularly violent, but his children certainly seem to.

Though Joseph did try to develop a relationship with his boys—by taking them camping and fishing on weekends or teaching them how to box to defend themselves—he never paid much attention to the girls. As a toddler, Janet liked to crawl into bed with her mother and father, but would have to wait until Joseph was asleep before she could do so.

"He wasn't easy to warm up to, and I don't know that any of us really ever knew him," Janet has said. "But I loved him. And I believe he loved us. I do believe that. I was closest to him, I think. I tried to be, anyway. But there was a sadness about him. . . ."

Katherine Jackson tried to keep peace in the family as best she could. She was devoutly religious—first a Baptist, then a Lutheran, and eventually, in 1963, a Jehovah's Witness. Katherine expected the rest of the family to accompany her to Kingdom Hall, her place of worship. Michael, LaToya, and Rebbie would eventually also become Jehovah's Witnesses.

In 1984, Katherine reflected on her religious feelings. "I sometimes wonder about society. Are we adults and parents providing the right environment for our children? By that I mean, do we respect our children enough to set ourselves up as examples they can live up to? It seems as if things are getting worse and worse. The Bible talks about that. Me, I try to serve God and I try to raise my children properly. That's all I can give. My children grew up learning about God and the Bible. But this isn't something we thrust on people. It's a personal, family matter with us, and people often misconstrue it."

"Mother was always very devout," Janet has said. "No matter what was going on, she had her faith to turn to. It kept her strong." But Janet was never very interested in being baptized a Jehovah's Witness, though she did read the Bible as a youngster and go door-to-door with her mother to talk to others about the faith. "I was never pushed into the religion by my mother or anyone else. I made up my own mind when I was old enough," she has said. "I am not a religious person, but I am spiritual. But I don't believe in things like guilt. I believe in a higher power. I believe in inspiration."

At this time, the late fifties, the era of so-called doo-wop music was happening; there were singing groups on every street corner. Eventually, Tito began sneaking Joseph's guitar down from the closet and he played while Jackie and Jermaine tried to sing.

This went on for a few months until Tito broke a string on the guitar. Suddenly the brothers' clandestine musicianship could no longer be concealed. "My father was so outraged that he just started beating Tito," LaToya remembered.

But after Joseph calmed down, he told Tito to play and, much to his amazement, realized the boy was good. He was also surprised at how the brothers had learned to harmonize. Joseph became thrilled; his boys had talent. "My father was totally amazed. He was in shock," LaToya recalled. "From that moment onward, he rehearsed with them every day."

"When I found out my kids were interested in becoming entertainers, I really went to work with them," Joseph Jackson would tell *Time* magazine. "When the other neighborhood kids were out on the street playing games, my boys were in the house working—trying to learn how to be something in life."

"Of course, I wasn't even born yet," Janet has observed. "But I've heard those stories so many times, I actually feel like I was there. In some ways, I wish I had been. It sounds like it was a wonderful time, a time when the family was really close."

By 1962, five-year-old Marlon and four-year-old Michael had joined Jackie, Tito, and Jermaine. As a group, they began to enter talent shows and it was clear that little Michael Jackson had star quality and knew what to do with it. He was an exciting performer at a very early age.

The boys' upbringing on the road was a time of confusion that would affect most of them as adults. That confusion even included such areas as sexuality, since they got a lot of mixed messages during that time about sex. Of course, Katherine taught that sex outside of marriage was sinful—that even to *think* about lust was a sin. She was ready to quote I Corinthians 6:9, according to which none of the unrighteous—"neither fornicators, nor idolaters, nor adulterers, nor effeminate, nor abusers of themselves with mankind"—

would inherit the Kingdom of God. Sex was reserved for marriage, and sexual choices were limited even then.

Joseph, however, apparently did not see things that way and booked his young boys into strip joints where they would be opening acts for strippers. Ordinarily strict, Joseph apparently gave the boys free rein at those times, allowing young Michael to stand in the wings and watch as men in crowded, smelly clubs whistled at voluptuous women who took off their clothes lasciviously, piece by piece, until they were naked.

But all of this may not have produced whatever effect Joseph had in mind. "That, to me, was the most horrible, disgusting thing," Michael would later say.

After these shows, the boys returned home to Katherine, who dutifully reminded them of their religious convictions.

By 1965, Joseph was making only about $8,000 a year working full-time at the mill, while Katherine was employed as a part-time saleswoman at Sears. "My father had to go to work at five o'clock in the morning," LaToya remembered. "And when he woke up at four, he got everyone else in the household up, and everybody had to work as well. He sent the guys outside and made them work, whether it was mowing the lawn in the dark, pulling weeds, or whatever else needed doing. He felt, 'If I have to go to work, so do you.'"

"Times were hard back then," Katherine has remembered. "There were times when my husband was laid off and we were down to our last penny. Jackie, Jermaine, and Tito shoveled snow in the wintertime; they had regular customers. We were all workers. In the old days I cooked what I had and the children loved everything. They all loved soul food. That's what we could afford, so that's what we ate."

By 1966, the boys were playing in clubs in Gary and as far away as Chicago, some twenty miles distant. Michael was eight years old and singing lead. Tito was on guitar, Jermaine on bass guitar, Jackie played shakers, and Johnny Porter Jackson (no relation; his family and the Jacksons were friends) was on drums. Marlon sang harmony and danced.

On May 16, 1966, Katherine gave birth to her last child, a girl, Janet Dameta—"a beautiful girl, the most beautiful baby in the entire hospital," she recalls.

The Jackson boys were becoming seasoned entertainers, their lead singer, Michael, more poised and professional. They won the amateur talent show at the Regal Theatre in Chicago on three consecutive weeks. In August 1967, the group performed at the famed Apollo, in Harlem, in that theater's amateur show. They won it hands down.

They still held rehearsals twice a day, before and after school. "He worked them too hard," recalled LaToya of her father. "He worked them eight hours straight, without stopping. And he'd have a switch, a branch from one of the trees, in his hand. He hit them with it if they weren't in step, if they weren't in synch. And at one point my mother said, 'Joe it's not worth it. If it's going to cause this, forget it; the children don't need to sing.' But my father was very devoted, very dedicated in that sense. Yes, I do give him credit for making them the Jackson 5. But the way he did it . . ."

"If you messed up during rehearsal, you got hit," Michael would remember. "Sometimes with a belt. Sometimes with a switch." Once, when Joseph was trying to convince Michael to execute a dance step a certain way, he swung at his son and smacked him across the face. Michael fell backward and hit the floor hard. "But I'd also get beaten for things that happened outside of rehearsal," he added.

Says LaToya: "Michael was very rambunctious, didn't agree with anything, and wanted to do things his way because he felt his way was the right way. However, he was very clever when he was young and his way usually *was* the right way, believe it or not. We had so much fear instilled in us because of our father, everyone else would take the beatings and just cry, but Michael would get a shoe and throw it back at him. Nobody else was that way."

Michael confessed to Oprah Winfrey, in his much-watched 1992 interview with the talk-show host, that he was so afraid of his father he would actually want to "regurgitate" whenever he saw him.

According to Joseph Jackson, this was news. When interviewed by the media after the Oprah special, he said that until he saw the program, he didn't know Michael had ever become physically ill at the sight of him. "If he did gurgitate [sic], he gurgitated [sic] all the way to the bank," Joseph said. "By me being strict with him a little bit, it made him a superstar. Look, he didn't just happen on his own. He had to have a beginning. All of them had to have a beginning."

Were there other kinds of violence? "I've never ever

seen my father hit my mother. Never in my life," LaToya has said. "However, Michael claims he has. He told me he'd seen him kick her in the stomach when she was pregnant with Janet. And I said, 'Michael, that's not true; he's never hit her in his entire life.' He said, 'LaToya if you don't believe me, call Rebbie right now and ask her.' I did call Rebbie, and she said, 'Michael's right. You just don't remember. He kicked her in the stomach when she was pregnant with Janet.'"

"That's not true," Janet told a friend later. "My mother would've told me that by now."

LaToya has her own bitter memories. She recalled one particularly ugly incident that happened when she was six years old. "After school, I brought home my report card. My grades were excellent. However, the teacher wrote, 'She never speaks in class. I'm sorry, I can't pass her.' I was happy, though, because my grades were great.

"But my father beat me so badly that he left bruises and cuts all over my body. And then he threw me into the bathroom, on the floor, tossed a book at me, and said, 'Now read this. You're an embarrassment to me.' That was my first beating. I lay there in the bathroom with the blood dripping, and my brothers and sisters came into the bathroom, stepped right over me, washed their faces and hands for dinner, and did not speak to me, because Joseph told them not to. He told them that if they did, they would be beaten, too."

"LaToya tried to stay to herself," says Jackson 5 keyboardist Ronny Rancifer. "She was real quiet, like mother's shadow. Whenever a guy would come around and talk to LaToya or try to take her on a date, Joseph would hit the ceiling. You had to scrape him off. It was wild. One time I was trying to teach her how to swim, and he went off. It was like, 'This is my girl, man.' As though you were dealing with a boyfriend more than a father."

"I don't date," LaToya told a reporter firmly when she was about fifteen. "I don't trust people. To be honest with you, I have no friends outside of my family. But it doesn't bother me. When I get lonely I read the Bible." She said she rarely goes out in public unless she is with other family members. She expressed no interest in marriage or in raising a family of her own. "I would never bring a child into a society like this one," she said simply.

"I do recall him [Joseph] not wanting me to do anything with anyone," LaToya recalled, almost twenty years later. "He just basically wanted me to himself."

"LaToya was always a little different," Janet has conceded. "She was a loner. She always dressed in long skirts with high collars and boots, all covered up. She was really shy, more shy than the rest of us, and we were pretty shy. No one understood LaToya, I think."

Jermaine, however, is quick to put the role of Joseph and Katherine in relation to their children in perspective: "If we didn't get anything else from them, the fact that they brought us out here from Indiana—nine kids, drug-free—and we became something . . . that's the most important thing. If we don't make another dime, that's what they gave us and we'll still have it."

Janet has concluded, "Who knows what would have happened to my brothers if they had been allowed to roam around the streets? Who knows what would have happened to LaToya and Rebbie? The streets were dangerous. I always say my parents made the best choices they could at the time. I believe that with all of my heart."

chapter
TWO

In 1968, when Janet was two years old, the Jackson family faced a crisis: eighteen-year-old Maureen—"Rebbie," a devout Jehovah's Witness—announced that she wanted to marry another young Jehovah's Witness by the name of Nathaniel Brown and move to Kentucky. She would be the first of a string of Jackson siblings to marry as soon as they were legally able to leave the house.

Katherine encouraged Rebbie to marry Brown, but Joseph was against it. Rebbie had a powerful singing voice and there was some talk of her becoming an entertainer, which is what her father wanted for her. But in the end, she decided to concentrate on raising a family. Rebbie preferred the comfort and security of a happy home life to the instability of show business.

"Rebbie is a most wonderful, level-headed woman," Janet said in a 1982 interview. "She's always had her own set of values, of feelings about family life, about ethics. She's most like my mother, I think. She knows what's important, what things really matter. She knows that family is the most important thing, a lot more important than show business."

For weeks, Joseph, Katherine, and Rebbie argued about the impending marriage. Joseph clearly did not want Rebbie to leave the fold. In the end, Joseph refused to walk his firstborn daughter down the aisle.

LaToya, however, says there was another reason her sister Rebbie left home at the early age of eighteen. In 1990, when LaToya was promoting her tell-all book *LaToya—Growing Up in the Jackson Family,* she made the startling accusation on numerous television and radio interviews that she and Rebbie were sexually molested by their father. She says that her mother knew of the abuse and, as she said on one program, watched many times "with a smirking smile" as it was happening. LaToya claims that this was why Rebbie married and left home. She further maintains that when Rebbie was sixteen, Rebbie asked Katherine to find a psychiatrist for Joseph, but Katherine refused. So Rebbie moved out of the house for a while, claims LaToya, and lived with an elderly woman of the Jehovah's Witness faith, confiding in her about the abuse.

Private investigator Jim Magilbrey, who spent time in Gary researching LaToya's claims, discovered that Rebbie had, indeed, moved in with an elderly woman for a while, but the woman was deceased at the time of his investigation.

"Of course, a lot of physical and mental abuse went on constantly. The sexual abuse started with my sister [Rebbie]," LaToya told talk-show host Jenny Jones.

"My sister and I slept in the same bed. My father would get out of his bed at night and get into bed with my sister; I would be in the same bed. When you're in the same bed and this is happening, you don't want to look. You don't want to see it; you don't want to know what's going on. But you do know what's going on, that something's wrong, that she doesn't like it, she's not in favor of it. And you hear Mother come out and say, 'Joe, not tonight. Leave the girls alone.'"

Rebbie, however, has denied that any sexual abuse ever took place.

"No. It is not true," she said in a 1992 television interview. "That never happened to me. It honestly didn't."

"And you are not corroborating any of these allegations [LaToya]'s made about sexual abuse?" the reporter asked.

"No," Rebbie said.

"Have you talked to LaToya recently?"

"No."

"Do you think you will?"

She answered quickly, "No."

LaToya asserts that her father then began molesting her when Rebbie married and left the house. Years later, according to LaToya, Rebbie noticed how withdrawn LaToya had become, and that she simply could not stand the sight of Joseph.

"[Rebbie] came to me," LaToya told Jenny Jones, "and said, 'LaToya, all these years after I left home I often wondered if he was doing the same thing to you that he was doing to me. Please tell me the truth. Did he sexually molest you the way he did me?' And I said, 'Rebbie, there are just certain things you don't talk about.' She said, 'Answer me this. Did he do it to Janet?' And I said, 'I can't speak for Janet.'"

"I couldn't deal with it anymore," LaToya has said. "Every day, everything I did reminded me of my father and what he was doing to me. I said to my mother, 'Mother, please tell me. I need help. Please help me. Why did he do the things he did? Why? Why did you allow him to do it?' She said, 'LaToya, your father did those things because something was wrong with him.' She added, 'Forget them. Forget it ever happened. And now it doesn't exist anymore. If you ever say anything about it, I'm going to deny it.' And I said, 'But Mother, I need help.'"

"It's not true. I think they're doing it for money," Katherine said on the television program "Day One." "I think the man she's with [LaToya's husband, Jack Gordon] is brainwashing her. I really think he's done something to her for her to get out there and tell lies, things that are not true. Something has to be wrong. I can't believe I have a daughter saying things like this. It's the worst thing that ever happened to me, besides the death of my mother."

"It is hard to hear these things, but life goes on," Joseph Jackson has said. "I can't sit down and build up stress over what LaToya is out there saying. I have to keep on going. I have a life to live."

As for LaToya's allegations, she gets no support from her younger sister, Janet Jackson. Janet—who was not yet born when Rebbie left the house the first time and who was about two years old when Rebbie married—says she doesn't believe a word LaToya has been saying. She calls it all "just a bunch of crap," and declares, "none of that went on."

"Janet was furious with her sister," says one family friend. "She was livid. She wanted to call her and give her a piece of her mind. But Katherine talked her out of it. She was afraid LaToya would use that phone call to generate more publicity, then hurt Janet in the process."

"When LaToya came out with these charges, Janet really didn't know what to make of it," says Jerome Howard, Katherine and Joseph's former business manager, who has also represented Janet. "Janet was too young to remember any of it. But she felt it wasn't true, that it couldn't have been true. She just held on to that. She had to be strong for her mother, but there was a lot of inner turmoil."

According to another friend, Janet telephoned Michael to find out what he knew about LaToya's accusations. Michael refused to discuss any of it with her. "Let's not talk about it, Janet," he told her. "Let's just leave it alone."

"I won't get pulled into this," Janet told the friend. "I know that's what LaToya wants, for me to come out and say, 'No, I was not sexually abused.' Then that would give her story more publicity. I'm not going to do it. All of this has hurt my family too much, and I'm not going to help LaToya hurt any of us any more."

One of the reasons the public is skeptical of most things the Jacksons have to say about their private lives is that they are known to waffle on important issues. In fact, either Joseph was abusive or he wasn't. But the family seems to want it both ways. For example, even though the television mini-series the Jacksons authorized and produced for ABC-TV depicted a horribly abusive father (portrayed brilliantly by Lawrence

Hilton Jacobs), Janet still holds her ground that this portrayal was not accurate.

"Yes, they did whip us," she told writer Steve Pond about her parents. "But they never touched us without our giving them a reason to. My parents were very strict and we were very sheltered, and I thank God for that. But my parents never mentally or sexually abused us; nothing like that."

Katherine Jackson has said she agrees with Janet. But then, she personally sanctioned Angela Bassett's ABC-TV mini-series portrayal of herself and the horror she felt watching Joseph hit the children. Downplaying what was depicted on the television screen, Katherine has said, "Whenever they did something wrong, we didn't jump right up and whip them, though Joe did punish them sometimes. But making him seem like a child abuser, that's not true. He was strict. That's the way it was back then. I imagine that's the way his folks raised him, and that's the way my parents raised me, and I really thank them for it."

It would seem—based on the mini-series, anyway— that the greatest abuse took place in Gary, Indiana, before the family left for Los Angeles in 1968—when Janet was two.

"She missed a lot of it, doesn't remember most of what she was around to see, and doesn't think *any* of it is anyone's business," says Jerome Howard. "Janet is very private. Even more than Michael, I think. I mean, even Michael has come clean about the abuse."

Janet recalls little about her life in Gary. As she confessed to writer Karen Glover in May 1983, "I don't remember much at all. Oh yeah, wait a minute. I do remember going to this party at my friend Rodney's house, and we all had on these weird glasses. Mine kept falling off my face because they were too big. I also remember my neighbor Gregory, because he was always sucking his thumb."

Indeed, Janet doesn't remember much.

She recalled being "whipped," but says it happened only once. In 1993, she told writer Angela Holden, "My father whipped me one time. Or as my brother [Michael] might say, 'My father beat me.' But it was a spanking. That's what it was.

"Like Eddie Murphy, who talks about how his mother took off her shoe and threw it at him. Today, that would be considered abuse. I'm not saying, 'Take this kid and keep beating him.' Like on television they had some video of some kid being hit on the head with a spoon over and over again. Now *that* is abuse."

Jermaine concurs. "I thank my father. Maybe certain family members are more sensitive to the way he was, but he was not a child abuser. He did not beat us. I mean, that's the term they may use, but any black family out there can relate to this. If you did something wrong, you got a whipping."

"What a lot of people don't understand is that it's cultural," Janet continued. "Like a lot of black parents, they say: 'Girl, if you don't stop, you're going to get a beating.' Or a 'whipping.' That's the way they talk, and what they mean is a 'spanking.' Like a lot of black parents, my parents were very strict. I'm happy my parents raised us like that. Nothing was handed to us."

To an impartial observer, it may seem that Janet Jackson is rationalizing, or that she simply doesn't want to admit to any of the apparently tragic circumstances of private life in the Jacksons' home. Perhaps she feels the past has nothing to do with her or the way she is today. But in actuality the past would seem to have everything to do with how she is as an adult. Though Janet probably wasn't abused as much as the rest of the siblings claim to have been, their reaction to that alleged abuse—and the subsequent stress it caused in the family—no doubt affected Janet's upbringing and also shaped the fiercely private and protective woman she is today.

If anything, Janet takes after her mother, who still insists, despite all evidence to the contrary, that the family is and was a happy one. "We are not feuding like the press has said we've been doing for the last fifteen years," she insisted to "Day One." "And we never did."

"It's all just so they can sell papers," Joseph concluded succinctly.

In May 1968, the Jackson 5 were invited back to the Apollo to perform, and this time they were paid for their appearance. Soon after, singers Gladys Knight and Bobby Taylor (who is also a record producer) brought the group to the attention of executives at Motown Records, the Detroit label that had launched the careers of such historic artists as Diana Ross and the Supremes, the Temptations, Mary Wells, Smokey Robinson and the Miracles, Stevie Wonder, and the Marvelettes, all young African-Americans who were plucked from the streets and transformed into international stars. The Jackson 5—seventeen-year-old Jackie, fourteen-year-old Tito, thirteen-year-old Jermaine, eleven-year-old Marlon, and nine-year-old Michael—

auditioned for Motown on July 23, 1968. They were signed to the label a couple of days later.

There would be a year of recording songs for Motown—attempting to find the right songs, producers, and sound—before, in August 1969, the boys and their father were asked by record-company executives to move to Los Angeles. The intention was that the boys would attend school on the West Coast while recording at Motown's new facilities there. (In time, the whole company would relocate to Los Angeles.)

Joseph, Tito, Jack Richardson, drummer Johnny Jackson, and keyboardist Ronny Rancifer drove to Los Angeles in the family's Dodge Maxivan. A few days after their arrival, Motown paid for Jackie, Jermaine, Marlon, and Michael to fly out. But Joseph Jackson did not want the whole family to relocate until he was certain their future in California would be secure. Thus, Janet would wait with Randy, LaToya, and her mother until Joseph gave the word that they, too, could move to Los Angeles.

"One of the biggest musical influences of my life," Janet said in an interview with writer David Ritz, "was Sly and the Family Stone's 'Hot Fun in the Summertime.' I was only three years old when that song had me jumping up and down. It made me so happy. There's also the Turtles' 'Happy Together,' the Association's 'Windy,' and Simon and Garfunkel's 'Feelin' Groovy.' Those are all precious moments to me. They're about just plain feeling good."

"Janet will probably be a singer one day," Joseph said at that time, assessing the family's future in the entertainment business. "She tries to sing now, but she's a little young at three. Randy is seven and thinking of joining the group, but he's still learning the congo drums. As soon as he gets tighter, he'll be in the group. LaToya, who is thirteen, likes show business but she really doesn't want to perform. She takes care of the fan mail. She'll probably get involved in the business end of the group soon."

Stardom for Michael and his brothers was just around the corner when "I Want You Back" was released in October 1969 and went to number one on the *Billboard* charts. It sold over two million copies. More hits followed, including "ABC," "The Love You Save," "I'll Be There," and "Mama's Pearl." The Jackson 5 would become the first act in pop-music history whose first four singles each became number-one hits on the *Billboard* chart.

Not since Sammy Davis, Jr., had the world seen a child performer with such natural ability. Both as a singer and dancer, young Michael Jackson exuded an amazing stage presence. "The pros have told us that no group has ever had a better start than we did," Michael has remembered. "Ever."

At the end of 1969, Motown leased a house for the Jacksons in Los Angeles. A month later Katherine, Janet, LaToya, and Randy joined the rest of the family. "When we arrived in Los Angeles, I missed Gary, but I was looking forward to the future. I knew we would all be happy there," Katherine said in an interview. "This was a new start. And, it was good getting LaToya, Randy, and Janet back with their brothers and sisters. Janet, especially, missed everyone. She sometimes would cry, she got so lonely for Michael."

After "The Love You Save" was issued, Motown

arranged for the family to move into a bigger home, in Beverly Hills. By this time, Janet was five. But she was fully aware that she and her family were different from other people.

"There was always so much stuff going on," she would say. "There were girls we didn't know wanting to come over and visit. There were interviews, television cameras all the time, people screaming, concerts, photo sessions. I mean, it wasn't what you'd call a normal household, let's face it. My brothers were teen idols, and sometimes we got sick of it. We had to have our phone number changed maybe once a week. And then these girls would still call. Who knows how they got the number? LaToya and I used to laugh because they made such fools of themselves over our brothers. And to us, well, they were just our noisy, smelly brothers."

The Jackson 5's next single, "Never Can Say Goodbye," was released in March 1971 and peaked at number two. A month later Joseph and Katherine bought a two-acre estate at 4641 Hayvenhurst Avenue in Encino, California, which is still the family home today. They paid $250,000 for the estate; by the early nineties, it was worth at least $5 million. Ever practical, Katherine asked her husband not to sell the two-bedroom home in Gary—just in case family fortunes took a turn for the worse and they had to move back to Indiana. Joseph agreed; the house in Gary was leased out to a relative.

Encino, a half-hour drive from downtown Los Angeles, is one of the wealthiest communities in Southern California. The Jacksons enjoyed the seclusion of the large estate and lived the Good Life there—or at least that's certainly how it appeared to outsiders. New, expensive family cars were parked in the circular driveway, including Jackie Jackson's 240-Z, Katherine's Audi, Joseph's gold Mercedes 300-SE convertible, and the family's van, which looked more like a minibus.

"I was about six when we moved into the house, but I remember it vividly," Janet has recalled. "There were lots of bathrooms, five I think. LaToya and I shared a room. There was a huge swimming pool, a tennis court, a recording studio. It was great. But the fans were annoying. They were always hanging around, trying to get in."

Indeed, fans were always congregating outside the gate, waiting to catch a glimpse of the famous brothers. Janet was annoyed by the lack of privacy. "She used to stand on the other side of the gate and curse at the fans," remembered one friend. "She wanted them to go away. I think a big part of her wished for a more normal life. She hated the scrutiny, even back then."

The group's popularity continued with "The Jackson 5 Show," a weekly animated series that began airing on Saturday mornings September 11, 1971. The Jacksons' actual voices were heard in musical numbers, but their dialogue was provided by young actors.

"I remember the cartoon series," Janet has said. She was five years old at the time. "I remember one Saturday morning; I had on my pajamas. The boys were out of town, on the road. I was sitting in my mother's bedroom, on the floor, waiting for that cartoon to come on. And when it finally did, I remember screaming and jumping up and down and dancing.

"My brothers' success was sort of inspiring. I knew at an early age I wanted to be an entertainer, but I didn't know how I would ever go about such a thing," she has said. "I just knew that if they could do it, maybe I had a chance, too. Every little girl wants to be a star, you know. I thought just maybe I had a better edge than most other little girls."

chapter

THREE

In 1971, Janet's thirteen-year-old brother Michael began recording as a solo act in addition to working with his siblings; his first release, "Got To Be There," was issued in October. It was followed by "Rockin' Robin." And then came "Ben," which went on to sell over a million copies. Janet was only five, but she recalls it well. "I remember there was no jealousy or anything like that between Michael and my other brothers," she says. "The press tried to say there was rivalry, but there was none. We always pulled together as a family first. Michael's success? Well, it was good for all of us. It just made the group bigger and better. I was happy that Michael was recording on his own. I loved those records."

But as the Jackson 5 became more popular, the family was under more stress than ever. The brothers and sisters were always overworked and complained in years to come that they "missed out" on their childhood. Michael and Marlon fondly remember the couple of years they spent in public schools as being high points of their lives. Michael attended sixth grade in Room 8 at Gardner Street Elementary School in Los Angeles—not consistently, because of his work schedule, but as much as he could. Soon Michael, Randy, Janet, Marlon, and LaToya began being tutored by Mrs. Rose Fine, who was accredited by the state of California as a children's welfare supervisor. During the day, because of labor laws, the five of them had to accumulate four hours of schooling as well as have time for recreation. "We always got the school time, but rarely the rest of it," Michael recalled.

"When I was little, I had such a hard time in school," Janet has said. "I was tutored off and on and attended a public high school in the San Fernando Valley, not a private one. I had a hard time. I just couldn't get the kids to accept me as being one of them. I was different, as far as they were concerned. But to me, inside, I was just like them and I wanted to be treated like them. That was impossible, I guess. Because, really, I *wasn't* like them at all, was I?"

The Jacksons preferred their private tutor to classroom learning. "We can learn faster with our own teacher," Randy said in 1975. "And we get more personal attention. Our teacher can take time to help with the hard stuff."

"When I was growing up, most of my friends were guys," Janet told *Rolling Stone*'s Anthony DeCurtis in 1990. "Maybe it's because growing up with my brothers, I was a tomboy. I got along with them so well, and

I thought the nails and the hair and that whole thing were so boring. I was always trying to play baseball and basketball and horseback ride and swim and climb trees."

When she was about six, Janet started playing the piano and violin. She seemed—and who would have imagined otherwise?—to have musical ability; Joseph and Katherine were impressed.

"I gave my first piano recital when I was seven years old," Janet remembered. "I'll never forget the dress I had on. It was blue with white dots—I called it my granny dress, because it reminded me of a dress a grandmother might have worn. Anyway, here I was, nervous as could be, with the entire family waiting for me to play—so I got up some nerve and ran up the steps only to have the whole side of that dress get caught on something and *rrriiippp*—there was a big hole in my dress. It was horrible."

Such are the disasters of being seven.

Michael's eighteen-year-old brother Tito was the first of the brothers to wed, when he married seventeen-year-old Delores (Dee Dee) Martes on June 17, 1972. This followed their secret seven-month engagement.

"Tito wanted out of the house," recalled Susie Jackson, who went on to marry and then divorce Johnny Jackson. "When he fell in love with Dee Dee, he was determined that they would marry, even though Joe and Katherine didn't like Dee Dee because she was from the ghetto. They were afraid she would turn out to be a gold digger." Dee Dee was asked to sign a prenuptial agreement, which she did.

* * *

In 1972, the Jackson 5's record sales began slipping, and the family blamed Motown, believing the company was no longer interested in promoting the act. In fact, some company officials felt the boys were growing up and their day in the sun as teen idols was over. Joseph refused to accept this. He firmly believed that all of the records that had been failures could have been successful if Motown had simply promoted them.

The next couple of years would be difficult ones for the Jackson 5/Motown alliance as Joseph tried in vain to convince the company that the group still had steam. Then, in December 1973, Jermaine married Hazel Gordy, the daughter of the founder of Motown. It's been said by friends of the family that Joseph thought the lavish $234,000 wedding and subsequent union would somehow secure the family's position at Motown. But it did not. The writing was on the wall and the group's future at Motown was limited, especially when the company was reluctant to allow them to write and produce their own material. There would be a few more hit singles—"Never Can Say Goodbye," "Dancing Machine," and "Get It Together"—but it was clear that the days of the Jackson 5/Motown merger were numbered.

Making matters even more complicated was the fact that by the time Janet was seven years old, Katherine and Joseph were having marital difficulties.

Because the Jackson 5 toured constantly, Joseph was away from home a good deal of the time with his sons. Temptation, apparently, was too strong for him to resist and he would openly date other women.

Marlon has recalled his father coming into the boys' hotel rooms with a bevy of shapely, giggling beauties on both arms. "G'night, fellows," Joseph would say to the boys. They, in bed in their pajamas, would watch as their father and his lady friends entered Joseph's room next door and closed the door. Everyone could hear the laughter from his room.

Some friends of Joseph Jackson's have indicated that he felt he was never really appreciated by his family. He felt he had given his family everything—fame, fortune, love—and got very little in return. Because of this, they report, his life was filled with immense sadness and loneliness. Some of his offspring couldn't even stand to be in the same room with him. They rarely showed him any affection. Of course, he rarely showed them any, either. It was a woeful situation all around, and perhaps explains why Joseph was inclined to wander outside of his household for appreciation and validation.

Of course, the boys knew what Joseph was doing, but they didn't know how (or whether) they should tell Katherine. Because they couldn't bear to hurt her, they kept Joseph's secrets. For these sensitive youngsters, this had to be tremendously difficult.

"The kids saw what their father was doing out on the road with the other women," recalled Susie Jackson. "They did not like it one bit. It made them feel bad for their mother, who was sitting at home. Katherine, of course, has never had a lover. She's always been faithful to Joseph. This only made the boys love their mother even more."

Eventually, in 1973, Katherine learned about one of these affairs. "I just didn't believe he'd risk all we'd worked for as a couple," she later observed.

Katherine was devastated by the betrayal. Rebbie talked divorce to her, but that just wasn't Katherine's way. Finally, though, Rebbie's viewpoint prevailed and she convinced her mother to leave Joseph. Katherine filed for divorce on March 9, 1973, at Los Angeles Superior Court. However, she continued living with Joseph, though the two of them slept in separate rooms. "This poor woman was trapped," said Susie Jackson. "She had nine kids. Where was she going to go with nine kids? She loved Joseph and just hoped he would stop screwing around."

And Janet? "Certainly she knew what was going on," says Susie Jackson. "I have always thought she was affected by what was happening at home between her parents when she was seven or eight years old, and that this is one reason she really doesn't trust men today. It's true, she is suspicious of all men. Who can blame her? She was so close to her mother, she must have known Katherine was hurting. All the kids did. There was no way Janet could have remained unaffected by this."

Three months later Katherine dropped her divorce action against Joseph.

By spring 1974, Joseph realized that his sons' appeal as teen idols was limited and that as soon as they grew up, they would be finished—unless they expanded. So his idea was to have them perform in Las Vegas before an adult crowd. Even though Motown disagreed with this plan, Joseph was adamant and proceeded to book the group at the MGM Grand in April 1974, as coheadliners with impressionist Frank Gorshin.

To make the pot sweeter for the Vegas patrons, he decided to add LaToya, who was seventeen, to the act, as well as Randy, twelve, and Janet, seven.

Joseph even convinced Maureen to perform, though she said it was against her religious convictions as a Jehovah's Witness. But Katherine didn't see anything wrong with Maureen's participating, and when LaToya agreed to be in the act, Maureen felt compelled to join as well. (Maureen sprained her ankle, however, so her debut was postponed a few months until June, when the family played Chicago.)

Janet remembered: "My father came to me one day and said, 'You want to be in the act?'

"I said, 'No way, I can't.'

"Then he said, 'Janet, you're in the act and that's that.'

"He knew I could do it, I guess. He knew a lot more than I did, or than I wanted to admit. I was always so shy, I couldn't imagine getting up on stage and performing. But I knew inside that this was what I really wanted to do. If it wasn't for my father, though, I would never have been able to get up on that stage. And, of course, my mother encouraged me, too."

As singers, both Janet and Randy left quite a lot to be desired, and Katherine's idea was to have them do mediocre impressions of pop singers Sonny and Cher performing "The Beat Goes On," of screen stars Jeanette MacDonald and Nelson Eddy singing a dreadfully off-key "Indian Love Call," and of rhythm-and-blues stars Mickey and Sylvia doing an amateurish "Love Is Strange."

Then another part of the act was developed, as Michael has explained. "Janet was always a clown," he said. "She was a great mimic, and she used to do this wonderful Mae West impression around the house. I thought that if audiences could see her do it, they would be impressed. So I told Joseph we should have her do that in the act, which we did. She was amazing."

But it wasn't all that easy for her. "She was growing gray hairs, worrying about everything," twelve-year-old Randy reported to *Jet* magazine. "You could just look at her and tell."

"As for the children's Las Vegas show, the highest of the high points was Janet's Mae West imitation," Katherine has remembered. "Night after night, she stole the show with it, the little ham. I knew then, she was destined for a career in show business."

Janet, in a backless, pink satin gown and feather boa, did a Mae West that *Variety* called "hilarious." It was really her first big success.

"And what a place to start," Jermaine has recalled. "I mean, Las Vegas. A lot of people work years and years to get to that point. You don't just start out working Las Vegas, but Janet did."

"Being in front of this huge audience for the first time, I could easily have gotten stage fright, but thank God I didn't," Janet remembered in 1990. "It would have ruined the whole show."

Most reviewers, and even Jackson 5 fans, were perplexed by the group's new nightclub act—with their impressions of groups like the Four Freshmen and the Andrews Sisters—fearing that the group had abandoned its African-American core audience in favor of a new, white "money crowd." But all of them—Jackie, Tito, Jermaine, Marlon, Michael, LaToya, Randy, and Janet—were a smash every night on stage. It was clear that they could be accepted by the adult crowd and that a new star had been born in the likes of Janet Jackson. Joseph was pleased.

The triumph almost took a nasty turn, though, when the newly popular Janet was asked to audition for a role in an African-American version of *Romeo and Juliet,* opposite then-child-star Rodney Allen Rippy. Katherine and Joseph thought this might be an interesting vehicle for their eight-year-old daughter. Thus, the two youngsters—Janet and Rodney—accompanied by their mothers, went to an audition at the Hollywood home of the producer.

Rodney Allen Rippy remembered, "The guy pulled out scripts, told our mothers we'd be more relaxed doing our parts without them, and shuffled them outside. Then he put the scripts aside and told us he'd have to take pictures of us kissing to see if we'd be suitable for the roles. He told me to take my shirt off, kiss Janet on the lips, and put my arms around her. I was only five, but used to orders from directors, so I unbuttoned my shirt and threw it on the floor. He also told Janet to lower the straps of her tank top, and she did."

Rippy recalled that he and Janet kissed "at least fifty times" while the producer took photographs. As he reloaded film the producer said to Janet, "Take off your top so I can get a picture of that." Janet apparently knew instinctively that something was wrong.

Rippy continued, "She stamped her feet and yelled, 'No, no, no! I'm not doing any more pictures. Where's my mother?'

"The guy stayed cool as he went outside and told

our mothers everything had gone great. They suspected nothing.

"But my manager found out later that there was no Broadway play and the guy wasn't a producer. He had just rented that house for the day to lure me and Janet there. He gave a false name and the police never found him. But I know he was out to get Janet and me in child-porn poses. Luckily, Janet's presence of mind saved us both."

It was a close call. "Joe and Katherine were livid when they found out what had happened," said Tyrone Wilson, a security guard for the family at the time. "They tried to find the guy, but he had disappeared. From that time on, they were more careful. It could have been disastrous. Janet, though, was not upset or emotional about what happened. She just very matter-of-factly said, 'No way was I gonna let that man take pictures of me without my top on.' She was a strong-minded, determined little girl, that's for sure. At an early age, she seemed to have learned not to let anyone mess with her."

In August 1974, the Jackson family was again booked into the MGM Grand in Las Vegas. While the kids were working, Katherine made the alarming discovery that her husband was having another affair, this time with a twenty-six-year-old Jackson 5 fan from Kansas. The woman was pregnant with Joseph's child.

LaToya explains, "This girl was in love with Jackie, my older brother, though he wasn't really interested in her. But my father was always competitive with Jackie, for some odd reason. If girls liked Jackie, my father would make it a point that he would get that girl."

Joh' Vonnie Jackson was born on August 30, 1974, at Centinela Valley Community Hospital in Los Angeles County. "Janet had just turned eight," said a family friend. "And now she had a half sister. She didn't really understand what was going on; she just knew she had a sister and she wasn't allowed to talk about her or see her. It was very confusing. She knew her father had done something wrong, but she didn't know what. They tried to shelter her from it, but how could they? There was so much unhappiness in the family."

"She's my half sister, but I've never seen her in my life," says LaToya of Joh' Vonnie. "I don't think any of us have ever seen her. Michael and I have always wanted to, but my mother told us we're never to see her, that she's a bastard child. And we would tell my mother Joh' Vonnie didn't ask to be brought into this world. We were curious to know what this little girl was like.

"However, I did speak to her on the phone. At the time I didn't know who I was speaking to. My father just handed me the phone and said, 'LaToya, I want you to speak to someone. She really admires you; she loves you a lot. She has all your pictures. Will you please say hello to her?' I said, 'Sure.' I thought it was another fan. And I got on the phone and she said, 'I can't believe I'm speaking to you! Oh my God! Do you know who I am?' That's when my mind clicked. I suddenly knew who she was. I said, 'It's very nice talking to you. I have to go now.' And I hung the phone up."

"Who knows why Katherine stayed with Joe,"

observed Joyce McCrae, one of the Jacksons' employees at this time. "Only Katherine knows. I guess she loved him. What else could it be?"

"At that point, Katherine just thought *all* men are like this, out there screwing around," said Jerome Howard, Joseph and Katherine's former business manager. "She was with him for over thirty years. Where could she go?"

"It's hard for me to talk about it," is all Katherine, with tears in her eyes, would say to a reporter from the TV program "Day One" when asked about Joh' Vonnie and the pending divorce.

"Yeah, love conquers divorce," Joseph added. "So there was no divorce."

"Let me comment on that," Katherine said to her husband.

The air was getting thick.

"You had a chance," Joseph responded.

There was nervous laughter from Jermaine, Rebbie, and Randy, who were sitting with their parents, listening.

"I guess he answered it," Katherine finally decided.

Remembered Jerome Howard, "Katherine told me she went into the grocery store one day and saw Joe's girlfriend and the daughter. She said she [Katherine] just stood there, frozen. 'Jerome, the girl looked exactly like Joseph,' she said."

"Yes, my mother had seen her on several occasions in stores," LaToya concurred. "She would say, 'I saw that little bastard today,' and we would say, 'How do you know you saw her, Mother? You don't know what she looks like.' And she would say, 'Because she looks just like *him*.'"

Recalls one of Joseph Jackson's former employees,

"When Janet was about sixteen and Joh' Vonnie was eight, Janet made it her business to find out about the girl. She started asking questions about Joh' Vonnie's mother.

"One day, I walked into Joe's office and found her rifling through Joe's address book. I was surprised and said to her, 'Janet, what are you looking for?' She was not at all embarrassed. She said, 'Look, I need the number of this woman Joseph had that baby with. I need to talk to her.'

"I was absolutely shocked and certainly not about to give the number to her. Joseph would have fired me immediately had I done something like that.

"Then Janet started asking me questions like, 'Well, why did he do it?' 'What's the woman like?' and 'What does Joh' Vonnie look like?' Then she wanted to know, 'How does Joseph treat that girl? Does he treat her better than he treats me?' That question broke my heart.

"I told Janet that she should ask her parents these questions, and she looked at me as if I was crazy. 'I can't ask *them*,' she said, really impatient with me. 'If you won't give me answers, I'll get them somewhere else.'

"She never got the answers she was looking for," concluded the former employee. "Years later she told me she's always been uncomfortable about the fact that she has a half sister she doesn't know. She said she'd seen the girl in a photo wearing a Rhythm Nation jacket, and that it made her want to cry. 'But what can I do?' she asked. 'It's too late now to do anything.'"

*　　*　　*

In September 1974, Janet and her brother Randy appeared on the cover of *Soul* magazine in a story entitled "Can Janet and Randy Survive the Rigors of Show Business?"

"She cheats at handball," Randy said of his sister Janet.

"I don't. *You* do," young Janet shot back.

"Sure, we argue," Randy noted. "All brothers and sisters fight when they're young, I guess. But everybody always thought Janet and I should do some kind of part in the act together, so we worked out our imitations."

"At home, the two of them argued about anything and everything," LaToya recalled of Janet and Randy. "And it was no different on the road. They squabbled before shows, after shows, and even between songs, turning their backs on the audience and fussing and tugging at each other's costumes. The crowd usually assumed this was part of the act and laughed all the more loudly."

Randy made it clear to the reporter that even though they were now stars, he and Janet were still kids. "We have our everyday chores to do," he said. "Like make up our beds, clean our rooms, and take out the trash. Then there are rehearsals and things like that. Janet eats a lot and likes to fool around in the kitchen."

The reporter asked Janet if, offstage, she ever played with the black Chastity doll she would hold during the Sonny and Cher bit in the act. "Oh no," Janet responded, aghast. "That's a prop. I have lots of dolls I can play with and lots I don't play with from my collection. The boys bring dolls home for me and LaToya from all over the world, but they're *collection* dolls, not *playing* dolls."

Now that she was gaining recognition as a "Jackson," Janet found herself doing a multitude of interviews. "I don't know about my astrological sign too much," she told writer Steve Manning in March 1975 as, nearing nine years of age, she colored in her coloring book. "But Mama did tell me I am a Taurus. Mother is a Taurus, too. A lot of people ask me when my birthday is, and when I tell them, they say my sign is a bull and all kinds of other silly things."

Later she added, "I can play the piano pretty well. I've been taking lessons from a teacher for over a year. I know the musical scale and everything. And guess what? I even had the chance to play for a little group of my classmates' parents at school.

"I like chocolate clusters very much," she allowed. "Randy and I, plus 'Toya, eat them all the time. Mother buys lots of fruit such as apples, oranges, and grapes every day so we can have them to eat. But eating too much candy is no good for you. So instead of eating candy every day, I'll have a piece of fruit."

As she colored she told the reporter, "I asked Mother if I could help her cook breakfast. She said okay. I ran into the kitchen. While Mother was getting dressed, I started mixing up some pancake batter. I thought I could make them, since I saw Mother cook them plenty of times. But by the time Mother walked into the kitchen, I had made a real mess of everything. Mama didn't get too mad, but she asked me to please wait until she's in the kitchen next time before I try to help her."

Such are the concerns of an eight-year-old entertainer. . . .

*   *   *

In December 1974, Michael's twenty-three-year-old brother Jackie made newspaper headlines when he suddenly married his childhood sweetheart, Enid Spann. Enid recalls that she had her first date with Jackie when she was fifteen. She was warned that night by the Jacksons' attorney Richard Aarons that if she had designs on marrying Jackie, she should know she would be asked to sign a prenuptial agreement to protect Jackie's finances. Enid responded by saying, "If a marriage license isn't good enough for him, then I don't need him and I don't want him."

Twenty-year-old Enid and Jackie finally began their romance anyway and were married three years later in a small, private ceremony in Jackie's room at the MGM Grand in Las Vegas during another family engagement there. According to Enid, Joseph was opposed to the marriage because he felt she had ulterior motives, especially since she, unlike Tito's wife Dee Dee, would not sign the prenuptial agreement.

When Motown released a fourth solo album by Michael, *Forever Michael,* in January 1975 and it was not successful, Joseph made the wise decision to have his sons leave the company. Negotiations were quickly carried out with a new label, CBS, and a lucrative deal was struck. (For years, there would be a certain distance between Jermaine and his brothers due to Jermaine's decision to stay with Motown.)

Meanwhile, personal matters for the family continued to spiral out of control. In January 1976, Janet's eighteen-year-old brother Marlon announced that he had been secretly married to eighteen-year-old Carol

Parker for four months. He had not told his brothers or sisters. Or Joseph.

"He could be married and I wouldn't know about it," Joseph told a reporter in January 1976. "These kids, they just slip off and get married. I wasn't even invited to the wedding. What can I say?"

While all of this family drama unfolded, an announcement was made that the Jacksons would star in their own television series, "The Jacksons," a thirty-minute program that ran for only four weeks beginning June 16, 1976. Though the series didn't serve the brothers well, it was a terrific showcase for Janet. As in the Las Vegas act, Janet, LaToya, and Maureen participated as "The Jackson Sisters." The CBS Jackson-family bio reported of Janet, "She's a former 'tomboy' who loves animals, drawing, playing cards, horseback riding, and eating. She would like to be a movie star, someday."

This was the first time an African-American family had ever starred in a television series, and the word was that if the show received decent ratings, CBS might pick it up in January as a midseason replacement.

"We're the Jacksons," Michael announced at the beginning of one show. "All of you who were expecting the Osmonds, do not adjust the color of your set." He then introduced "the sexy side of the family: ladies and gentlemen, our sisters," Rebbie and LaToya.

The act continued. "Okay, let's go," Michael yelled out as the family prepared to reprise their opening number, "Forever Came Today."

"Hold it right there, dude!" came a voice from off stage.

Nine-year-old Janet stomped onto the stage wearing

a long blue skirt and matching boots. Her hair was pulled up into a little Afro puff.

"Nothing goes till *I* say it goes," she announced with mock "attitude."

"Oh, I forgot," Michael joked. "This is our little sister, Janet Jackson."

After big applause, Janet announced, "That's right. I'm Janet Jackson and nothing goes until I say 'go.'"

Pause . . . one, two . . .

"Okay," she announced with a snap of her finger. "Go."

More laughter and applause.

Indeed, the Jacksons' series was a launching pad for young Janet Jackson's singing and acting career. The format of the television show interspersed musical numbers with comedy sketches, which meant the youngsters had to learn lines as well as music. Some were quicker studies than others, but it's doubtful that anyone could have topped Janet.

In one episode, she, Rebbie, and LaToya performed a rendition of "Save the Bones for Henry Jones," made popular at that time by the Pointer Sisters. The three of them dressed in tacky but colorful thrift-store clothing; Janet was positioned in the middle and sang lead. She was a natural, especially compared with poor LaToya, who did everything she could just to keep up with her other two, obviously more talented sisters. ("It was always harder for 'Toya," one family friend allowed. "She had to work twice as hard just to be half as good.")

Another episode demonstrated the entire family's tap-dancing skills with a lavish Busby Berkeley–style number, "Stepping Out with My Baby." Janet and Michael were surprisingly adept, as were the rest of the youngsters. Even LaToya seemed to be in her element; a big smile played on her face as she dutifully went through her routine.

In still another episode, Janet premiered her Mae West impersonation for the TV audience. Dressed in a pink satin hourglass-shaped gown trimmed in tulle with a matching parasol and picture hat covering her platinum-blond wig, Janet sashayed onto a bar set where Ed McMahon was W. C. Fields pouring himself a generous shot of (alcoholic) medicine.

One of the most difficult tasks for an actor to learn is the art of timing (some professionals claim it is impossible), but Janet seemed to have a natural instinct for it.

"Hi, big fella," she said. "I'm Mae West."

"My goodness!" McMahon exclaimed.

Janet fixed him with a long, baleful look and patted her blond curls. "Goodness had nothin' to do with it," she purred in her Mae West voice. It brought the house down.

When Randy, as Cab Calloway, made his entrance onto the stage, he asked "Mae, is this fellow bothering you?"

"Unfortunately," Janet drawled, "no."

The kid was nine. She probably didn't even know what she was talking about. But she was funny, and believable as well. It was obvious to anyone watching that Janet Jackson was on her way.

When she strolled out on "Cab Calloway's" arm, Randy said to her, "You're good, baby."

Janet rolled her eyes. "When I'm good, I'm very good," she said with a sexy purr, "but when I'm bad, I'm better."

chapter FOUR

Most industry observers were impressed with Janet Jackson's work on the Jacksons' series, and word of her performances eventually reached noted television producer Norman Lear of "All in the Family" and "Maude" fame. At that time Lear was revamping the popular African-American situation comedy "Good Times," which had been spun off of "Maude." Esther Rolle and John Amos, who portrayed the parents on the series, had both departed, leaving the future of the show in jeopardy. In order to keep it on the air, Lear intended to recreate the series as a vehicle for Ja'net DuBois, who played the sassy neighbor, Willona. He was searching for a young actress to play DuBois's foster child, Penny—a girl who had been physically abused by her natural mother. Lear telephoned Joseph Jackson's office to ask if Janet might be available.

Joseph thought the idea was a terrific one; Katherine, of course, agreed.

Katherine drove Janet to the production company, where Lear personally auditioned her. Before he had the youngster read the script, he asked her a simple question: "Can you cry?" Janet said she thought she could. So Lear presented her with an improvisational scenario in which she had given him a tie he didn't like. He said some unkind things about her and the tie, and as if on cue, Janet began to weep. Lear was impressed. "You've got the job," he said.

Janet was thrilled. On the way home, Katherine stopped at a toy store and bought her a new Barbie Dollhouse doll as a congratulatory present.

Janet's two-year stint as the battered child on "Good Times" showed the world that she had great ability as an actress, both comedic and dramatic. "It was probably my greatest learning experience," she has said. "I knew nothing when I started the show. I had picked up a little on the Jacksons' series, but in terms of real rehearsal, camera blocking, and learning a lot of lines, I was really green. Everyone was patient with me. It was good."

Ja'net DuBois once recalled, "I was very nervous about having Janet in the show. It was an important time for me because they were planning to give me my own show, a 'Good Times' spin-off and they were going to have the Penny character go with me. So the girl who played Penny was going to have to be great, or it could ruin everything I had been politicking for.

"When I first read with Janet, she was nervous. I thought I was sunk. But then, after a few rehearsals, she started to relax. And before we even taped the first show, I knew she was going to be wonderful. Of course, she was. I actually became very attached to her, started feeling like her mama. She even used to call me Mama, just as if I was her real mom. She was a warm, completely unaffected child."

Many scenes called for complicated emotions, especially those during which the young girl was torn between her love for an abusive mother (Chip Fields) and affection for the DuBois character. To many observers, the accuracy of Janet's performance was an absolute surprise. "What does this kid know about child abuse?" one astonished reporter asked. "Not much, I'm sure. But, amazingly, she acts as if she does."

To those who knew what was going on at home, it wasn't so amazing at all.

Actually, Janet claimed she did not draw from personal observation when preparing for the role. The ten-year-old explained to one writer, "I had watched a television special on child abuse a few months before I went to audition for 'Good Times.' It was very sad. It was all about this young boy who was beaten by his mother, and when people asked him how he got hurt, he made up stories about falling down and things like that. I'm sure seeing that show helped me when I was playing Penny."

"She's a cute kid," comic Jimmie Walker, who played the obnoxious J. J. ("Dy-no-mite") Evans character, remembered at the time. "We don't know her well, though. She's quiet. Secretive, maybe."

"I remember her as being a precocious child, but there was also a sadness about her," noted one "Good Times" crew member. "She got along with the cast, but stayed to herself mostly. Her mother would come down to the set with a Bible and sit in a corner quietly and read. Then, during breaks, Janet sat by her side and the two of them would whisper to each other in a conspiratorial manner, pointing at cast members. They were rather odd, mother and daughter were."

While Janet was busy on "Good Times" she continued work on the Jacksons' family series. The ratings for the Jacksons' show were strong enough for CBS to order more episodes to begin airing in January 1977. But in time, the show plummeted to the bottom of the ratings, number seventy for its last broadcast in April 1977. Even though Michael was glad to see the show end—he never wanted to do it in the first place—Janet was disappointed. "I loved doing it," she said. "It was the most fun I'd ever had. I knew then that I really wanted to be in show business full-time. I started to have dreams."

These were traumatizing years for Michael Jackson, and he confided in only two people—Janet and his mother. His face was breaking out, and the resulting pimples made him miserable and increasingly shy. He began to withdraw even more, keeping to himself and spending time with Janet. He was so ashamed of the way he looked that going out in public was almost impossible for him.

"I became subconsciously scarred by this," he has confessed. "I got very shy and became embarrassed to meet people. The effect on me was so bad that it helped mess up my personality."

"This was the worst time of all for him," Janet would say years later. "But, in a selfish way, it was one of the best times for me. I got to spend all my time with Michael. We did everything together. We'd wake up in the morning and decide what we were going to do that day. Then we'd make a schedule, and throughout the day we'd accomplish everything on the schedule: write songs, watch old movies, feed the animals, read books, practice dance steps. It was a good time."

Michael and Janet withdrew into their own world, and though Janet would eventually emerge, it could be argued that Michael never did.

When Michael was offered a role in the movie *The Wiz,* it provided him a temporary avenue of escape from his family. He moved to New York in July 1977 to begin preproduction on the film and asked LaToya to accompany him. She did, and the two resided in an exclusive $2,000-per-month high-rise apartment on Manhattan's expensive Sutton Place. This marked the first time the two Jacksons were away from home and their family—if only for three months, from October 1977 through the end of December.

LaToya, nervous about being away, turned to chocolate for comfort. "She ate chocolate the whole time she was in New York," said Susie Jackson. "She became absolutely addicted. She told me it got so bad, she had such chocolate fits, that she would take Hershey's cocoa and mix water with it and drink it. That's how addicted she was. By the time she came back, she had gained twenty pounds."

Without Michael at home, Janet was tremendously lonely. "Poor Janet," recalled Susie. "She and Michael were so close, and then he was gone. LaToya was gone. Janet knew she'd have to make it on her own for a while. She missed her brother badly."

"She felt absolutely deserted," said another family friend. "She was beginning to realize that being

Michael's shadow and mother's little helper wasn't going to get her far. She had big dreams and wanted to make something of herself, even at this early age. She was a lonely child when Michael wasn't around. She spent her time daydreaming."

"That was traumatic," Janet has recalled of Michael's leaving home to do *The Wiz*. "He was my best friend and I couldn't stand the thought of his leaving. I cried my eyes out and begged Mother to take me to visit him in New York. I remember when we arrived, he took me over to the stereo and put on 'How Deep Is Your Love?' by the Bee Gees. Funny how you remember moments like that. I was entranced. That same night, I went to my first nightclub, Studio 54, and I was *down* for all the dancing."

In January 1978, eleven-year-old Janet took part in one of the family's press days at the Encino home. Reporters from different publications spent the day at the house interviewing various family members in alternating shifts. Janet was never an easy interview, since, like her siblings, she had practically nothing to say.

"I try to be nice," Janet told *Soul* magazine's Rita Cash. "You know, you can't go around with a big head."

And what did Janet like best about her role on "Good Times"?

"It's fun." She giggled. "I just like it."

Since her Cher impression was such a success, had she considered doing impressions of other stars?

"Farrah Fawcett would be easy," Janet said, laughing. "All I'd have to do is shake my hair."

What are her ambitions?

"I want to do a lot of things," she answered.

"One time I was at a store and this lady told me how she had seen me on TV and how much she liked me. Then she said she was sorry about what happened to my father. The lady was talking about Danielle Spencer [a young actress who appeared on the program "What's Happenin'"], and so I had to tell her that it wasn't my father who was in the car accident. I was a member of the Jackson family."

To another reporter, Jason Winters of *Black Stars* magazine, Janet fretted, "I love to eat. But now, being on television, I have to be careful. I don't want to gain too much weight."

Janet, who confessed that she loved horseback riding and playing gin rummy, added, "I would really like to be a movie star. I want to do a film that would be very dramatic. I think I like drama a little bit more than comedy—but I love them both.

"I see myself as a career girl," the eleven-year-old concluded. "As I said, I want to do movies, but television and records, too. I'm going to try everything."

The Jacksons' next album, *Destiny,* would sell over a million copies and reach number eleven on *Billboard*'s album chart—not bad for a group that hadn't scored with a major record in some time. But then came disappointment when *The Wiz* was released, in October 1978. It was a box-office disaster.

Michael was torn about what his next move should be. There were a couple of film offers as a result of his work in *The Wiz.* Sidney Lumet (who directed *The Wiz*) offered him the part of a transvestite in the movie version of *A Chorus Line.* Michael was ambivalent about taking the role, feeling people would identify him too strongly with it. He confided in Janet, who told him she thought he should take the part. "It'll be great for you," she said enthusiastically. But in the end, he turned it down and decided to concentrate on a solo album, much to the chagrin of his brothers, who hoped he would devote his attention to a group effort.

Michael went on to record the fabulously successful *Off the Wall* album, produced by Quincy Jones. The first single, "Don't Stop Till You Get Enough," went to number one and became Michael's first solo chart topper in seven years. The *Off the Wall* album was released in August 1979.

When "Rock with You" also made number one, and "Off the Wall" and "She's out of My Life" both went to number ten, Michael became the first solo artist ever to have four top-ten singles from one album. No one was more thrilled than Janet. "I was proud," she said later. "He was achieving everything he had worked so hard for. It was inspiring."

The album had a fine start, so when *Off the Wall* won only one Grammy (in an R&B category), Michael was crushed. "It bothered me," he said. "I cried a lot. My family thought I was going crazy because I was weeping so much about it."

Janet told a friend, "Mike came home from the Grammys and I had never seen him so miserable. He came into my room and just cried. He felt so slighted. I didn't know what to say to him. To me, the album was such a success; I didn't understand why he was so upset. But he wanted more. 'I sold fifteen million records worldwide. It was totally unfair that I didn't get that award,' Michael said. He wanted that final recognition and didn't get it. I felt bad for him."

Michael got hold of himself and said to Janet, "You

watch," he said angrily. "The next album I do, you watch. . . . I'll show them."

"I believed him," Janet recalled. "I really did."

In September 1980, Janet began appearing in a recurring role as Charlene, Todd Bridges's girlfriend on the television sitcom "Diff'rent Strokes." Unlike her "Good Times" role, the part of Charlene was relatively nondescript; any young African-American girl could have played it.

Of Janet, Todd Bridges said years later, "She was a sweet, kind of unassuming, really shy girl. But she was getting interested in boys. I sometimes felt she had a crush on me and she didn't know what to do about it. But Jan was the kind of girl you wanted to protect, not have sex with. She was such an innocent, you didn't want to mess with her."

"I was very embarrassed when I had to do romantic scenes with Todd," fourteen-year-old Janet recalled at the time. "But you just have to block all that out. I socialize with Todd sometimes. We talk a lot on the phone, and sometimes we go to movies. Todd is a sweetheart, but as I said, we're just good friends."

"I know she was having some problems at home," Bridges remembered. "She told me that when she came to the studio, she was happy to be able to leave those problems behind for a minute. I thought there was some pain there, that no one knew the real Janet. She opened up to me a little, but mostly she didn't talk much to anyone. She would stay in a corner, reading her script. Sometimes her mother would come and they'd sit on the sidelines with the mother reading the Bible and all kinds of religious pamphlets, and Janet just sort of watching things going on around her."

Remembered one crew member, "You couldn't talk to Janet Jackson. No way. She wanted nothing to do with anyone. It wasn't that she was stuck-up as much as she was this tremendously insecure kid who didn't know how to relate to anyone. It was as if she was raised by wolves; she was that antisocial. You'd walk up to her, she'd see you coming, and—whoosh!— she'd turn and disappear. Once, Michael came to the set and it was the only time I saw her actually have an animated conversation with a person. But he was a mirror reflection of her. Try to approach him, and he, too, would make a quick getaway."

To Cynthia Horner of *Right On!* magazine, Janet explained the contrast between her "Diff'rent Strokes" character and her real personality. "In some ways, Janet and Charlene are the same, but the difference is, she [Charlene] comes out and says whatever she has to say, and I can't. She shows her feelings, but if I'm upset and angry, I just can't come right out and tell the person. It takes me quite a while. That's the main difference. She speaks up and I don't."

At about this time, the family heard rumors that Joseph was having an affair with his nineteen-year-old secretary, a girl of Mexican-English-Irish descent by the name of Gina Sprague.

All of the children were extremely upset. No one wanted to see Katherine hurt again. "It's not fair," Janet told one relative. "I don't understand how he can do this to Mama. What's wrong with him? What's going on?"

"Janet was absolutely crushed," said the relative, who would speak only upon condition of anonymity.

"She'd had it with her father. She said she would never marry, and made a point of saying so, because prior to that time she talked about getting married and having babies. But I saw Janet beginning to develop a real distrust of men. She felt she had pretty good reason.

"But she was also a girl going through puberty. She was curious. She was surrounded by sex and by men: her brothers, her father. The subject came up all the time. We knew it wouldn't be long before Janet would start to experiment. As it turned out, James DeBarge was the one she chose."

James DeBarge came from a family of ten children in Grand Rapids, Michigan. He and his brothers (Marty, El, and Randy) and sister (Bunny) were Motown recording artists, performing as "DeBarge." In fact, Janet's brother Jermaine had assisted them in obtaining their deal with Motown.

Janet and James first met in a Detroit recording studio when Janet was thirteen. Thereafter they corresponded as pen pals for two and a half years before meeting again on the set of the television program "Soul Train." Janet was then fifteen.

"She started calling the house when LaToya began dating my other son, Bobby," recalled DeBarge's mother, Etterlene DeBarge Rodriguez. "As time went on, the relationship got stronger and stronger. I liked Janet. We got along beautifully; she's such a sweet girl. But she was moody. She didn't always seem happy or at peace with herself. I knew Janet was very much in love with James—she had confided that to me—and I knew he felt the same way about her. They related to one another."

"It was a puppy-love thing that really got out of hand fast, and no one knew a thing about it," says a Jackson intimate. "Janet kept it from everyone. She was embarrassed by the relationship, didn't know how to explain it, didn't know what it was. You could say that James took advantage of the situation."

James—who has never claimed to be a model of chivalry—says that "within two weeks" after their meeting on the set of "Soul Train," he and Janet were "lovers." And he added, "Let me tell you, the lady loved."

According to James, the couple spent a day lounging with LaToya at an apartment in West Hollywood that the Jackson family maintained as a "getaway." James wistfully recalled, "We went into the apartment's sauna and just sat there holding each other. I wanted to kiss her so badly, and I did. Wow! This was love."

When LaToya decided to leave the apartment discreetly, Janet and James went into the bedroom. "Janet was underage by a few months," he recalled. "But I didn't care. We made beautiful love and she was so passionate. She said to me after that first time, 'Thank you for taking my virginity and making me a woman.' That was what her family would never accept, her being a young woman, not a little girl anymore. Janet's parents had brainwashed her into thinking sex was dirty and to be feared. I taught her that it is lovely, beautiful, and wonderful."

According to James, when LaToya returned to the apartment, she immediately noticed a change in her younger sister's demeanor. "You're different," she said to Janet. Then, after studying Janet's reaction, she came to a startling conclusion. "You've finally done it," she exclaimed. "Haven't you?"

Janet could only blush.

"She was different from that time on," a relative of Janet's remembers. "Some of the innocence was chipped away. She was a 'woman' now. She started talking back to her mother sometimes. She started having her own say about things. She was clear about how she felt about Gina Sprague; she disliked her a lot. In fact, she made it clear that she resented all of her father's dalliances. Prior to the romance with James, she would mostly keep her mouth shut about them. Janet was getting tougher. Maybe she was growing up."

To this day, Gina Sprague denies having had a romance with the Jackson patriarch. She insists that trouble started when Joseph confided in her about the existence of Joh' Vonnie Jackson.

Gina recalled that Joseph took her to a "secret place." "We went up to this building and this woman, not a very friendly one, answered the door," recalled Gina. "And all I remember is this little munchkin running out saying, 'Daddy, Daddy, Daddy!' And Joseph's whole face lit up."

It was rare that any family members discussed the child. "Michael didn't acknowledge her at all," said Gina. "Unless you were a child of Katherine's, you were not anything to him. And even though that's Joseph's child, that's all it is. And all it will ever be . . . Joseph's child. Janet also had no interest in the girl, really. None of them did."

Gina claimed that perceptions of her association with Joseph as a romance were actually misinterpretations of her efforts to assist him in his effort to see Joh' Vonnie by covering for him and making excuses to his family as to his whereabouts. However, it did seem to most observers that Gina and Joseph were closer than just friends. (According to LaToya, she and Janet were in their father's office one day listening while Gina was on the telephone ordering expensive clothing from a catalog. LaToya notes that when Gina was asked for the name on her credit card, she responded in a loud voice, "Joseph Jackson." LaToya says she and Janet were appalled at her audacity.)

Katherine was distraught about this latest apparent affair. It was more than she could take. Her children have recalled that the stress of her crumbling marriage was making her feel desperate, perhaps even a bit irrational.

Gina claims that Katherine Jackson telephoned her at the office one day and threatened her with bodily harm if she did not quit her job. When Gina told Joseph of the phone call, he said he would take care of the matter. Apparently, he did not.

On the afternoon of October 16, 1980, Gina was behind her desk at Joe Jackson Productions—which was housed in the same Sunset Boulevard high rise as Motown Records—when Janet, fourteen, and Randy, eighteen, walked into her office.

According to Gina, "Randy socked me in the face, hard. And Janet was next to me, covering up my mouth. They pulled me out of the office—and there was Katherine. Katherine didn't waste any time. She just lunged at me and started hitting, hitting my face, my chest, anything she could. Then Randy threw me down and Katherine sat on top of me. She's no light cookie, okay? And she was slugging and slugging and slugging."

Jim Krieg, an office security guard, heard Gina's

screams and ran over to assist her. According to the police report subsequently filed by Gina, when Janet saw the guard, she said, "Leave, mister. This is a family affair."

"Janet could be violent," says Etterlene DeBarge, who would one day be Janet's mother-in-law. "She could slap your face if she wanted to."

"That was the flip side of her personality," observed one former associate. "She was this quiet kid—but with a temper, exactly like her mother. Push Katherine and she would react strongly. The same with Janet."

Gina Sprague was taken to Hollywood Presbyterian Medical Center, where she was treated for multiple cuts, bruises, and a head injury. The Jackson family, however, was skeptical about the seriousness of Gina's injuries. "[She] wasn't hurt as much as scared," recalled LaToya.

According to Gina, the only member of the Jackson family who visited her there was Jermaine. "He apologized for his father and his family," she said.

Why did Katherine bring her youngest daughter along to witness such an incident? "She probably didn't ask Janet to go with her," says Susie Jackson. "Janet probably volunteered when she heard what was about to go down. Janet idolized her mother and would do anything for her. Randy, too. They worshiped this woman, just as the rest of the family did. They were mad at Joe for pushing their mother over the edge. They were mad at the victim [Gina Sprague]. But never at their mother."

Another friend of Janet's recalls, "Being a witness to or participant in this kind of incident wasn't as upsetting to young Janet as one might think. Basically, Janet felt Gina got what she deserved.

Janet is a street-tough kid. She's had many a rude awakening as a child. She's never fooled herself into thinking life was easy. 'Sometimes people get hurt, especially when they bring it on themselves,' Janet once told me. She thought Gina brought that beating on herself."

Indeed, in their answer to Sprague's complaint, Katherine, Randy, and Janet said Sprague would never have been injured if she had exercised "ordinary care in her behalf."

Having filed a $21-million civil lawsuit against Katherine, Janet, and Randy, Gina Sprague showed up for a court date with her close friend Susie Jackson. The family was shocked that Susie had taken Gina's side. "I was so nervous that day in court," Susie Jackson said. "I hadn't seen the family in a while, only once in two years, and that was when I went to visit Randy in the hospital after his accident."

Susie says that she walked over to Katherine Jackson and greeted her by casually saying, "Hello, Mother." Janet and Randy just stared at her. Katherine was stunned.

Said another friend, "Throughout this whole ordeal—the court thing, the litigation—Janet was very upset. She knew she had done something wrong, and she was sorry she'd done it. But how could she get out of it? Katherine told her things would be all right, but even Katherine was sorry she let her emotions go unchecked and dragged Janet into it. This was a terrible ordeal, something no fourteen-year-old should have to go through."

Eventually, Gina Sprague reached an out-of-court settlement with the Jacksons. She says she is not at liberty to discuss the terms of the settlement.

"But I didn't get anything out of it except a lot of harassment," she says. "I got blackballed in the record industry. I never got any money. I never got anything. If I could talk to Mrs. Jackson right now, I'd tell her the next time your husband is hoochie-scooching some other woman, hit him, not the woman."

chapter FIVE

Having cosmetic surgery has been a hallmark of the Jackson family's behavior for years. They have never understood the public's curiosity about it. As Katherine has said, "If you are unhappy with your nose, you just have it done." The fact that many family members have obliterated traits characteristic of African-Americans does not faze them. "I look in the mirror and I know who I am. I know I'm black," Janet has said. "And I'm proud of that."

Each of the Jacksons with the exception of Jackie has had a rhinoplasty (a nose job), even the mother and father. Several of them have had additional work as well.

Michael got the ball rolling. He was considering a nose job, but before he could decide one way or the other, he tripped and fell during a dance routine in 1979 while he was on a concert tour. When his face hit the floor, he broke his nose.

Now Michael had no choice. He had to have his nose fixed—and while he was at it, he decided he should have some work done to make it narrower. He flew to Los Angeles and, in the spring of 1979, had his first rhinoplasty. Says Gina Sprague, "Joseph doubted that Michael would ever have had the nose job if he hadn't been forced to because of the accident. That was the first. But after the bandages came off, Michael liked what he saw. No one ever dreamed what that nose job would lead to."

However, the doctor who performed Michael's surgery—even if his work looked good—did not create a medical masterpiece. As a result, Michael had trouble breathing. He was referred to plastic surgeon Dr. Steven Hoefflin, who suggested a second nose job. Hoefflin performed that surgery, and all others Michael eventually had.

Janet, now, was unhappy about her figure, as are most girls at the age of fourteen. She, LaToya, and a childhood friend would commiserate about their shapes. Remembers a relative, "Janet was like all girls her age. She wanted breasts and she didn't have them. But because looks were so important in that family, and because her sisters were amply endowed, Janet was even more sensitive about it than she probably should have been. She used to stuff her training bra with Michael's socks just to have some kind of figure.

"Michael only made things worse," said the relative. "He used to tease her all the time, calling her flat-chested. All the Jackson siblings ribbed each other mercilessly about the things they were most sensitive about. For instance, they called Michael 'Big Nose.' Marlon was 'Liver Lips.'"

Michael was twenty-one when he had his first rhino-plasty, his first attempt to be physically what he envi-sioned himself to be. Janet, though only fourteen, followed suit.

"It was a big thing," recalled Marjory Van Valkenburg, director of the Valley Professional School, which Janet attended. "A lot of kids were getting their noses done."

"[Janet] hated her nose," recalled Enid Jackson, her former sister-in-law. "She really wanted it done. But even when she had it done, she wasn't that happy with it.

"What inspired her was Michael's surgery. She was so close to him, she wanted to be like him in every way. She discussed it with him, and he said, 'Do it if it will make you happy.' But he also cautioned, 'Don't do it just to copy me.'

"Then Janet asked her mother for permission. Katherine thought it over, discussed it with Joe, then agreed to let her do it. She thought it would make her daughter happy. Janet was so shy. Maybe, Katherine thought, this would help bring her out of herself.

"Katherine and Joe have never really been against plastic surgery. Whatever you can do to make yourself better—stricter rehearsals, a better diet, plastic surgery—that's what you do in the Jackson household. It might be a big deal in most homes for a fourteen-year-old girl to have a nose job, but in the Jackson house it was perfectly acceptable. Michael broke the ice, so to speak. And then the rest followed.

"Janet had her second nose job when she was eighteen."

But the nose job did little to "bring her out," Enid explains. "She was as shy as ever, except when she got herself riled up. She was most furious when Katherine was being hurt by Joe. But, usually, she was a fairly introverted child, like all of them. She was extremely self-conscious about her appearance."

"Want to know what I see when I look in the mirror?" Janet asked writer Debi Fee in 1980. "Well, I'll tell you. I see too much face. Look at these jaws. No matter how thin I might get, my face will always look big because I inherited these jaws from my grandmother. I have a round face and people tell me that's good, but I don't think so. Now LaToya is beautiful. Face it, the girl is gorgeous."

Janet was obviously unhappy about her appearance, and maybe a little envious of LaToya's. "And thin? I'll *never* be as thin as LaToya," she continued. "We are definitely built differently. I'm just chunky. That's the best way to describe me. My thighs are too big, too.

"I'm short, and oftentimes short people have to watch their weight," Janet said in 1980. "The problem is, I like food. I like Italian, French, and good old McDonald's fries. Like the rest of my brothers and sisters, I don't eat meat now, but there was a time when I used to pig out on steak.

"I know I need to lose weight," she said with a resigned sigh. "I'm good at starting my diet tomorrow, if you know what I mean. Of course, if I gain too many extra pounds, there's always someone around to tell me and then I have to do something about it."

"She was only fourteen, for goodness' sake," said Gina Sprague. "But she had this great preoccupation with her weight. It was heartbreaking. She simply never felt that she looked as good as Rebbie and LaToya. And the rest of the family made it hard on her."

Indeed, Janet said in 1980 that her family constantly reminded her to diet. "Michael gets on me a lot. Or LaToya will say, 'Janet, I think you're gaining a little weight.' Or my dad will tell me to lose it. I'm glad they do, because sometimes I have absolutely no willpower."

Another friend added, "I think having her weight always thrown in her face hurt Janet, just as it would anyone. It made her unnecessarily self-conscious. And she wasn't really fat. But she would end up dealing with this 'weight problem' for years and years, never really believing she looked as good as LaToya, never recognizing that she was thin when she did lose the weight. She's been absolutely obsessed with dieting in the past, with working out, with pushing herself to the point where she'd end up in the hospital as a result of these weird low-calorie diets. I wouldn't be surprised if Janet looks in the mirror today, now that she is thin, and sees a fat girl staring back at her. That wouldn't surprise me at all."

By April 1981, plans were being made for Janet's brothers to embark on a thirty-nine-city concert tour of the United States to support their new *Triumph* album. Michael didn't want to go. He just didn't want to do another tour with his siblings, but he *was* ready to start touring as a solo act. If he had to go, however (which he did because he was outvoted), he had one request.

He wanted Janet, LaToya, and Rebbie added to the act. In fact, what he actually wanted was Janet on the road with him to keep him company. The brothers didn't agree with this idea at all.

"They thought Janet and LaToya would be out of place on the tour, and of course, they were right," says J. Randy Taraborrelli. "It had been a long time since the Las Vegas family act, and the girls hadn't progressed much as entertainers. Janet was crushed, though. She really wanted to go out on the road and was angry at her brothers for holding her back. There was a lot of whining and crying amongst the sisters. So in order to placate them, Katherine decided that Janet, LaToya, and Rebbie should form their own group, a new trio in the grand tradition of the Supremes.

"Bad idea."

From the beginning, Janet, LaToya, and Rebbie simply could not get along as a trio. Rebbie has explained, "We did a few things in the studio, but the group never got off the ground. There were debates between us over who should be the lead singer."

Janet didn't care who sang lead—she certainly never considered herself a lead singer—as long as the group came together and was taken seriously. She hoped Michael might produce their album; Michael said he was interested. But LaToya and Rebbie fought bitterly; each wanted to be the next "Diana Ross."

In the end, the sisters couldn't agree and the group broke up before it really even got started. "My personality and LaToya's didn't click," Rebbie has recalled. "Although I really tried to make things work, I got tired of bending."

Now that her sisters had, in effect, canceled each

other out, Janet made a decision that would have personal and professional consequences more far-reaching than she could possibly have imagined at the time. "All right," she concluded, "I'm just going to have to make it by myself." It was a fateful moment. The thought was to echo in her mind again and again. *"I'll do it on my own."*

But there was more family confusion to navigate through before Janet could think seriously about her career plans.

Michael and Rebbie had been encouraging Katherine to leave Joseph. None of the children ever got over their dad's infidelities; watching their mother endure an insufferable marriage was heartbreaking. Finally, Katherine decided the children were right; she should leave Joseph once and for all.

On August 19, 1982, Katherine filed for divorce again. Somehow, the family managed to keep this news from the press.

There was only one snag in Katherine's declaration of independence. Jerome Howard, her former business manager, remembered, "She told me that after she filed for divorce this time, she expected Joe to move out of the house. But he refused to leave. What could she do? She didn't want to make a big legal scene, so she let him live there while the proceedings were going on."

At this same time Janet's brother Marlon filed for divorce from Carol, his wife of seven years. The couple had three children, including a one-year-old boy, Marlon, Jr. Marlon hadn't done as well financially as his brothers. In court records, he listed his monthly income as only $3,218, yet his monthly expenses totaled $16,664.

Meanwhile, Jackie and his wife, Enid, were still having marital problems.

In August 1982, Michael Jackson and Quincy Jones began work on a new album at Westlake Studios in Los Angeles. To be entitled *Thriller,* it would consist of nine songs the two had pared down from three hundred selections. It was scheduled to be released December 1, 1982.

At its sales peak, CBS reported that *Thriller* was selling an astounding 500,000 copies a week. Indeed, this was one hot product. It went on to sell forty million copies—the biggest-selling album of all time.

"I knew it the first time I heard it," Janet has said. "I wasn't at all surprised. I just knew I wanted to have an album that big myself. I didn't know how I was going to go about it, but that's what I wanted."

At the end of that year—1982—Janet got her chance at recording stardom when her father had her record a few demos and then signed her to a deal with A&M Records. "He asked me if I would like to start singing again," Janet recalled. "But I never saw myself as a solo artist like my brothers and sisters. 'Do you think I'm ready?' I asked him. 'What if people don't like my voice?' 'Believe me,' my father said. 'You're ready.'"

She wasn't.

Her debut album, *Janet Jackson,* was a weak affair with eight songs that did little to camouflage the fact that she wasn't much of a vocalist. But thanks to her television exposure, the album (produced by Foster Sylvers, Jerry Weaver, and the songwriting/producing team of René and Angela) managed to sell a quarter of a million copies. Janet's decision was that none of her family members would participate in the record. "I didn't want people to buy it because Michael wrote a song or LaToya sang background," she told a reporter. "I wanted it to be something that's mine alone. So I'm proud of it."

Neither of the single releases from the album, "Young Love" or "Day You Do," nor the album itself, was successful.

On March 12, 1983, the comanagement contract Michael Jackson and his brothers had with their father and with Weisner-DeMann expired. Industry watchers expected twenty-four-year-old Michael to renegotiate and sign a new deal. However, he decided not to. Instead, he hired his own attorney (John Branca) and accountant (Marshall Gelfand) and went on to have another number-one single that month: "Billie Jean."

Neither did the other brothers resign with Joseph. Clearly, they no longer wanted him as their manager. Rebbie, LaToya, and Janet were shocked. (LaToya said she would "never be so mean to Joseph, even though I don't like him, either.")

"I guess business is business," Janet told one relative. "But I don't see how Michael can fire our father. Even though he makes me mad sometimes, he's still our father."

"There's a little more to that decision than met the eye," said Michael's first cousin Tim Whitehead.

(Whitehead's mother is Katherine's sister Hattie; his father is Joseph's stepbrother, Vernon.) "Michael was extremely upset about the way he perceived his father as treating his mother. It hurt him. The whole family knew that. He apparently was saying to Joseph, 'You cannot do this to Katherine and get away with it. She is a wonderful woman and she doesn't deserve it.' Michael hit him where it really hurts, in the pocketbook. That's how I saw it, anyway. At least now the money Michael generated for the family wouldn't be spent on women other than Joe's wife, Katherine."

Joseph was hurt that his sons had abandoned him. His credo was, "I was there when it started, and I'll be there when it ends." Apparently, however, that was not to be the case.

Also in March, Michael was persuaded to appear on the "Motown 25—Yesterday, Today and Forever" television special, where he made an indelible mark on show business with his compelling, dynamic performance of "Billie Jean." Without exaggeration, Michael Jackson's was quite possibly the single most captivating pop-music performance in television history.

"After the 'Billie Jean' performance, everything changed," Janet has said with enthusiasm. "The next day, our whole house was buzzing with people calling, coming back, congratulating us on how great Mike was. It was wonderful."

By the summer of 1983, everyone who lived at the Hayvenhurst estate—Michael, Janet, LaToya, and their parents—existed in a state of emotional siege.

Even though he and Katherine were separated, Joseph still maintained a bedroom suite in the house, much to his children's dismay. "I wish he'd just leave," Janet said at one point. "Either you're separated or you're not!"

Michael and Joseph argued incessantly. LaToya tried to keep out of her father's way. Janet just stayed in her room, out of sight. "She lived in that room," said Enid Jackson. "She was afraid to leave. Who knew what would happen? It was a tense time."

The year 1984 started out with a bang when Michael's hair caught on fire during the taping of a Pepsi-Cola television commercial in January. (He sustained second- and third-degree burns and is still treated regularly for complications as a result of that accident.) And then, by the end of February, it was time to plan his appearance on the telecast of the Grammy Awards, scheduled for the twenty-eighth.

Shortly before the ceremony, eighteen-year-old Brooke Shields—who had been a friend of Michael's for two years—came by the Encino house unexpect-edly to ask Michael if he would consider taking her to the awards show. She had already accompanied him to the American Music Awards in January (when Michael won eight awards) and to the Guinness Awards in February. But Michael was lukewarm about taking Brooke to the Grammys. He felt she was getting too attached to him, that she per-haps felt more strongly about him than he did about her.

Janet and LaToya were in another room when Michael came back and told them of Brooke's request. He told his sisters he wanted to turn her down, but didn't know how to go about it. This was fine with Janet, who never liked Brooke and referred to her as "Giraffe Butt."

"Janet was jealous of Brooke," said Steve Howell, who worked for Michael Jackson. "She never liked any girl who was attracted to Michael. Number one, she was afraid Michael would be taken advantage of. And, number two, she felt Michael already spent too little time with her. Brooke was competition. Janet didn't even like to give Michael telephone messages from Brooke. She sort of worked to keep them apart."

Janet suggested that Michael just level with Brooke and tell her he wasn't interested in taking her to the show. He left the room, went in to see Brooke, then returned—only to announce to Janet and LaToya that he was taking her to the show after all.

A while later Michael showed some photographs of himself and Brooke to Steve Howell, explaining that he only took her to the show to "help her out." He added, "There was no romance. Not at all. We're friends. All of this was strictly for her, for the sake of publicity. It was good PR for her to be seen with me."

The night of the Grammys, Janet's older brother made history by winning eight awards.

"I was so proud," Janet said. "Finally, Michael got the recognition he deserved."

In the summer of 1984, Janet graduated from Valley Professional School. She has said that she never really enjoyed high school, that she couldn't relate to the students. Oddly, she felt *they* were spoiled. In a 1993 interview, she said of her former classmates, "You turned sixteen and you'd get a Porsche for your birthday. Or some kid would drive up in her Mercedes. It was like [the television program] 'Beverly Hills 90210.' In my family, I didn't learn to drive until I was seventeen. I was the oldest one in the class, and I didn't know how to drive. The kids used to make fun of me for it. But that's how it was in my family. If you wanted a car, you had to buy your own. But we couldn't buy one until we were eighteen.

"When I was in high school," Janet remembered, "my mother used to say, 'Oh, Janet, you're so lazy.' It was because I used to come home from school, go straight to my room, and right as the sun was setting, put on jazz records and practice kissing my pillow and the back of my hand. I didn't have anybody to kiss, but I was getting ready for when that person did come along."

For graduation ceremonies, the seniors were requested to wear white. Janet went to the principal and pleaded with him to permit her not to wear that color. "I look horrible in white," she said. "It'll make me look fat. Please!"

When she began sobbing, the principal recognized that she was serious. Either because Janet is a member of the Jacksons and, as such, was deemed as deserving of special treatment or, perhaps, simply because he just felt sorry for the poor girl, the principal decided that she could wear a different color. So on graduation day, Janet Jackson didn't have to wear white. One wonders, however, if the principal was prepared for what she *did* wear—which just happened to be a red, strapless ruffled gown.

In July, Michael embarked with his brothers on the ill-fated Victory tour, which would continue through December 1984. During that tour, there was a tremendous public backlash against the brothers because of their well-publicized infighting. There was also a heated controversy, played up by the press, about the high price of concert tickets. Indeed, during this tour, all hell cut loose, not only on the road but also at home—with Jackie (who didn't make the tour because of a broken leg) and Janet (who would find true love despite strong objections from her family).

chapter SIX

The Jackson siblings have often complained that they were sheltered from the real world as a result of their tremendous fame. They have also complained that because of their high visibility as recording stars and stage performers, they were not able to socialize with youngsters their own age, thus missing out on growing up, on experiencing the freedom of youth. In some ways, that may be true. None of the Jackson children really had the carefree adolescence they may have craved; then again, few adults anywhere ever reflect on their youth as having been ideal.

Many Jackson historians would agree that those youngsters actually experienced *more* of the so-called real world than most kids their age, and their lives were none the better for it.

Further, in the tradition of their parents' marriage, the children's relationships were anything but tranquil.

In 1984, Jackie began having an affair with vivacious dancer-choreographer Paula Julie Abdul, who was twenty-one years old at the time. Jackie had hired Paula to choreograph the Jacksons' video for their song "Torture," in which Michael did not participate. (In years to come, Paula Abdul would choreograph excellent award-winning videos for songs from Janet's *Control* album—including "When I Think of You," "Control," and "Nasty." Eventually, of course, she would go on to become a major recording and video star herself.) Jackie's romance with Paula would eventually lead to the end of his marriage to Enid Jackson.

While Jackie's marriage was breaking up, eighteen-year-old Janet was on her way to putting a marriage together.

Janet had continued her relationship with James DeBarge over the previous couple of years, though her family never knew much about it. The two would sneak away, have dinner, and spend romantic time with one another. They were not an "item," but they did date from time to time, and he would always hold a special place in her heart.

As they got older Janet became more attracted to James because of his sensitivity; he seemed to understand her like no one else ever had. She was feeling particularly lonely at this time because Michael was off with his brothers on the Victory tour. Actually, her relationship with Michael had not seemed quite the same since the release of *Thriller* and the onslaught of so-called Michael mania. Her brother's tremendous international success had begun to monopolize all of his time; though Michael tried to make time for Janet, there was little time left. She knew her brother still cared deeply for her, yet she couldn't help feeling somehow abandoned.

"After all, we did everything together, everything under the sun," she had said of Michael. "But then after *Thriller*, it was 'See you later, Michael' for me. He was so busy."

Because of her fame, Janet also found that making friends was difficult. "A lot of people, someone I might think was my friend, might be using me to get to know my brothers or my sister LaToya," she told writer Gary Jackson at that time. "They might not really want to know me. It hurts, but I get over it. I've been disappointed a couple of times—just recently, too.

"I only have two friends," she admitted, "one of whom I've known for eight years. It took a little while for me to see that she is a true friend, because usually a person's true intentions come out after a while." Apparently, Janet Jackson had a difficult time not being suspicious of people.

James was able to communicate with Janet about the dysfunction in his own family; she was certainly able to understand it and even offer constructive suggestions.

Katherine and Joseph—who had reconciled again by this time—were not fond of James DeBarge. They had heard he was involved with drugs, but couldn't be certain. Nevertheless, the possibility raised a legitimate concern. Also, Joseph felt that DeBarge was using Janet to become associated with the Jacksons, thereby furthering his career in some way. Neither Joseph nor Katherine trusted him and they wanted Janet to break off the romance, but she would have none of that. She felt her parents were simply trying to control her life, as she had seen them manipulate (or attempt to manip-

ulate) the lives of her siblings. She was determined to
be treated as a grown-up.

The more Joseph and Katherine attempted to separate
her from James, the more determined Janet was to be
by his side. James felt the same way about her. "I
loved her like nothing on earth and nothing was going
to keep me from my baby," he said years later.

Since Janet had never given Joseph and Katherine a
moment of trouble in the past, they were at a loss as to
how to deal with this unusual situation. Why was she
so adamant about being with James DeBarge? they
wondered. Since their worst nightmare was that Janet
would run off with him, they decided to back off and
handle the emotionally charged situation by attempting to demonstrate subtly that James was not the right
man for her, while also seeming to allow her room to
make her own decision—hoping all the time that she
would come to her senses. But despite every effort
they made to appear diplomatic, Janet could not help
feeling that her parents were interfering in her life.
This interference was certainly not unusual, but now,
for the first time, Janet resented it. She wanted
Katherine and Joseph to keep their opinions about
James to themselves. Perhaps, she thought, she and
James could find true love together if her parents
would only stop meddling.

James did not want to lose Janet. "He wanted her
badly," said one DeBarge family member. "He was
afraid that, given time, Katherine and Joseph would be
able to get to Janet. He didn't want to take a chance on
losing her. He had grown to depend on her, and was
becoming more desperate by the hour. At one point he

said he felt her slipping away, giving in to the family pressures. Finally, he convinced her of what he thought had to be done."

They suddenly eloped on September 7, 1984. Janet, eighteen, and James, twenty-one, were married in Grand Rapids, Michigan. "She was shaking in her shoes at the ceremony," he recalled.

"Immediately, Janet regretted what she had done," said the DeBarge family member. "She realized that she had been pressured into the marriage. But she did love James, so she decided to make the best of it. She knew, though, that she would be in for it when she got back home."

Janet telephoned LaToya to tell her what she and James had done. LaToya thus had the unenviable task of breaking the news to her father and some of her siblings, none of whom took it well. Joseph then called Katherine, who was accompanying her sons on the Victory tour. She was, understandably, upset.

Michael was particularly distressed and was in constant communication with Motown's director of publicity, Bob Jones, to find out what was going on with Janet and James (who, we must remember, as a member of the DeBarge recording group, was a Motown artist). "She's gone!" Jones said of Janet as he walked through the Motown offices after a phone call from Michael. "Janet's gone off and eloped. Married one of those TV babies. Raised on television; doesn't even know his own social security number."

James booked himself and his wife into an expensive suite at the Amway Plaza Hotel in Grand Rapids, which, he says, "cost me a small fortune." No sooner had the newlyweds checked into their room than James went out to socialize with some friends. He promised Janet he would not be long. But then he got, as he recalled later, "rotten drunk."

Janet stayed up nervously waiting for her new husband to return, afraid that perhaps something terrible had happened to him. This probably was not the honeymoon she had anticipated. Then, at three in the morning, James came stumbling into the room. "Janet was waiting up for me with tears streaming down her face," he recalled.

That night, James rocked his new wife to sleep in his arms.

When Janet got back to Encino, Joseph was at the door waiting for her, though the acrimonious scene she anticipated did not materialize. Janet would recall later that her father embraced her, kissed her on the cheek, then congratulated her. "I wanted to give you away, walk you down the aisle one day," he told her.

Janet was speechless.

Then, with tears in his eyes, Joseph went upstairs to his bedroom. Janet was left in the foyer with her suitcases at her side, looking up the stairs at her father. She must have wondered what the hell was going on.

Because she felt so guilty about what she had done, Janet decided the newlyweds should live with the Jacksons in the Encino mansion. "But my son wanted them to have their own place," recalled James's mother, Etterlene. "He felt they needed to be alone to give themselves a chance to grow in their marriage. He was very certain about that. But Janet didn't want to leave home. She was still like a little girl who never wanted to leave her bedroom. At least that's what James said about her. Also, James said she felt bad about what they had done. She thought maybe she could make amends."

Etterlene DeBarge said of Janet's parents, "I liked

Katherine. We would talk girl talk, about how we were going to take more weight off, that sort of thing. She never discussed anything personal with me. Never anything about Joe. And Joe never spoke to me. He was very cold.

"James always used to be upset about Joe's womanizing, and it upset Janet, too. She wanted to be very close to her father, but said it was difficult. When she saw him, she didn't know whether to hug him or shake his hand, because they had such a turbulent relationship. It was not a warm relationship like a father and daughter should have. He was a stranger to her."

"The whole thing was weird from the start," said James, recalling his life with Janet in Encino—which included Joseph and Katherine, Michael, and LaToya. "Once I was inside [the house], I felt they were poisoning Janet's mind against me."

"One immediate problem was that my son didn't get along with LaToya," observed Etterlene. "I think she wanted him for herself."

DeBarge concurred. "Her room was next to ours," he said of LaToya. "And she would make personal remarks when she knew we had made love. She had just ended the affair with my brother, which made things difficult for us. She hated everything to do with the name DeBarge. One night I almost decked her when her vicious tongue ran away with her. She was accusing me of cheating on her sister. She even insinuated I was gay. She went to drag her long painted nails across my face, and I just ran. I jumped out the window. I knew if I had stayed I would have flared up and knocked her out."

In her own defense, LaToya has said she had nothing against her new brother-in-law and found him to be "sensitive and charming," but that she didn't trust him because she believed him to be too immature for marriage. She feared he would hurt her sister, "and I just couldn't allow that to happen."

When James moved into the house, Janet's parents, Michael, and LaToya all made an alarming discovery—something Janet would later admit she had known for some time but never confided to anyone. James, as Joseph and Katherine suspected and feared earlier, had a serious drug problem.

"You always think you can change people," Janet admitted later. "And I knew he wanted to change so badly. He was trying—but he wasn't trying hard enough."

Now, more than ever, Katherine and Joseph didn't want Janet to have anything to do with this young man. However, they were powerless to do anything.

"Janet," says Etterlene, "wanted to help my son in any way she could. James began to depend on her, and that probably was no good. He should have been depending on himself more and on Janet less."

Steve Howell has recalled, "The guy would be completely out of his mind on drugs. He would be so high on coke and alcohol that twice the guards tried to stop him from going into the house. 'If you go in there, Mr. [Joseph] Jackson will kill you,' they'd tell him. But he was pretty belligerent and didn't care. Funny thing was, when he wasn't high he was the nicest guy in the world. He was like Dr. Jekyll and Mr. DeBarge."

Katherine didn't want her daughter involved with James, but she sympathized with the young man just the same. "Whatever drove him to this, he has to get over or he'll never be right," she told Etterlene. "I want to help him. We all do. But we're afraid of what he's capable of. We're worried about our family."

Katherine offered to enroll James in a rehabilitation center, but he refused to go. "He thought that during that time away, Katherine and Joe would convince Janet to annul the marriage," said a DeBarge family member. "He was paranoid. Plus, he didn't want to lose Janet. So he said no. Even LaToya offered to pay for his rehabilitation. He turned her down as well."

At night, according to LaToya, James's tortured screams echoed eerily through the hallways of the Encino mansion. "I can't help it. I need it," he bawled. Janet attempted to help him, but she was at a complete loss as to how to deal with her husband's dilemma. "Sometimes I heard slaps," claims LaToya. "It was heartbreaking."

Janet steadfastly refused to admit that James had a drug problem. Perhaps she thought his addiction was a personal matter, to be handled between the two of them. "He's not on drugs," she screamed at LaToya one day. "And don't you ever say he is. Just butt out!"

"Janet was infuriated that her family had a point of view about what was happening," noted Etterlene DeBarge. "She wanted them to leave her and James alone, and she would always blame a lot of her troubles on their 'meddling.' But what else could they do? Janet brought this huge problem into Katherine and Joe's household and laid it at their feet. They had to react."

Certainly Janet had learned to follow Katherine's example of absolute discretion, of never admitting to a single soul the torture she, Katherine, had endured in her own long and troubled marriage. And until these problems began to actually affect her children, Katherine's decision was to act as if they simply did not exist. But it was so painfully obvious to everyone that James had a drug problem, Janet could no longer deny it with any credibility. Instead, she tried to cover it up. At her insistence, she and James began to venture outdoors without security, just so the guards would not report back to any family member anything she and her husband discussed. "They all thought I was the AntiChrist," says James DeBarge of his in-laws.

Indeed, Joseph—who was justifiably concerned about his daughter's welfare—had developed an intense dislike for his son-in-law. Katherine valiantly tried to keep her husband's temper in check, and most family members would agree that the only reason Joseph had not thrown James out of the house was that Katherine convinced him Janet would leave as well. Katherine felt the only way to keep an eye on her daughter—and also to protect her from James's "druggie" friends—was to have Janet living at home. But Joseph could only take so much of James's insolence and defiant drug abuse. After all, this was his home, not James DeBarge's.

Eventually, Katherine's worst-case scenario came true when James insisted on leaving the Encino home and Janet agreed to go with him. The couple moved into a condominium in the fashionable, upscale Los Angeles community of Brentwood.

"Frankly, they moved out of the house because Joe was going to kill the guy," said Steve Howell. "He had threatened him, and we felt he was going to follow through. Janet was scared to death."

"They were enemies," Etterlene DeBarge concurred

in regard to her son and Joseph Jackson. "It was just terrible. I cannot tell you how terrible it was."

In Brentwood, James's behavior worsened as his monster drug habit all but consumed him. He would disappear for days at a time, leaving Janet to fear the worst had happened. She simply did not know what to do.

"I needed help," James admitted later. "I was hurting bad. I needed understanding. I depended on Janet too much. It was hard for her, but I loved her, no matter what anyone thinks."

"'My God,' I wondered, 'where is he? What's going to happen to him?'" Janet remembered later. "I felt like I was the only one who cared." According to Joseph and Katherine's former manager, Jerome Howard (who negotiated recording contracts for Janet), Janet received terrifying telephone calls in the middle of the night from friends telling her that her husband was helpless, stoned out of his mind somewhere. Janet would get dressed and drive into the dangerous ghetto areas of Los Angeles to rescue him.

"She got to know the ghetto better than any other Jackson," says Howard. "She loved that man and would do anything for him."

Michael was always amazed and full of questions for Janet when he learned she had been in the ghetto. "What was it like?" he'd ask. "What did you see? Weren't you scared?" It was as if he was living an exciting adventure vicariously, through his sister's experiences. Both he and LaToya felt they had never really seen the harsher realities of the world outside the walls of the Encino mansion. But Janet, who had enough on her mind already, was not especially patient with Michael's probing.

Matters became more heartbreaking when, according to James DeBarge, she became pregnant. DeBarge claims his young wife had been taking birth-control pills, but that she stopped because they were causing her to gain weight. He says that Janet did not share the news of her pregnancy with any member of her family except, perhaps, her mother.

"Personally, I wouldn't have minded a child, but it had to be her decision," he says.

"How could she bring a child into this marriage?" asked a DeBarge family member. "I think she had already decided she couldn't take any more. I think she was trying to find a way out."

James DeBarge says Janet opted for an abortion. They made an appointment at a clinic in Los Angeles—deciding to go use the back door in order to avoid being seen.

"We sat down together and the doctor told us about the risks," he recalls. "I paid for the operation. Around five hundred dollars. Then I took her home and held her in my arms. I told her everything would be okay."

Janet denies ever having been pregnant and has never publicly addressed the question of whether she had an abortion. James's mother, Etterlene, says, "I heard she was pregnant, that she'd had an abortion. But I really can't say it's true or not."

Rumors of an existing daughter would haunt Janet for years to come. The singer Vanity—of whom Etterlene DeBarge insists Janet was quite jealous—confronted Janet one day saying, "Hey, I heard you had James's baby."

"I told her that was *old* news," Janet said later.

She noted to one reporter: "A few months ago this guy stopped me on the street to say he heard I really had my baby in Europe and was paying somebody to raise it for me. God, that's so stupid."

In fact, Janet gained so much weight during her marriage, it did seem to many observers that she was pregnant. "She may have had an abortion at one point during the marriage, but I swear to God she was pregnant again," said a "Fame" crew member. "I saw her pregnant myself, with my own eyes. She was big, too. Not just a couple of months. That girl was pregnant."

Indeed, Janet's former sister-in-law Enid Jackson insists, "I have not seen the baby, but she and James do have one. A little girl. Her family didn't even know she had the baby. She went in and acted like she was having her tonsils taken out, but she was really having a baby. She gained a lot of weight."

It all seems so unlikely, yet the rumor persists even to this day. Why would Janet keep the existence of a child a secret? Enid speculates, "I believe the reason she didn't say anything is that the family is so cruel, and they did not like James. They would have been the types to start a rumor saying James wasn't the father. And Janet has learned from being around the family, growing up as a little kid, to keep her life private, because she knows how the family is. She knows how her mother is. She knows how they all are. And they will rip you apart if they do not like you or think you're doing what they don't think you should, and they can't have control. So she did the best thing, which was smart. And that was to be private.

"You have to understand. Michael, Randy, and Janet, since they were young, were exposed to this kind of family behavior," Enid continued. "Every week, two or three times a week, they used to call family meetings. Everybody in the family had to come—I always called it 'the round table'—and everybody talked about each other, lied about each other, cried, cursed each other out. It got to the point where I stopped going.

"Michael never went. Randy never would go. Janet never would go. As she got older they asked Janet to attend the meetings and she said, 'No, I don't want to get in the middle of whatever is being discussed. Keep me out of it.'"

The strain created in Janet by her marital turmoil was obvious to everyone who knew her. "I couldn't take it anymore. Do you know what it feels like to have a ton of bricks in your head every day?" she said years later, when reflecting on her marriage. "And to lie awake at night unable to sleep?"

She was always nervous, never sleeping, and had gained a great deal of weight. When she's under stress, Janet has said, she tends to overeat. Rebbie has noted that her sister was "endangering her own health, risking a nervous breakdown." At one point Janet collapsed while taking a walk with James and had to be rushed to a hospital's emergency ward.

Each family member tried to persuade her that it would be best if she left James, but in the end it was Michael, during an emotional telephone conversation, who finally managed to convince her.

"Janet was a good girl," Steve Howell observed. "She just got in too deep. Michael knew how to talk to her, not down at her. He respected her. The feeling was mutual."

"God, I felt like my whole life was falling down. And I could see him going down, but there was nothing I could do," Janet admitted years later. "And James said to me, 'Well, you haven't tried to help me,' but I thought, 'What about helping yourself, too?' I felt myself going down with him and I thought, 'I can either go down with him and that's the end of my life, or I can just let go and continue on by myself.'"

Janet left her husband on January 7, 1985. She then filed for a petition to nullify the marriage and restore her former name, Janet Dameta Jackson. (In court papers, she claimed she was earning only $3,000 a month, and that she did not know how much her husband earned.)

When she returned from the courthouse, she immediately telephoned her friend René Elizondo and said, "God, I can't believe what I've just done."

The annulment would be granted on November 18, 1985.

Though Janet still resented her parents' intrusion in her life, nothing could ultimately interfere with the deep feelings she had for Katherine. She moved back home and took solace in her mother's protective arms.

"My mother was always there for me when I was feeling lonely and depressed," she recalled. "'Don't hold it inside,' she'd tell me. 'Let it out. Then let it go. Life is going to be like this at times. You just have to know how to deal with it.' Just to hear her say those soothing words and hold me meant so much."

"It wasn't easy for her," recalled Katherine. "She still loved James. I shared her pain."

Janet was stung by the criticism of some intimates who thought she should have stuck by James during this difficult time in their life. "Some people have said I was selfish," she acknowledged. "But there was nothing more I could do."

The end of the marriage was a great relief for the Jacksons, but a crushing letdown for the DeBarges, who, perhaps, felt Janet was to be James's savior. Says Etterlene DeBarge, "Part of me feels they could have made it, then another part of me feels they never could have made it because the odds were against them."

James has opted to blame the Jacksons—not himself—for the turmoil in his marriage to Janet. He insists that all of the couple's problems started when they moved into the family home, and that they were never able to rebound from that experience. "Moving in was the biggest mistake I ever made," he has concluded. "If I could have kept her out of there, everything would have been fine between us. But I was a fish swimming up the waterfall. There was no way I was going to win. It was them against me, and I lost."

chapter

SEVEN

It had been a demanding year. By early 1985, as a result of her tumultuous marriage and unsettled home life, eighteen-year-old Janet Jackson had matured in many ways that would be slowly revealed over the next several years. Above all else, she was proud to have survived such a ghastly time. She told friends that meeting these challenges head-on had encouraged her to believe that she was, indeed, a strong, self-reliant person.

"I had been sheltered," she admitted to reporter Lisa Robinson, "and there was good and bad to that. The good was not getting into drugs and alcohol. The bad was not being ready to deal with the real world.

"The first times I faced it were when I was on 'Fame' and when I got married. Being around kids on 'Fame' opened me up so much that when I was around my family, they'd say, 'Jan, you're so outgoing now.'

Actually, I was not really that outgoing, but compared to everyone else in my family, I guess I was."

"I survived really tough times," she told another reporter. "It amazed me. I didn't know I was that strong. I just never dreamed it. I'd be surprised if I ever again got as low as I did during that period."

In line with the Jacksons' tried-and-true tradition of image making and public relations, however, Janet Jackson would not dare publicly disclose the true reason behind the breakup of her marriage. Instead, she blamed the external pressures of her and James's careers. To *Interview* magazine, she said, "I just never got a chance to see James, and that was the major problem. A lot of people thought I was selfish to annul the marriage because I couldn't see him as much as I wanted to. But I feel that when two people are married, they have to spend time with one another, get to know each other more, share things with each other.

"At that time," she continued, "I had to leave at four in the morning to be on the set of 'Fame' to start shooting at six, and I wouldn't get home until nine-thirty at night. Sometimes we'd shoot on weekends. James would be in a recording studio at night and he'd be coming home just as I was getting up. It wasn't working right at all."

To another reporter, an exasperated Janet explained it this way: "There were people who didn't like it that James and I got married. So we decided to get an annulment so everybody would just shut up. . . ."

Janet apparently still had intense feelings for James, and in months to come, she acknowledged being distressed when girls told her they were dating him. "But I'm happy he's dating and getting out. I feel he's over it now. Even though," she added, "I spoke to his mother a while ago and she says he isn't. I think she wants us to get back together again. . . ."

"Oh, yes, I wanted them back together," James's mother, Etterlene DeBarge, confesses. "But I don't know that they could have made it. Other women were always in James's face, and Janet was very jealous.

"The big misconception about the Jacksons is that they are perfect. And, of course, that's not true of any family. The Jacksons have always tried to make it appear that they are one hundred percent pure, but they have the same kinds of problems any other family has. Katherine is strong, though, as are all the women, I think. And Janet was a stronger person after the marriage. That's for certain."

Though she obviously was more adult now than before, Janet chose, paradoxically, to move back home into the Encino estate—which the family now called "Hayvenhurst"—rather than stay on her own. She rationalized to one reporter that her intention was to move into a condominium, but that Katherine persuaded her to move back home.

"Even if you get married, you can come back here," she says Katherine told her. "You don't have to move out just because you're eighteen. You can be fifty-five and still live here." Janet said she was happy to move back, "because Michael and LaToya are there."

LaToya says that in retrospect, she was astonished at Janet's actually moving back home. "Most of us did whatever we could do to get out of there. And Janet moved back *in*." LaToya, who was single into her thirties, has said she tried a number of times to win her independence and move out onto her own. The problem was that Joseph was her manager, as he had been all of his children's.

*   *   *

Not every moment after Janet's return was smooth. For example, while she was always considered the family's tomboy, she felt more feminine after her marriage and often intentionally tormented male guests at Hayvenhurst by coming downstairs from her room wearing nothing but a long, sexy T-shirt. Michael was aghast at this kind of conduct.

"Just look at those fat, funky thighs," he would scream at Janet. "Now go back up and put something on. You never know who is going to be down there."

Janet usually countered with a barb directed at "your girlfriend, Brooke," who, Janet would pronounce, "looks like a cow."

Michael loathed it when Janet spoke derisively about Brooke Shields—a woman his sister clearly did not like or trust. "She's a goddess," Michael insisted of Brooke.

"Yeah, right," was always Janet's wearied response.

"Janet always had this good angel/bad angel thing going for her," says LaToya. "She liked to act innocent, but also liked to turn on the guys when she could, especially after her marriage. I think she was just experimenting, trying to find out how much she could get away with. She had become more aggressive."

(After her marriage, Janet did have experiences of love and sex that Michael and LaToya no doubt only fantasized about. Today, in 1994, both Michael and LaToya are approaching forty and seem, at least by some accounts, to be virgins. LaToya, who has been married nearly five years, says she never allowed a man to touch her prior to the marriage, and that the marriage itself has never been consummated.)

There were many fiery and troublesome scenes in the Encino home during the next couple of years. It certainly seemed to most observers—and this has been verified by both LaToya and Michael—that Joseph and Katherine simply did not want their children to leave the nest, and that most of them married at early ages in order to get their "release."

Sadly, Joseph was extremely insecure about his relationships with all of his children, except his illegitimate daughter, Joh' Vonnie, who he knew adored him. Joseph felt he had not only created the Jackson family, but had also made them quite rich and famous, and he believed all of his offspring were profoundly ungrateful to him. In fact, they seemed to resent him more every day.

But Joseph's children felt they had been badgered and intimidated by their father for years, as well as having been abused physically, emotionally, and, according to LaToya (where she and her sister Rebbie are concerned) even sexually. In fact, it would seem that the Jackson siblings never really got over their dysfunctional upbringing. "They have all been damaged beyond compare," longtime friend Joyce McCrae has said. "You have to feel terrible for all of them. They were such great kids and things could have been different."

In 1983, Michael and the brothers had severed their managerial relationship with Joseph in a bitter and, for Joseph, a sorrowful way. Now that his sons were gone, Joseph seemed to hold on to Janet and LaToya with a vengeance. LaToya says he threatened to ruin her if she tried to break her contract with him, that he said he would hunt her down if she ever dared leave home.

"You fool with me, you're messing with your

career," she says he warned her. "If you don't want me to manage you, nobody will know about you. You're *history.*"

At one point, LaToya packed her bags after a tremendous dispute with her father. Janet begged her to reconsider, but LaToya resolved to make her move. She was about to walk out the door when an enraged Joseph Jackson confronted her in the doorway.

"Just try to get past me," he told her menacingly. "Just try it."

A hair-raising verbal battle between father and daughter ensued, and just when it seemed matters were going to become physical between the two, Janet intervened. Telling her sister, "it just isn't worth it," she convinced her to stay.

"I felt like I'd died inside," LaToya later admitted. "Just a few feet away from freedom—*all I had to do was walk out that door*—yet I couldn't do it. Joseph's physical threats, Mother's planting fears in my mind, and Janet's pleas all held me back like some supernatural force."

Janet has indicated to friends that she felt LaToya was simply unprepared to go out into the "real world." Because her sister had been so sheltered all of her life, it was difficult for Janet to envision her fending for herself.

But even as she was urging LaToya to remain at home, Janet recognized that she herself was fully primed for life on her own, and that when the time came for her to leave Hayvenhurst, no one would be able to prevent her from doing so. "If he thinks he can bully me into staying, he has another thought coming," Janet said of her father. "There's no way he can make me do anything I don't want to do."

Joseph was not at all hectored by Janet's tough-girl stance. "She may think of herself as a little rebel," he told one reporter, "but she's still my daughter. She's always been just Janet Jackson to me."

"Janet was much stronger than Michael and LaToya when it came to dealing with Joseph," says one family friend. "Mostly, she just seethed at Joseph's behavior and bided her time until she was ready to make a move. She did not loathe her father as much as Michael and LaToya did, but she wasn't overly fond of him, either.

"Once," the friend continued, "LaToya told Janet that Joseph had said he loved her [Janet]. Joseph was never one to make those kinds of statements to his children, and Janet simply couldn't believe her ears when LaToya told her he'd said that. It seemed incomprehensible to her. She said never once did her father utter those words to her. 'He makes me sick,' she said of him. 'I wouldn't believe a word he has to say. I just pray for him, that's all.'"

Janet did not make that statement lightly, as she apparently became open to a new acceptance of spirituality after the annulment of her marriage. As she told her sister-in-law Enid Jackson, "I have a sense now that I can't go wrong, that I'm being protected somehow by a higher power. That's why I don't worry about Joseph and what he's going to do to me. Even if I stumble, I still find my way eventually. It's the one thing I learned for sure during the frightening time with James."

Interestingly, Janet decided during that period—1985—that she no longer wished to be considered a member of the Jehovah's Witnesses. Prior to their turning eighteen, Katherine had insisted that all of her children attend the Witnesses' local place of worship, Kingdom Hall in West Woodland Hills, California, on Sundays. At the age of eighteen, they were permitted to make their own decision about whether they wanted to continue as Witnesseses. All except Michael, Rebbie, and LaToya decided to drop out.

"I'm not a religious person," Janet told a reporter. "But I am spiritual. I certainly believe in God, but I want to respect God in my own way. I don't know that I believe in organized religion."

A well-known, and often criticized, manner in which most Witnesses present and explain their beliefs to others is by going door-to-door. Janet says she only did this twice, but was not happy with the results. "A lot of people made fun of it. I got upset if they slammed the door in our faces; I think it's very rude," she said. "I don't think that's the way you should treat a person. And I'm not just saying this because my family is in this religion. If it was another religion coming to my door, I wouldn't do that to them."

A family friend adds, "Janet told me about the first time she and her mother went door-to-door with their pamphlets and other reading material. It's called doing 'fieldwork.' She was about thirteen, and she really believed people would welcome the good news she and Katherine had to share about Jehovah. Well, she was in for a rude awakening. Most people felt they were being intruded upon and they slammed their doors in Janet and Katherine's faces. Katherine is used to this; she's been doing fieldwork for years. But Janet was extremely upset and even angry. She went one more time, but never again. As I recall, she told me that out of twenty homes, only two people would actually talk to her and Katherine. It was demeaning."

Michael continued as an extremely devout Jehovah's Witness; on the Victory tour he even hired someone whose only function was to locate a Kingdom Hall in each city so he could attend services. However, Jackson had a difficult time remaining a Witness after he became internationally successful with the *Thriller* album. When the church's elders heard about the video to the album's title track, in which, via masterful special effects, Michael is transformed into a werewolf, they insisted that he dispose of the footage, because it contained "verbal and visual references to witches, demons, and devils." After they met with Michael and told him he would be drummed out of the denomination if he defied them, he was so distraught he decided the fourteen-minute "Thriller" video—which cost $600,000 to produce—should be destroyed, never to be seen by his public. His attorney, John Branca, convinced Michael that this destruction of art was unnecessary and that a disclaimer at the beginning of the video (stating that Michael "in no way endorses a belief in the occult") would placate the church's elders. Michael discussed the matter with Janet and LaToya. Both agreed that Branca's idea would help mollify the Witnesses' higher-ups, so Michael allowed the video to be released with the disclaimer, which, in fact, did nothing to help matters and, instead, made Michael appear to be defiant.

"As if he doesn't have enough stress in his life," Janet complained privately. "He can't win."

The day after Michael won an unprecedented eight Grammy Awards (in February 1984) for *Thriller,* he was flying high with joy. But that same morning, the church brought him back to earth by issuing an ultimatum: he had to choose between his career and his religion because, as they saw it, he was encouraging people to "idolize" him. Michael invited an elder from the church to tour with him so it would be understood that he really was doing his best to live within the church's guidelines. What the elder saw on the road only served to make matters worse for the singer—his brothers and the group's musicians are not exactly saints.

The final, pivotal incident occurred in the spring of 1987. LaToya had stopped attending services because she was told she could no longer speak to a close friend who had been "disfellowshipped" (meaning expelled) from the faith. It was a difficult decision for LaToya to make—she says she had, and still has, strong religious convictions.

Then, one day, Michael came home from a meeting at the church and ran up to Janet's room, crying. Janet has recalled that her brother would not, at first, explain what had caused him to be so upset. Finally, she was able to understand that he had been told he could no longer speak to LaToya, since she herself had been officially disfellowshipped, though no one knew exactly why. To Janet, the church's edict seemed impossible to believe.

"That's crazy," Janet remembered telling her brother. "She's our sister."

Michael could not bear to explain any of this to LaToya—he was that unhinged—but Janet insisted he do so. When he complied, LaToya was incensed that her brother had been put into such a difficult position. Michael eventually decided he could not allow the church to keep him from his own flesh and blood, so he shot off a letter officially dissociating himself from the Witnesses. He was not kicked out, as reported by the press, although, from the Witnesses' standpoint, it might have been better for Michael had that been the case. Gary Botting, coauthor of *The Orwellian World of Jehovah's Witnesses* and a Witness himself, has stated that choosing to leave the religion is "worse than being disfellowshipped or kicked out." He said, "If you willfully reject God's only organization on earth, that's the unforgivable sin."

Rebbie and Katherine remained devoted to the strict, God-fearing faith; both are still Witnesses and say they are strengthened and empowered by their faith. Janet, however, went her own way. She told one friend, "I don't claim to understand all of the rules of the faith, but I believe in freedom of religion. Michael does, too. This particular religion just doesn't work for me or any of my siblings, except for Rebbie, who is married to a Witness. I have nothing bad to say about Jehovah's Witnesses, though, and I never will."

Katherine did not talk with her children about any problems they had with the Jehovah's Witness faith, and she has said she doesn't know why any of them dropped out of the religion. As she once explained, "Witnesses do not discuss spiritual matters with persons who have disassociated themselves from the Witnesses, including family members."

After her annulment, Janet was determined to get her career back on track. Her second A&M album, *Dream Street,* had been issued during the marriage. Produced by Giorgio Moroder, Pete Bellotte (famed for their work with Donna Summer), and Jesse Johnson, former lead guitarist for the Time, *Dream Street* was a passable album that sold a respectable 200,000 copies.

But Janet was disgusted with making records no one cared about. When she thrashed out the matter with Joseph, he told her she had nothing to say about this situation, that he would choose her writers and producers because he knew what was best for her. All he wanted from Janet was for her to be on time in the studio.

Behind her father's back, Janet telephoned executives at A&M and lambasted them because other female artists had records on the charts and she didn't. When Joseph heard about this, he was incensed with his youngest daughter.

"Stay out of it, Janet," he ordered her. "It's none of your damn business."

"I hate it when he acts as if I don't know anything, as if I can't do anything," Janet complained to a friend. "I want to be in charge. I am *ready* to be in charge. It's just a matter of time."

Janet was competitive and had no problem with being in a race to the top against complete strangers. But vying for top-dog position with her brother Michael was not easy. Though admitting it was difficult for her—and years were to pass before she would openly discuss it—deep down inside she really wanted to be as famous, as renowned, as Michael Jackson. "It was a secret goal," said a family friend, "one she dared not verbalize because she was afraid of how it would make her look."

John McClain, a twenty-nine-year-old vice-president of A&R (Artist and Repertoire) at A&M Records, had taken a special interest in Janet's career. She trusted him implicitly, for she had known him a number of years. (McClain, a family friend since 1968, used to change Janet's diapers. At one point, he attended the Walton Academy in Encino with several of Janet's brothers.) When Janet was trying to figure out what to do about her ill-fated marriage, she turned to John for counsel. In fact, it was McClain who first brought up the idea of an annulment. In the end, Michael convinced Janet that annulment was the appropriate step, but it was John who first planted the seed in her mind. "I did pry into her business a bit," he admitted. "I didn't think the marriage was a good move for her."

At first, McClain's involvement with Janet was strictly platonic and professional. He was the first to get her to admit that she wanted to be as successful as Michael, and in interviews he has acknowledged encouraging her in that regard. "She experienced guilt about admitting she felt competitive," McClain told writer J. C. Stevenson. "She was also scared that she'd try and fail. Well, Michael may not want her to be as big, but it's no sin for *her* to want it."

Also important in Janet's life after her marriage was René Elizondo, a young dancer with whom she shared a special friendship that flourished into an on-again, off-again romance. "Everyone loved René," Enid Jackson remembered. "He was a breath of fresh air after James. He was levelheaded and sensible; even Katherine and Joe liked him. He and John McClain helped convince Janet that it was okay for her to want to be a success, that competing with Michael was healthy."

But her ambitions weren't a hit with everyone. One day at home, for example, LaToya overheard a telephone conversation Janet was having with an A&M executive, one that startled her. Janet was telling the person on the other end of the line that she would not only be as great as Michael, "but I'm going to do a record that's going to be even bigger than *Thriller*. Wait and see."

LaToya felt obliged to run down the hallway to Michael's room to tell him what Janet had said. "How could she be that way?" Michael wanted to know. His feelings were hurt, but apparently neither he nor LaToya ever discussed the matter with Janet.

Both of Janet's siblings completely misunderstood her meaning. Every artist in the recording industry was competing with Michael Jackson, striving for an album that would outsell *Thriller*. And finally, Janet admitted that she, too, was one of the many artists out to beat his sales record.

"It was nothing personal," Jerome Howard, Janet's attorney, observed. "It had nothing to do with Mike, Janet's brother, and everything to do with Michael Jackson, the artist. Janet was determined to kick his butt on the charts. Michael wasn't really concerned," Howard added. "Mostly because he didn't think such a thing was possible. He didn't necessarily like the idea of Janet wanting to be bigger than he was, but he most certainly wasn't afraid she would be."

John McClain took Janet under his wing; he felt she had great possibilities. The first thing he did was send her to a "fat farm" to lose weight. He also insisted that she take dance lessons, and he began sending her to a vocal coach on a daily basis.

Janet was—and still is—insecure about the quality of her singing voice. She always longed for it to be stronger, more full-bodied, but that just wasn't in the cards for her. "A lot of people say, 'You know why your voice isn't strong? Because you didn't grow up in [an African-American] church,'" Janet has noted. "Now, Whitney [Houston] and Patti Labelle, *they* grew up in the church.' I don't know. Maybe that has something to do with it—my not growing up in the church—but I don't think it has *that* much to do with it," she mused. "I think the feeling comes from within. When you hear those gospel singers sing that way all the time, you try to pattern yourself after them. But I listened to Frank Sinatra and classical music when I was little.

"The majority of the people in my family have soft voices," Janet added. "Especially my grandfather. His voice is very high and soft."

John McClain recalls, "I've told her, 'Let Whitney [Houston] and Patti [Labelle] sing their lungs out. Just concentrate on being a female Michael Jackson and you'll give the people something even more exciting. After all, Luther Vandross is a better singer, but Michael's a bigger star because of the way he dances, because of the visual concept.'"

John McClain's presence in Janet Jackson's life was changing everything, including her stormy relationship with her father. "When I talk to Janet," McClain observed, "I'm her father, her brother, her shrink. She trusts me." Whereas Joseph didn't seem to care about Janet's opinion, John not only cared about it, he *encouraged* her to express it. "Janet has so much potential. She has cards she hasn't even showed yet," he said proudly.

None of this was music to Joseph's ears. "People know I'm the backbone of the Jackson family," he said. "As for Janet, I was putting her on stages in Vegas when she was still a little girl."

Indeed, Joseph seemed to regard Janet as a puppet. When he pulled the strings, she would give a convincing Mae West impression, sing what she was expected to sing, wear what he wanted her to wear. But to John, Janet was a diamond in the rough, a superstar in the making, a gifted, ambitious woman who knew what she wanted—fame—but just didn't know exactly how to get it. John McClain's objective was, as he put it, "to make her the queen of the music industry."

By the end of 1985, Janet Jackson also had a goal: to do anything she could to help John McClain achieve *his* goal.

chapter
EIGHT

Most observers didn't seem to feel Janet Jackson would ever realize the level of accomplishment John McClain envisioned for her. Considering all of her achievements in recent years, it seems difficult to imagine that back in 1985 most people perceived her as just another one of the more incidental Jackson kids, one with marginal talent. Indeed, Janet was thought of as nothing more than Michael's little sister, a sometimes convincing actress, half-decent dancer, and barely adequate singer.

But John McClain felt he had something special on his hands. "Janet's kind of quiet and shy, and the company didn't know how dynamic she is," he once recalled. "At the same time, I knew that Michael, Jermaine, Tito, Marlon, and Jackie are also real quiet—but when the red light is on in the studio or when the spotlight hits, they turn into different people. Basically, I had an idea of what Janet had in her."

John McClain wanted Janet's third album with A&M to be produced by Jimmy "Jam" Harris and Terry Lewis, former members of the Morris Day group the Time—all protégés of Prince—who were struggling to make a name for themselves as writers and producers. The duo had an infectious sound, an aggressive rhythm-and-blues approach, that McClain felt Janet needed to counteract any deficiency in her singing voice. (Janet, then sixteen, saw the Time perform in Chicago when she and Katherine attended a concert. She recalled that even though she enjoyed the show tremendously, she was mortified because the group was "s-o-o-o nasty." She said she had to move a few seats from her mother just to be able to enjoy it.)

Joseph Jackson was against having Harris and Lewis produce anything for his daughter. He wanted a more pop sound for her, something commercial enough to cross her over to a so-called white, or pop, audience. But because John held such an authoritative position at A&M, and because he had Janet's confidence, Joseph was overruled by the record company. John also determined that Janet should record the album at Flyte Tyme Studios in Minneapolis, far from her father's supervision.

At first, Janet was reluctant. She remembered, "Jimmy and Terry said, 'We want to take you out of the environment of having everyone do everything for you.' I said, 'But no one *ever* does anything for me!'"

In the end, Janet agreed.

This decision did not please Joseph and Katherine at all; it seemed that what they feared most was beginning to happen: they were beginning to lose their hold on another one of their children.

In August 1985, nineteen-year-old Janet, accompanied by close friend Melanie Andrews, left for Minneapolis to record her next album. "I come from a sheltered background," she observed to writer David Ritz. "And then suddenly I'm off to Minneapolis, and these guys, Jimmy Harris and Terry Lewis, are running around cursing like crazy. That made me so uncomfortable, I wanted to go home, until I saw they meant no harm or offense. They were merely talking the way they talk. They were being funny. They were being *real*. The problem was with my perception, not with their hearts. I was this little prude, I guess. I was uptight.

"I knew I wanted control—I believe strongly in creative control—but I soon saw I'd have to give in order to get: give myself over to a creative environment that was different from anything I'd ever known, and even a little dangerous."

The danger was not just in the studio's creative atmosphere. It was woven into the fabric of the big city, which was not exactly the same as life behind those big gates in Encino.

"It hit home when a couple of guys started stalking me on the street," Janet continued. "They were emotionally abusive. Sexually threatening. Instead of running to Jimmy or Terry for protection, I took a stand. I backed them down. That's how some of the songs were born, out of a sense of self-defense. Control meant not only taking care of myself, but living in a much less protected world. And doing that meant growing a tough skin. Getting attitude."

Many of the album's instrumental tracks were already recorded, but needed to be completed with lyrics and vocals. In fact, the instrumental tracks had originally been submitted to A&M recording artist Sharon Bryant, former lead singer of the rhythm-and-blues act Atlantic Starr. Bryant rejected them, leaving the door wide open for Janet Jackson.

"This was a new beginning for Janet," says her former attorney, Jerome Howard. "She really began to soar, being away from home like this, working with those guys so closely, having an input in the music, sharing her ideas with them, and being listened to. She would never be the same after this experience. She talked to the guys about her life and problems, and a lot of her feelings were incorporated into the lyrics."

Janet remembered, "I told them my whole story, what I wanted to do. I told them about things that happened in my life and what I really wanted this album to be about. I said, 'I need you guys to help me express how I feel, to help me get my feelings out.'"

Two months later Janet returned home with the tapes of the new album. She played them for Joseph, who promptly dismissed most of the songs as inadequate. He hadn't been permitted to hear the music prior to this time, and now that it was complete, he didn't like it, especially one of the tunes, "Control" (in which Janet declares her liberty from her father, saying, "When I was seventeen, I did what my father said, but that was long ago").

Janet was not particularly disheartened by Joseph's reaction, and neither was John McClain. "I would have been scared if Joe Jackson *had* liked what we did," said McClain boldly. "I wasn't trying to get a fifty-year-old audience. I was trying to get the kids. And because I'm a lot younger than Joe Jackson, I have a clearer vibe on how to do that."

The tone of the *Control* album, its biting boldness

and cocky swagger, made it appealing to younger audiences. On its January 1986 debut single, "What Have You Done for Me Lately?", the only thing funkier than Janet's tone—in the song, she mercilessly lambasts her boyfriend with all manner of reasons why he is a substandard mate—is Harris and Lewis' insistent, underlying groove, which took the record straight to number one. It was almost impossible for Janet to believe such a thing had happened, that she had a record on the top of the charts.

"She was walking around with her head in the clouds," remembered Jerome Howard. But John McClain was not surprised. "It's a great tune, Janet did a great job, and Harris and Lewis are phenomenal," he remembered. "Why shouldn't it have gone to number one?"

The *Control* album was released soon after the single. Indeed, much of *Control* had a bit of a male-bashing quality to it, which was not surprising considering the melodrama Janet had been through with her husband and was experiencing with her father at the time of its production. (Janet's influence on the material was direct, and her having contributed ideas and lyrics to the songs was acknowledged by her receiving cosongwriting credit on seven of *Control*'s nine songs and coproducing credit on all of them.)

During the album's funkiest song, the beat-heavy "Nasty," she demands that any male in hot sexual pursuit of her call her "*Miss* Jackson, if you're nasty." Janet's young followers had never really seen this type of hard-bitten attitude from a young, female R&B act, let alone a Jackson. Before *Control*, female confidence like this prevailed only among "old school" R&B artists, such as the controversial Millie Jackson.

Between Jackson's sauciness and beauty, and Harris and Lewis's irresistible beat, the public was immediately intoxicated by practically everything on *Control*. The album went to number one and would sell more copies—about seven million—than anything previously released on A&M Records.

The songs, either relentlessly dynamic or melodically romantic, were the perfect vehicles for music videos. Like Janet's career, the clips at first started out simple, with "What Have You Done for Me Lately?" emerging as a rather routine dance ensemble piece. On the record, Janet declares that anything a man did for his woman in the past isn't enough to sustain her interest in him in the present; what really matters is what he's doing for her *now*. However, by the time the black-and-white video "Let's Wait a While" was issued (featuring martial-arts expert/actor Taimak as her boyfriend), Janet found herself in an on-screen romantic mode, finally with an opportunity to call upon her acting skills.

The strategy of the long-form "Control" video, which featured a Harris-and-Lewis-led band behind an onstage Janet, was to establish the notion of Jackson as a confident stage performer. Meanwhile, the purpose of the video accompanying the relentless single "Pleasure Principle"—Janet alone, hoofing it up in a stark loft—was to present her as a prodigious dancer, able to captivate an audience by herself, without accompaniment. Both succeeded handily at meeting their objectives, though, to Janet's discontent, she is forever on videotape just a bit overweight in the clip of "Pleasure Principle," as she was in the album's third video, the throbbing "When I Think of You."

"I've been on diets since I was two years old," Janet

has admitted. "When I get depressed, I eat. Or, I can be eating the same way and my body totally changes and I gain weight. So for ten days I went to a resort in Arizona [Canyon Ranch] and worked out with some instructors. Then, once I came home, I kept up the program—walking every day for four miles, an hour a day. Then I started gaining it back, and by the time of that third video, 'When I Think of You,' I was pretty plump."

Control's unyielding quality as a quintessential mélange of R&B, pop, and funk is what made it tremendously successful. The album was so vibrant, so deep in strong tracks, that some of its best musical moments—such as the sexy, sensual ballad "Funny How Time Flies" and the rollicking vamp "You Can Be Mine"—didn't even see the light of day as singles.

The air of *Control*, its musical dynamism, its lyrical assuredness, is often credited to Janet and her coming-of-age as a young adult during its production. While this is partially true, the music also unmistakably reflects the hunger and bristling talent of Jimmy "Jam" Harris and Terry Lewis, who, before the album, were anxiously trying to prove themselves as hit writers/producers. *Control,* the musical platform on which Harris, Lewis, and Jackson based their future careers, worked well for everyone involved. At one point the album was selling 250,000 copies a day (in comparison with Janet's *Dream Street* album, which sold 200,000 copies total).

The album also established Janet's independence from her brothers. On *Dream Street,* Marlon produced two of the tracks; Jackie, Michael, and Tito contributed background vocals on one song; and there was a photo of the brothers on the inner sleeve. "I wanted the public to like *Control* because of me, not my family," Janet explained to writer Cary Darling of *Bam* magazine. "I didn't want them to say, 'Michael produced this song' or 'Jermaine or the rest of the brothers and sisters sang with her, so I'm going to buy it; it must be good.' I wanted it to be successful because of me and I wanted to prove that to myself."

For her simply to have held that ambition in theory or abstractly, as an ideal, might have garnered some respect from observers. "She's got an independent streak," they might have said. But for her actually to put everything on the line, do the album without her brothers' help, and be willing to take the professional consequences when she could still have played it safe—that was the mark of true courage, of genuine independence, of her as a free woman.

With the astounding success of *Control,* the battle lines were officially drawn between John McClain and Joseph Jackson. For months, the two hardly spoke without bellowing at one another. Janet didn't make matters between them any easier, because she had figured out that one way to survive in the Jacksons' home was to have John do her dirty work with Joseph. He did so gladly, but this did not ingratiate him with Joseph.

"Janet had people to fight her battles," LaToya has said. "If things got rough with Joseph, she could call on John [McClain] or on Jerome [Howard] to intervene. She was smart that way. She would just stay in her bedroom and wait until the shouting was all over before coming back out. I, on the other hand, had to fight my own battles."

"We're the dog with the bone that all the other dogs are trying to get," Joseph Jackson complained to writer

J. C. Stevenson for a *Spin* magazine cover story entitled "Damn It, Janet." "And the pressure is always on you to hold onto what you've got. I've worked hard for my family," he continued. "The problem comes, though, when others move in behind you and try to steal them away. Others tell them: 'We can do this for you, we can do that.' But the wheels had already been set in motion for Janet Jackson; anyone who jumps on now will be getting a free ride. And I don't intend to let that happen.

"I take nothing away from John McClain," Joseph concluded, somewhat bitterly. "But he works for a record company and he gets paid to do what he's done for Janet Jackson. He has no control over her. He's not in business to have control over her. Others try to jump on the bandwagon. I *am* the bandwagon."

And as for Janet's claim in the press that her parents treat John "like a son," Joseph retorted, "No, he is not like a son to me. John McClain has his own daddy."

Joseph Jackson had been down this troubled road before. He hired managers to handle Michael's and the Jacksons' career in the early eighties, and the next thing he knew his sons were taking direction from those outsiders and not from him. The sons generally regarded Joseph as having shrewd managerial ability, but no "people skills." Unfortunately for Joseph, the music industry is full of "people," all of whom have fragile egos and practically none of whom like to be browbeaten. Janet realized that her career would thrive at A&M if her father wasn't hanging around the offices intimidating everyone in sight, even if he was doing it with her best interests at heart. Not to mention the obvious: she didn't want him bullying her, either. Joseph Jackson's time was running out as far as Janet was concerned.

"It's family, but *I* take out my dad's percentage. After all," Janet reasoned to one reporter, "even though he is my dad, he's my manager and he works for me."

"If Janet listens to me and works a little harder," Joseph had said, "she'll be as big as Michael."

With the possible exception of Janet, all of the Jackson siblings have presented themselves in interviews as being intensely insecure, no doubt a result of tremendous emotional abuse heaped upon them during their lifetimes. Michael, with all of his money, fame, and power, seems perhaps the most insecure of them all. He had striven to be number one for years, always with an eye on the competition. Now, suddenly, his chief competition was sleeping down the hall from him—his baby sister, Janet. He did not handle it well.

"This was a tough time for Michael," remembered one family friend. "First, there was an awards show that Michael was supposed to attend with Janet. But he canceled at the last possible minute because he didn't want to be seen with her. He was afraid she would get more attention. Janet ended up going with René Elizondo.

"Then there was a nasty incident having to do with some choreography he had shown Janet that she inadvertently—or maybe not so inadvertently, only she knows—stole from him and used in one of her videos. He was livid about that and stopped speaking to her. For about a month, Michael wouldn't speak to her. When they passed in the halls, he snubbed her."

"I remember that," said family friend Byron Moore. "It was a difficult time. At first Michael was thrilled with her success; he loved the *Control* video when Janet screened it for him. But the more famous Janet got, the more threatened Michael felt. Finally, he didn't know how to handle it, so he just stopped talking to her. Janet was more annoyed than hurt by Michael's behavior."

"Michael and I are no longer close," Janet conceded in an interview in 1986. "Once a month, our family has a meeting and we're together then, but mostly we keep to our own areas in the house."

Janet had to admit that a certain pressure did exist, if only in her mind, about comparisons to Michael. "I keep imagining that everyone is looking at me, thinking, 'She doesn't dance as well as Michael,' or 'Her videos are not as exciting as Michael's,' or 'Is she going to be as successful as Michael?' They expect so much and I get very tired of it."

Michael's reaction to Janet's sudden fame seemed to most observers not to be vindictive but rather a very human response from someone of his temperament. "He didn't know whether to think of Janet as his sister or as someone he couldn't trust," LaToya observed. "It wasn't malicious as much as it was just confusion."

"Plus, the father didn't make things any better by pitting him against her," said another friend, "telling him Janet was on his tail, that he'd better come up with a strong follow-up to *Thriller* or he'd be finished."

Many observers felt Joseph had a vested interest in rubbing Michael's face in Janet's success. After all, Michael had fired him as his manager, indicating a lack of confidence in his father's judgment and in his wisdom. But, technically, Joseph was still Janet's manager. In other words, Michael's own father was managing his most formidable competition, his own sister. It seemed, at times, to be more than Michael Jackson could endure.

"He spent a lot of time in his room," said one of Michael's cousins. "He played Janet's album over and over and over again. Then he played *Thriller* over and over and over again. Then one cut from *Control* and one cut from *Thriller*, over and over. He became obsessed by trying to determine the value of each product. The family just left him alone to work this out. Really, you can't tell Michael what to do or how to feel. He's his own person."

Michael informed one of his advisers that he would delay the release of his next album until Janet had cooled down on the charts. "I can't compete with her," he fretted. "What if I lose? How will that look?"

But suddenly Michael changed his point of view. "Janet said he knocked on her door one night and had tears in his eyes," recalled Byron Moore. "He apologized for being such a jerk. He said he had prayed and prayed and come to the conclusion that there was room on top for both of them. He said he wanted her to become even bigger, and that he would never be anything less than supportive of her from that moment on. The two of them spent the whole night listening to each other's new songs and making comments about them. They had always been close, and it must have felt good to them to have that old feeling back."

"She's very serious," Michael Jackson said of his sister at the end of 1986. "People don't know that about Janet. You don't mess with Janet Jackson."

*　　*　　*

Sporting a black leather jacket, matching slacks, high-heeled boots, and hot orange lipstick, Janet Jackson pulled up to the security entrance of A&M studios in Hollywood one afternoon in December 1986. "What Have You Done for Me Lately?" blared out of her sleek Mercedes's sound system. Though she slowed down, the guard didn't stop her. He just waved her on with a big smile. Janet hit the gas pedal and the car screeched into the parking lot and glided into a space.

"Hey, girl," someone shouted at her as Janet got out of the car. "What's up?"

"Business," Janet said as she walked with a determined strut toward one of the A&M executive offices. "Business is up. And that's what I'm all about."

Indeed, Janet Jackson had arrived.

chapter
NINE

Reporters who have interviewed Janet Jackson or spent any time with her at all often comment that she seems to be "the normal one in the family." That observation may seem, by implication, to be characterizing the rest of the Jacksons unfairly; after all, who's to say what is normal and what is not in human behavior?

Nevertheless, it is true that Janet exudes a calm confidence and sense of security that appear to have eluded her siblings, many of whom seem bashful and skittish in public. Janet has been subjected to a considerable degree of familial and show-business pressure—at least according to best-selling published accounts of the family members' lives by Michael, Katherine, and LaToya, as well as the portrayal of the family on the ABC mini-series produced by Jermaine—and has managed to rise above it all.

Perhaps it's because she, as the baby, was sheltered by her brothers and sisters from much of the madness. Who really knows why or how Janet Jackson turned out the way she did—a sharp-witted, level-headed, usually rational young lady? The fact is, she did, and her inner strength and deep resolve are as much a part of her true personality as Michael's extreme sensitivity and LaToya's extreme fragility are parts of theirs.

By early 1987, Janet Jackson's brother Michael, now twenty-eight years old and a master media manipulator who, when it pleased him to do so, used the mechanisms of public relations to his greatest advantage, had fashioned a Peter Pan–like, fantasy image of himself for public consumption. "This is going to be my Bible, and I want it to be yours," Michael told his manager, Frank Dileo, and attorney, John Branca. He handed them a copy of P. T. Barnum's biography, and added, "What I want is simple: I want my life to be the greatest show on earth."

Janet didn't necessarily approve of the approach Michael was taking, but she conceded nonetheless that it was his business and none of hers. Janet has said, "Generally, I don't offer him advice. I think he knows what he's doing, even if I don't agree with whatever it is."

If anything, however, time would show that Michael was giving his kid sister some valuable lessons on what *not* to do if one wanted to be taken seriously as an artist.

First, Michael posed for a photograph in a futuristic-looking hyperbaric chamber at Brotman Memorial Hospital in Culver City, near Los Angeles. He instructed Frank Dileo to have publicist Michael

Levine submit the photograph to *The National Enquirer.* The tabloid was given permission to run a cover story about Jackson and the chamber in its September 16, 1986, issue—with the headline MICHAEL JACKSON'S BIZARRE PLAN TO LIVE TO 150 and a color photograph of Michael lying in the chamber in his stocking feet. Part of the deal with the tabloid was that the article include words such as *wacky* and *weird.* According to the story, Michael was sleeping in the chamber so he would live to an extraordinary age, whereas he was actually hoping, even if indirectly, to promote his $20-million, seventeen-minute, three-dimensional film, *Captain EO* (in which he starred for Disney Studios) by fostering an eccentric science-fiction image of himself. (*Captain EO* is still featured at Epcot Center in Orlando, Florida, and at Disneyland in Anaheim, California.)

Recalled reporter Charles Montgomery, who wrote the feature, "I had no reason to think it was untrue. Michael's manager, attorney, and his plastic surgeon all confirmed it. In other words, Michael put one over on us.

"In time, I realized that Michael Jackson likes to see himself portrayed in an absurd, bizarre way. In years to come, I did the biggest number of stories on Michael in the *Enquirer.* Before I ran anything, I always checked with his camp. I almost always had the full cooperation and support from Jackson's people."

When Michael Levine set up an interview for Frank Dileo with the Associated Press, Dileo confirmed the report, feigning great concern. He declared, "I told Michael, 'That damn machine is too dangerous. What if something goes wrong?' But Michael won't listen. He and I are in disagreement about this. He really believes this chamber purifies his body and that it will help him accomplish his goal of living to be a hundred and fifty."

When Joseph Jackson read about Michael's chamber in *Time* and then *Newsweek,* he ran up to his son's bedroom to see if the contraption was there. "But I didn't find anything," he said.

"I don't think I'd let Michael have it in the house anyway," Katherine added.

Obviously Michael's parents were not let in on their son's shenanigans.

And neither was LaToya or Janet. "I took a look in his room and there was no chamber gizmo," Janet said. "When I asked Mike about it, he just kind of giggled."

After the hyperbaric-chamber hoax, Michael released the equally preposterous story that he was intrigued by the ninety-seven-year-old skeletal remains of John Merrick, the so-called Elephant Man, and that he wanted to purchase the bones from the London Hospital Medical Center. At this time Michael was apparently trying to get publicity to promote *Bad,* his follow-up to *Thriller.*

"What's he going to do with the skeleton, Frank?" a reporter asked Dileo.

"I don't know, except that he'll probably put it in the room when I'm trying to have a meeting with him."

Katherine Jackson was concerned about the fact that Dileo was assisting Michael in "looking like an idiot." Upset, she met with Dileo. But her feelings didn't seem to matter.

Soon, as a result of these unusual stories and the firestorm of accompanying rumors, attention had shifted from Michael's artistry and showmanship to his alleged eccentricities. The tabloids had a field day with

Jackson, publishing so many false stories that determining which originated from Jackson's camp and which had been fabricated by unethical journalists became impossible. According to the tabloids: not only did Michael have a shrine to Elizabeth Taylor in his home, but he also wanted to marry her; he was concerned that Prince was controlling Bubbles the chimp with ESP; he had seen the ghost of John Lennon, who told him to allow Nike to use the Beatles' song "Revolution" in a television commercial; he refused to bathe in anything but Evian water (this one turned out to be true, when Michael actually tried it and liked it); he was having plastic surgery so he would look like Diana Ross (when Diana Ross heard that Jackson was refashioning his face to look like hers, her reaction was: "I look like *that*?"); he was having an affair with Princess Diana; he and LaToya were the same person (it was all done with mirrors— shades of "The Patty Duke Show"!); and so on, ad nauseam.

When *Playboy* magazine reported, "Rumor has it that the descendants of the Elephant Man have offered $10,000 for the remains of Michael Jackson's nose," Janet was bewildered by what Michael had wrought. "No gimmicks for me," she announced to her associates. "I don't know what Mike is doing. Maybe it works for him. Not for me, though. My personal image and my music will speak for me." (She later made the mistake of calling Michael an "oddball" in an interview with a London publication, which she quickly regretted.)

Michael was equally upset by how the onslaught of preposterous stories about himself seemed to explode out of control, but in the truest of Jackson traditions of image making, he blamed the media, not himself. "I don't know how they can write these untrue stories about me," he said. "It's all lies, and it hurts."

Of the hyperbaric-chamber situation, he told Oprah Winfrey during his much-publicized February 1993 interview with her that the story was "a complete lie."

Of the Elephant Man's bones story, he told Winfrey, "Another stupid story. Where am I going to put some bones, and why would I want them?"

"It's just part of showbiz behavior to deny knowledge of anything that reeks of the sensational," said one Jackson associate. "Michael's not about to admit that he threw the first punch with those early tabloid stories and that he's responsible for his own image. But he's also used all of this to his advantage. He's smart that way. In the end, the music will out."

"I don't know that Michael needed to do those things to get attention," Janet has said privately. "He's so brilliant, anyway. Why did he start all of that?"

Just before the hyperbaric-chamber story broke in 1986, Michael underwent yet another operation to make his nose slimmer. This was his fourth—and, as of early 1994, his last—rhinoplasty, or nose job. (He has also had a number of other corrective surgeries on his nose—each of which has been more a minor alteration than an actual rhinoplasty.) Now he was telling his family he wanted to have a cleft surgically dug into his chin. Katherine was so alarmed by this that she asked Janet to talk to him. Janet did, but got nowhere. Apparently, Michael's mind was made up.

It was clear to Janet, as she would tell friends, that

the reason for all of this plastic surgery was Michael's determination not to look at all like his father (as adults, the boys inevitably ended up resembling Joseph). "The trouble is," observed longtime friend Joyce McCrae, "no matter how much Michael tries to scrub Joseph off his face, he's still there."

Janet herself certainly has no problem with plastic surgeries; she's had several and been content with the results—the nose job at fourteen, then another (and, as of early 1994, her last) four years after that. Rumors, which she has denied, also have it that she underwent a significant amount of liposuction as well as some work on her breasts.

"I think if more people could afford it, they'd do it, too," she has said in reference to rhinoplasty. "I see nothing wrong with it." But still she felt Michael's behavior was excessive and compulsive.

All things considered, having had plastic surgery— or even several such surgeries—does not provide conclusive evidence that one grew up in a dysfunctional family. But it may be a pointer, a hint, an indicator that things were not as well balanced as they might have been.

Janet has told friends that she was saddened to see the apparent psychological damage done to Michael and LaToya by their upbringing. "I'm sorry it got to them the way it did," she told another family member. "I'm just glad it never really got to me. I've had to be strong; it's taken everything I have to get through it all. Sometimes I had to pray to God, 'Please help me keep my temper, please don't let me break down, please give me strength.' I was fortunate."

*   *   *

Among the Jackson clan, problems persisted. In 1987, the wives of two of Janet's brothers were divorcing them.

One of the greatest contributors to Janet's early success, singer/choreographer Paula Abdul, figured in the divorce of Janet's brother Jackie from his wife, Enid. Abdul was a twenty-one-year-old "Laker Girl," a cheerleader for the Los Angeles Lakers basketball team, when she was discovered by Jackie Jackson in 1985. Jackie felt she would be the ideal choreographer for Janet's early videos, inasmuch as Abdul had already proved herself by working on the Jacksons' "Torture" video. Janet liked Paula tremendously at first and felt she was genuinely talented. The two worked well together, and the results speak for themselves on Janet's exciting, early videos from *Control*—including "Nasty," "What Have You Done for Me Lately?", and the title track.

In time, Jackie began a romance with Paula, despite the fact that he was married to Enid and they had two children. As it happened, Enid Jackson was one of Janet and Michael's favorite sisters-in-law; the two spent most of their Christmases at Jackie and Enid's, since Joseph and Katherine did not celebrate the holiday.

"Janet and Michael were always at our house," says Enid. "They were two of the greatest kids, and we got along terrifically. I always felt a special kinship to them; they thought of me as a sister. Janet was, is, a very warm, sensitive person. She was always the first to *give*. She was never a 'taker,' but rather a 'giver.' And not just of material gifts, but of her love. She was a loving child."

Devastated by Jackie and Paula's relationship, Enid

decided to file for divorce. Unfortunately for all concerned, the divorce proceedings were particularly rancorous.

"I admit that my feeling about Jackie at first was, 'If you have one single penny left when I finish with you, that will be one penny too much,'" remembers Enid. "But after a while it was, 'Whatever it takes to get you and your girlfriend out of my life so I can go on, take it.'"

By the time the final decree was handed down in August 1987, the family had been divided between those who sided with Jackie and those who supported Enid. Janet supported Enid.

"Janet has never been one for infidelity," says Enid. "It's one of the things she has always held against her father, the fact that he cheated so openly on her mother. Janet has admired her mother for surviving that marriage, but said she would never tolerate that kind of behavior herself. Janet has said that when she settles down, it will be with a person she trusts will never betray her. I think, perhaps, she is more suspicious of men than most young girls are, because of what she has seen in her parents' marriage. That has to have an effect on a girl. I believe it's one of the reasons she sided with me."

The love shared by Jackie and Paula caused Janet to have serious second thoughts about working with Paula in the future. "Ultimately, Janet let her go and replaced her with some young guy [Barry Lather]," Enid says. "I don't know if it was because of what happened with Paula and Jackie, but I suspect, and I had heard, that it was.

"It wasn't all Paula's fault, however," Enid hastens to add, when speaking of her divorce from Jackie.

"She was wrong for breaking up my marriage, but Jackie was the older one. He had the commitment. Nobody forced him to do anything." Enid says she now realizes that beneath all of Paula's bravado— apparently Paula and Enid had a couple of physical altercations—she was just a bewildered young woman who had fallen deeply in love with a married man and didn't know what to do about the situation.

Publicly, Janet didn't offer much of an explanation as to why she replaced Paula as her choreographer. "I wanted to get a little bit funkier," she told *Jet* magazine. "Paula is a wonderful choreographer, but I wanted to do something else."

"The truth is that Janet was distraught at what was happening between Paula and Jackie," Marcus Phillips, a friend of the family, has said. "Janet and Paula never really got along after the first video anyway. They were like oil and water. Janet tried to be professional and overlook what was going on with Paula and Jackie, but it was difficult. However, LaToya often referred to Paula as 'Jackie's girl,' but Janet wouldn't hear of that, out of respect for Enid. In the end, Janet just didn't want to work with someone who was partially responsible for causing a certain amount of stress in her family. Janet was also very disappointed in Jackie.

"So was Michael, for that matter," says Phillips. "Michael liked Paula Abdul, though he didn't know her well. He thought she was talented. He figured his brother was probably to blame for the situation. Mike was busy anyway at this time with the *Bad* album promotion and preparing for his tour, so he didn't spend much time thinking about the situation.

"Paula's point of view was that Jackie's marriage

was in trouble long before she came along, and she shouldn't have to sacrifice the way she felt about Jackie for a marriage that didn't work. To Janet, that wasn't a good reason to get involved with a married man."

"It's none of my business," Janet told one friend. "But I just can't condone what's going on with Jackie and Paula."

After Paula had become a star in her own right— beginning with the 1988 album *Forever Your Girl,* which was in the top ten for a dizzying sixty-four weeks and yielded a string of number-one singles, including "Straight Up"—Janet said to writer Anthony DeCurtis, "I'm really happy for the success she's had. She's a very ambitious girl and I know that's something she's wanted deep down. I kept telling her she should pursue a singing career, and she kept saying, 'No, not just yet.'"

And as for being in competition with Abdul, Janet reasoned, "It's all competition out there. We're all reaching for the same spot. But I don't feel we're really competitors, I guess because I know her and love her. She's more like a sister than a competitor. We don't talk to each other as much as we used to, only because we've been busy."

Of Janet's professional relationship with Paula Abdul, Jimmy "Jam" Harris has said, "[Janet] had the ability to take someone like Paula, who was basically an inexperienced choreographer who'd done the Laker Girls, to take what Paula did and make it 'the thing' . . . not just another set of dance moves, but *the thing*. She takes what people give her, and she *sells* it."

*   *   *

For a period of time after the release of *Control*, there was a perception by some critics that Janet was little more than an assembly-line product: created by John McClain, choreographed by Paula Abdul, produced by Jimmy Harris and Terry Lewis. But such was not the case at all. In fact, McClain, Abdul, Harris, and Lewis were all novices, just starting out in show business. None of them had impressive track records. In a sense, Janet Jackson was taking a chance on all of *them.* "The question can be brought up: who raised who to what level?" observed Jimmy "Jam" Harris. "Bottom line: none of it would have happened without her."

Indeed, Janet's own drive, artistry, and creativity are what made all of those neophytes work so well together. René Elizondo told Robert Hilburn of the *Los Angeles Times,* "Anybody who has been around Janet for any period of time will tell you the same thing: that she is humble to the point of fault. She will not take credit for the things she is responsible for. She will always say, 'We did it' instead of 'I did it.' That's what we've been trying to point out to her. It's the way she was brought up. I've told her, 'Part of the perception people have is your fault because you won't tell them what you did.'"

Janet has countered with, "It sounds so selfish to say *I, I, I.* But it bothers me that there are people who think someone gave me an image or told me what songs to sing or what clothes to wear. I'm not a robot. I want people to know I'm real."

Certainly Paula didn't make things any clearer when she told *People* magazine, "Janet Jackson is my prize pupil. She worked her butt off for me."

"I'm happy for her success," Janet said of Paula. "But

I get upset when people say things like, 'Paula Abdul taught me how to dance.' You cannot teach someone how to dance. All you can do is show them some moves. We worked on the choreography *together*."

In October 1987, two months after Jackie and Enid were divorced, Hazel Gordy filed for a divorce from her husband, Jermaine, after nearly fourteen years of marriage and three children. Jermaine, too, had apparently become involved with another woman, Margaret Maldonado, whom he met one night in a restaurant. Both Hazel and Margaret were pregnant by Jermaine at the same time, much to Hazel's consternation. Jermaine's lady friend had her baby in December 1986; his wife had hers only a few months later, in March 1987.

Hazel seemed to have had a deep and abiding love for Jermaine, as she even offered to adopt the baby his girlfriend had given birth to. Jermaine, however, opted to stay with Margaret; the subsequent divorce from Hazel was heartbreaking and emotionally wrenching for all involved, as it was for any family member who was witness to it.

Eventually, Jermaine and Margaret moved into Hayvenhurst with their child, then had another baby. At first, Katherine was opposed to their moving into the Encino home on what she cited as "moral grounds." Perhaps it was difficult for her to handle the sad truth that her son had emulated her husband's conduct and fathered a child out of wedlock. In the end, though, Joseph insisted that Jermaine be permitted to move back home.

"I don't think any of the boys are happy with the things their father has done in the past," Jerome

Howard has observed. "But some of them certainly turned out to be just like him. Let's face facts. What's that saying about the apple not falling far from the tree?" One could put it charitably and suggest that both Jermaine and Jackie reached adulthood with a certain amount of confusion about marriage and fidelity.

"Janet was extremely disheartened by Jermaine's behavior," says one of her confidants. "She said she just couldn't understand what would possess him to treat his wife the way he had. But deep down inside, she probably understood that these boys were raised with skewed ideals. It's not surprising that, as adults, they would be somewhat confused."

Certainly, given Jackie and Jermaine's divorces, life at Hayvenhurst was filled with turmoil. "There was a lot of craziness going on," remembered Steve Howell. Howell, an excellent photographer, was employed at first by the Jacksons as a maintenance and repair man. Soon, though, he was hired by Michael as his personal videographer—which meant he shot videotape of the family around the house, tape that would be saved for posterity. Thus he observed a lot of the Hayvenhurst goings-on.

"I thought LaToya was a bit schizophrenic," he recalled. "One second, she was her age and rather nice. The next she was very young and spoiled. She would *make* you do things for her. 'Go park that car' or 'Get me some food.' Never 'please.' It was just the way she was raised. You couldn't really blame her, you know? She was a little princess.

"Once, she ordered me to go into her room and fix her TV. I had a weird feeling I was being set up. I went in and she was standing there in a sheer robe with lots of cleavage showing. This was unlike LaToya. She was always covered from head to toe. So I immediately got nervous.

"'My TV doesn't work.' She pouted. 'Fix it. Now.'

"I was a nervous wreck, wondering what she was up to," Howell continued. "This is the way everyone felt who worked in that house. You were always wondering what they were up to. It made you paranoid. I didn't give her ten seconds to cause a problem. I put blinders on, as if I was riding in a New York subway, then fixed her TV as quickly as I could. I swear, the whole time I was up there, I was waiting for her to start screaming, 'Rape!'

"Janet had a little more heart," Howell remembered. "She was less conceited, but still a diva. For instance, she and her sister thought of the guards who worked at the house as kind of lower class. They treated them badly.

"Janet was very demanding and obviously over-indulged. If you did something wrong, she'd fire you on the spot. If you were a grounds person, for instance, and you said something to Janet that she didn't like, she'd call you on it and fire you so fast your head would spin.

"They tested you a lot," he remembered. "Janet, LaToya, and Katherine had a big walk-in closet full of furs and jewels. Sometimes they would disconnect the alarm, just to see who would go in there. Then they'd all stand in the corners, out of sight, and keep watch. It didn't make any difference. No one dared go near the damn closet anyway.

"Once, someone was ripping off money. Janet thought it was the maid. So she and Katherine started leaving money around the house. Then they hid and

Daddy's little girl. Janet, age two, in 1968. With her father, Joseph.

Mommy's little helper. Janet, age three, in 1969. With her mother, Katherine.

A family photo of the Jacksons, taken in June 1970. Top row: Jermaine, fifteen; LaToya, fourteen; Tito, sixteen; Jackie, nineteen. Bottom row: Michael, eleven; Randy, eight; Katherine; Joseph; Janet, four; and Marlon, thirteen.

Janet's brothers, horsing around on the basketball court in late 1969. Clockwise from center: Michael, eleven; Marlon, twelve; Jermaine, fifteen; Tito, sixteen; Jackie, eighteen; and Randy, eight.

June 1971. Michael, twelve; Randy, nine; Marlon, fourteen; and Janet, five.

Janet has said she always felt closest to her brother Michael, pictured here at the age of twelve.

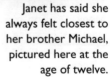

In September 1971, Janet's brothers, The Jackson 5, starred in their own cartoon series.

The Jacksons at the end of 1972. Well, they certainly *looked* happy . . . Top row: Jackie, twenty-one; Katherine; Joseph; Janet, six; Jermaine, eighteen; Michael, fourteen. Bottom row: Marlon, fifteen; Randy, eleven; Tito, nineteen; and LaToya, sixteen.

After the family became successful, Katherine took on a more glamorized look. Here's Janet's mother on a shopping spree during a tour of Japan in 1973.

His children have said they rarely saw him smile, but here's Joseph Jackson at son Jermaine's wedding to Hazel Gordy in December 1973.

From left to right: Janet, seven; Katherine; Marlon, sixteen; and LaToya, seventeen. With Jermaine, nineteen, at his wedding, December 1973.

Janet made her performance debut with The Jackson 5 at the MGM Hotel in Las Vegas, but received no marquee billing.

On opening night, April 9, 1974, seven-year-old Janet and her twelve-year-old brother Randy were the hits of the Las Vegas show with their impression of Nelson Eddy and Jeanette MacDonald . . .

. . . and Groucho Marx and Mae West . . .

The Jackson kids in April 1975. Clockwise from bottom center: Janet, eight; Randy, thirteen; LaToya, eighteen; Michael, sixteen; Jackie, twenty-three; Marlon, eighteen; Tito, twenty-one; and Rebbie, twenty-four.

. . . and Sonny and Cher.

Janet, nine; and Randy, thirteen; in June 1975.

Janet at home in Encino.

Janet and Randy in August 1975.

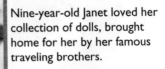

Nine-year-old Janet loved her collection of dolls, brought home for her by her famous traveling brothers.

The Jackson girls in October 1976, from left to right: LaToya, twenty; Janet, ten; and Rebbie, twenty-six.

When the Jacksons left Motown to sign with CBS, the family held a press conference on June 30, 1975, in New York, to make the announcement. From left to right: Joseph; Katherine; Jackie, twenty-four; Tito, twenty-one; Marlon, eighteen; Janet, nine; Michael, sixteen; and Randy, thirteen.

Janet, age eleven, in December 1977.

What a face!

In September 1977, eleven-year-old Janet became a regular on the popular CBS-TV situation comedy, "Good Times." She portrayed an abused child, Penny Gordon. Here she is pictured with her "TV Mom," Ja'net DuBois.

Janet's sister, twenty-four-year-old LaToya, in a glamour shot from 1980.

7810
24
1956

In happier times, LaToya shares a dance with older brother Jackie, while father, Joseph, watches.

Some of the Jackson women in June 1980. Left to right: Carol Parker Jackson (Marlon's wife); Janet, fourteen; Enid Jackson (Jackie's wife); Tana Terrell (Enid's sister); and LaToya, twenty-four.

Three months after this photo was taken in July 1980, fourteen-year-old Janet and eighteen-year-old Randy were accused of joining forces with their mother, Katherine, in assaulting Gina Sprague, a woman they suspected of having an affair with their father, Joseph Jackson. From left to right: Janet's grandmother, Chrystal; Joseph; Gina Sprague; Marlon, age twenty-three; Janet; and Randy.

On the set of the "Fame" TV series in July 1984, eighteen-year-old Janet seemed troubled . . . and with good reason. She had fallen in love with and married James DeBarge, who had a serious drug problem.

Janet and husband, James DeBarge, at the American Music Awards, January 28, 1985.

Janet, twenty, with her boyfriend, René Elizondo, in January 1987.

Janet performed at Madison Square Garden in January 1987. By this time, she had taken control of her life and was a new, independent woman, promoting a hot new album entitled, appropriately enough, *Control.*

On April 20, 1990, the Hollywood Chamber of Commerce honored twenty-three-year-old Janet with a star on the Walk of Fame. By this time, her *Rhythm Nation 1814* album had already sold in excess of five million copies.

Janet's sixteen-year-old half-sister, Joh' Vonnie, poses with a Janet Jackson Rhythm Nation tour jacket in 1990. If she's looking for a letter from Janet, she can forget it. She and Janet have never even met.

In November 1990, *Billboard* magazine honored twenty-four-year-old Janet with eight Billboard Awards for her *Rhythm Nation 1814* album.

On February 24, 1993, twenty-six-year-old Janet presented
her thirty-four-year-old brother, Michael, with a Grammy
Lifetime Achievement Award. The affection she feels for
Michael is evident.

spied on the maid. Sure enough, they saw the maid put the money in her pocket. Janet jumped out and said, 'Aha, gotcha!' They fired her ass so fast, she didn't know what happened; her head was spinning.

"Janet and Michael got along well," Howell continued. "They were always together, doing things, planning what they would do next. They were inseparable, and LaToya always felt left out.

"LaToya and Michael would fight a lot. 'Your voice is extremely irritating,' Michael used to tell her. 'You sound like Carol Burnett.' Sometimes I'd see Janet and LaToya together, and when I did, it was odd, because they weren't together that much. I think they were close, but it was hard to tell by watching them.

"I seldom saw Katherine and Joe together," he recalled. "He'd come and go. When he left, there was always a big sigh of relief and everything was mellow. When he was around, it was tense and uneasy. As for Janet and Joe, they didn't say much to each other. Mostly, they ignored each other. At least that's how it appeared to me."

Many people who have worked at the Jacksons' Encino estate recall that fans who stalked the Jacksons constantly—congregating outside the front gate— sometimes broke into the grounds and terrorized its occupants. Occasionally, girls stripped naked at the front gate, hoping to entice the Jackson men as they drove in and out of the property. Once, a woman was found living in the premises' recording studio. She'd been there for days, her only sustenance being sweets from the Jacksons' own candy store (which Michael had built on the property, near the studio).

"There were a lot of times when they got too close," Steve Howell recalls. "A couple of times I really was worried. Once, a woman actually snuck through the gate, met Michael in the driveway, and got him in a bear hug. Security hustled her out of there fast. Some of them were wacky. The Jacksons were like prisoners. 'Don't let any of them get to me,' Janet and LaToya used to say. 'As long as they're on the other side of that gate, we're fine.'"

One former estate security guard remembered, "Once, I was at the front gate when Janet came racing up the drive in her car from the outside, through the open gate, and up to the house at what seemed like a hundred miles an hour. She hit the brakes so hard when she reached the end of the driveway, we thought she must have hurt herself. Three of us raced to the car. Inside, Janet was sitting at the wheel, crying, babbling that someone was after her. 'He's been following me,' she said. 'He's after me. I don't know who he is, but he's after me.' I could never make heads nor tails of it, but we reported it to the police anyway. Janet didn't leave the house after that for about a week.

"Another time Janet was lying out at the pool in a bathing suit, soaking up the California sun, when a young stranger suddenly approached her. Janet absolutely freaked out. 'How did you get in here?' she demanded.

"He was obviously deranged. He said he was sent from God to save her, and that he was going to take her to heaven with him. Then he started stripping off his clothes. As I was running to her aid Janet let out a scream so loud you could hear it around the world.

"The other guards and I were at her side in no time. 'How did you let this guy slip in?' Janet hollered at us as we hustled the intruder out of there. 'I could have you all fired,' she screamed. 'In fact, I will. That's what I'll do,' she threatened. 'I'll have all of you fired.'

"She was distraught, and with good reason. 'I'm not even safe behind these gates. This place is a goddamn prison. And I'm not even safe in it.' She went on and on.

"Just as she was letting us have it, Joe came out. Janet ran to him like a five-year-old going to Daddy and he held her in his arms for several minutes until she calmed down." For those brief moments animosities and family tensions were forgotten as something more primal was experienced. *A father was protecting his daughter,* and that surely was nourishing to both of them—perhaps in a deeper way than either might have consciously recognized at the time.

Despite any fearful thoughts about the outside world, twenty-one-year-old Janet decided in late 1987 that the time had come for her to leave Hayvenhurst and move into her own place, a condominium in Bel Air she would share with René Elizondo. "I can't be behind these gates forever," she said.

"But it's dangerous out there," Katherine warned her. "What if something happens to you?"

Janet has said she told her mother she had to try, and that René would take care of her if anything happened.

There was no argument or discussion about it. Just as Janet had once unemotionally predicted, Joseph and Katherine had little choice but to let her go when she decided the time had come. And just as coolheadedly, Janet instructed her attorneys to work out an agreement whereby Joseph would no longer manage her career. "She's no dummy," says Joyce McCrae. "She knew there was a reason why Michael and his brothers left Joe, and she didn't trust her father's management, either."

It seems difficult to believe, considering the angst that surrounded similar occurrences between Joseph and his children, but the split with Janet was relatively peaceful. Janet thought it would be easy to tell her father that she no longer wanted him to manage her. She probably rehearsed her "going-away" speech a dozen times. But in the end, when she was finally face-to-face with Joseph and had to strike the same blow that Michael and her brothers had delivered, Janet found herself practically speechless. She actually started to sob.

"It would have been easier for Mother to tell him for me, but that was something I had to do for myself," Janet has remembered.

As she sat there with Joseph in his den, her remarks seemed to get caught in her throat. "I couldn't say the words," she has remembered. "I was bawling like a baby. And finally he just said, 'You don't want me involved in your career? Is that it?' 'Yes,' I finally found the nerve to say. 'That's it.'"

Firing her father was much more emotional for her than Janet had ever dreamed it would be. That was a surprise, since she doesn't think of herself as weak or emotional. But suddenly there she was, ten years old, telling her daddy she didn't want him around anymore.

Letting Janet go was difficult for Joseph, but inexplicably—considering how difficult he made it for his sons to defect—he decided not to fight her.

"It broke his heart, I'm sure," said Joseph's friend Larry Anderson. "Janet was his baby, so he put a lot of love and care into her career. He only wanted the best for her.

"Look, if it wasn't for him, I don't think she would ever have started singing. He pushed her out onto that stage. She was scared to death. It wasn't as if she had this terrific drive in the beginning, this goal to be a star. She was just a kid; singing was a hobby. Joe encouraged her, groomed her, made her rehearse when she'd rather be out there playing. And then when she got big, really big, she started listening to outsiders tell her she could be even bigger if it wasn't for her father.

"Joe isn't always the best businessman," Anderson concluded, "but no one cares about his kids as much as he does, and that's a fact."

"I believe Janet was [Joseph's] favorite," said Susie Jackson. "I saw his face light up a couple of times because of something she did or said. If there was a disagreement between the kids, he'd side with Janet. Because she was the youngest, I think he felt she needed to be watched over."

"You have my blessing," Joseph told Janet. With tears in his eyes, he hugged her. Then, dejected, he slowly walked out of the room, leaving her to wonder what had just happened.

"I will always give Joe a percentage of my royalties," Katherine recalls Janet saying. "I just want to do that."

To *Rolling Stone* magazine, Janet explained, "I needed to grow and do things myself. It becomes real difficult, when your family is your business, if you've hired a family member to do a job for you. I don't think it's something I would ever do again. Because they're relatives, sometimes they feel they should get breaks. You can't yell at them—that sounds so awful—and you can't really get after them if something has gone wrong."

To another friend, Janet described their parting this way: "I just packed up and left. I hated to leave

Mother. But the time had come. As for Joseph, well, it was harder than I thought it would be. He just watched me walk out the door. He didn't try to stop me, as he had done to LaToya. Maybe he knew I would not allow it. I refuse to suffer in this life like poor LaToya."

LaToya, by this time, thought she had finally found her knight in shining armor. She was beginning to depend on Jack Gordon, a businessman who had been put in charge of her career by Joseph. In 1981, Jack served four and a half months in prison for a bribery conviction in Nevada. Joseph and Katherine knew about his arrest when they allowed him—he always seemed to be a caring and well-meaning person—to work with LaToya as a manager in a position under, *way under,* Joseph.

Eventually, Jack began sincerely to care about what happened to LaToya on a personal level. She always seemed so dispirited; he wanted to assist her in some way.

LaToya suffered from severe insomnia. "Sleeplessness brought about the breakdown of my body," she recalled. "My blood was not circulating properly. Soon my hands, fingers, and arms were numb, cramped all the time, and they became almost paralyzed."

"I walked the halls at night," LaToya has said. "When Janet was living at the house, I would peek into her room and see her sleeping like a baby. I envied her so much. It was as if she had no problems, or they were all under control. I wondered what her secret was. . . ."

"Something is wrong with my sister," Janet once

told Celia Lopez, a woman who worked in the Jacksons' house in a domestic capacity. "I want you to keep an eye on her today. Don't let her out of your sight. I'm afraid she might hurt herself. Do you understand?"

"Miss Janet was extremely worried about Miss LaToya," recalled Lopez. "She cared about her deeply and felt, I think, that Miss LaToya was hiding something, that she had secrets. Miss Janet said she was determined to find out what they were.

"She and Miss LaToya took long walks, and Miss LaToya would cry and cry. I never knew what they were discussing. I watched from the window as they played with the animals, talked, and cried.

"Once, Miss Janet came running into the house, tears streaming down her face. 'Miss Janet,' I said to her, 'what's wrong? What can I do for you?'

"'Just leave me alone, you,' she screamed. 'My life is a mess. My sister's life is a mess. My brother's life is a mess. I hate what's going on here. I can't take it another second.' Then she slammed the door in my face. For hours afterward, I heard sobbing coming out of her room.

"Then, suddenly, the tables were turned," recalled Lopez. "I was working in the kitchen later that day when Miss LaToya came over to me and said, 'Hey, you. You keep an eye on my sister, do you hear me? I'm afraid she might hurt herself. If anything happens to her, it will be your fault. I'm going to bed.'

"It seemed as if I was on a suicide watch. Before I retired, I knocked on Miss Janet's door to see if she was okay. There was no answer. I knocked again. No answer. So I became very concerned. 'Oh my God,' I thought, 'she's killed herself.'"

Rather than go into Janet's room—"I was told never to open the door to any of their rooms, under any circumstance"—Lopez ran to LaToya's room. The door was open; LaToya was pacing the floor in the dark. The television was on, a test pattern glowing on the screen.

"Something's wrong with Miss Janet," the domestic told LaToya. "Come, quick. Please!"

"What? What's happened?" LaToya screamed.

The two of them ran across the hall to Janet's room and LaToya burst in. "Miss Janet was in bed, on her back. She looked dead. My heart stopped," Lopez recalled.

"Miss LaToya started shaking her. 'Janet! Janet!' she screamed. She was frantic.

"Then, suddenly, Miss Janet came to. It turned out that she'd been sleeping the whole time. And she was sleeping so soundly, it was as if she was dead. She had worked herself into such an emotional state that day, she just knocked herself out. She was that exhausted.

"'How can you sleep like this?' Miss LaToya screamed at her, shaking her by the shoulders. 'What's wrong with you? How can you sleep like this when so much is going on around here? I can't sleep at all! How dare you! How dare you!' She was practically hysterical. I felt terrible for both girls. I wanted to hold them, as if I were their mother. They needed love. It was so clear to me. They were so afraid.

"Miss LaToya ran out of the room, sobbing. She went into her bedroom and slammed the door.

"Miss Janet just sat in bed, dazed.

"Working there was an unusual experience," the

domestic concluded, in what seemed like one of the great understatements of the decade. "There was always so much stress. When I left, I was a nervous wreck. I saw LaToya once in a drugstore about a year after I left, and she didn't even recognize me. She didn't have the vaguest idea who I was, and I worked there for two years."

Jack Gordon suspected that something was troubling LaToya, that she had been affected in a deep way by some traumatic event in her life. In fact, he suspected the worst. When he asked LaToya if she had ever been beaten by her father or abused in any other way, she said no. However, he didn't believe her. Soon he was setting up appointments for her without Joseph's involvement—all in an effort to pry her from her father's tight grip. It was obviously what LaToya, who was in her late twenties, desperately wanted.

Though Jack was inching his way into her personal life, LaToya was still being managed by Joseph; therefore, the battles between Joseph and LaToya and Joseph and Jack raged almost daily. Soon Joseph and Jack were having violent altercations. ("Joe, you're going to kill him," Katherine screamed during one particularly nasty run-in.) All of this conflict and anger was more than LaToya could stand, and at one point she actually considered suicide.

"Miss Janet and Miss LaToya were sitting at the kitchen table," recalled Celia Lopez, "and I heard Miss LaToya say, 'What would you do if I just killed myself?' I had my back to them. I didn't dare turn and face them, but I couldn't help listening.

"'How can you ask that?' Janet wanted to know.

'Nothing is so bad. Believe me, when I was married, there were times when I thought I'd like to be dead.'

"I was shocked to hear this conversation.

"'I had some pills,' Janet said. 'I got them from Mother's medicine cabinet. And one night I decided to take them all. I just wanted to be dead. I couldn't take it anymore. So I prayed that night and didn't take the pills. The next morning when I woke up I was glad to be alive. Things pass, LaToya,'" Lopez remembered Janet saying. "'You'll look back on all of this one day and be proud of the fact that you were strong.'"

Finally, much to LaToya's relief, Joseph agreed to comanage her with Jack. But it became clear that Joseph still wanted to control his daughter's life and career, and that he was just placating her by allowing her to think he wasn't really involved in her career. Actually, he was still pulling the strings.

"You're the only Jackson I'm managing now," he said to her. "And I'm not letting you go!"

"It was hardest for Joe to release LaToya, because she was the last one who wanted to leave," Katherine has said. Indeed, it would seem that LaToya's move was just as difficult for Katherine, who also discouraged her daughter from leaving home.

LaToya leaned on Janet for help. "There must be a way out of this mess," she told her sister. "Help me. You did it. How did you do it?" she pleaded. "Please, tell me."

On a radio interview show, LaToya remembered Janet telling her, "You absolutely cannot let them get to you. You have to find that place deep down inside where they can't touch you, LaToya. And then you have to draw upon that for strength."

At this, LaToya recalled crying and saying, "I've tried. But they're too strong for me. I just can't do it."

" 'Toya, as long as you feel you can't," Janet told her sister sadly, "you won't."

chapter
TEN

The year 1988 saw the defection from Hayvenhurst
first of Janet Jackson's superstar brother Michael (who
was thirty in August) then of her sister LaToya (who
was thirty-two in May).

Michael subsequently purchased a 2,700-acre ranch
estate in Los Olivos, California, in Santa Barbara
County, for $17 million, changing its name from
Sycamore Ranch to Neverland Valley (early reports
that he paid $28 million for the property turned out to
be untrue). His parents first heard about the extrava-
gant purchase on the television program "Entertainment
Tonight." Michael hadn't exactly been in a commu-
nicative mood of late.

"It was like a Howard Hughes situation," Joseph
noted. "We had to go in his room every so often and
see if he was alive."

Michael was on the road when escrow closed on his

property; upon his return, he moved in immediately. He didn't invite his parents to his housewarming party or to the fete celebrating the kickoff of the European leg of his tour, which would keep him busy practically all of 1988.

"That hurt us," said Joseph of the obvious snubbing. "Of course, I can always go drag him out of there. He's never going to get too big for me to go get him. And he knows I'll come get him, too. But we wonder why things have changed like they have, why he doesn't seem to care about his family."

Both Katherine and Joseph were already upset about Michael's 1988 autobiography, *Moonwalk,* in which the superstar charged that his father had physically abused him. Being snubbed just added insult to injury.

"I don't know if I hit him or not," Joseph said in his own defense. "But if I did, he deserved it."

Janet observed: "Mike was wrong to say he was physically abused. That's not really true. He was *whooped,* but not abused. People just don't get it. African-Americans use the word *beat,* but that's not always what they mean. I have black girlfriends who will say to me, 'We got *whooped* as kids,' but they don't mean *beat up*."

One friend remembered, "Janet tried to get in touch with Michael when he moved into the new house, but he wouldn't return her telephone calls. Finally, she tracked him down. 'What's the matter with you, Mike?' she told me she asked him. 'How can you not call me back?' Michael told her he was afraid she was just calling to spy on him, to report back to their parents on what he was doing. Janet was hurt. She said she would never do that, that the two of them were soul mates and needed to stick together."

Three days after Michael moved out, Janet received a phone call from LaToya.

"I'm moving out," LaToya said.

"Well, good for you, 'Toya," Janet responded. "Good for you, girl."

"I'm going with Jack," LaToya told her.

"Oh, no," Janet exclaimed. "You're not!"

Janet certainly wanted LaToya to move out of the Encino home and become independent, but she felt her sister was jumping from a bad situation to a worse one by leaving with Jack Gordon.

Celia Lopez, the family's onetime domestic, picks up the story: "Miss Janet came running into the house one day. I was standing in the foyer in front of the staircase with a large crystal vase of flowers in my hands. 'Outta my way,' she screamed at me. She pushed me aside, and I almost dropped the vase."

Janet bounded up the stairs, two at a time. Fearing there might be trouble, the domestic followed.

"When I got to the top of the stairs, I heard Miss Janet screaming at Miss LaToya. 'Are you crazy? Are you crazy?' she was shouting at the top of her lungs. 'Have you lost your mind? You are not leaving with that man. I won't allow it. I just won't let you go. He'll ruin your life.'"

According to Lopez, LaToya told Janet, "You cannot run my life. Jack cares about me. He's going to get me away from here. And don't you try to stop me. You're as bad as Mother. All you want is for me to be miserable and live here for the rest of my life. I want out."

"That's not true," Janet said, defending herself. "I love you. Don't you know that? I want what's best for you. But this man is going to destroy you, then all of us. I can just see it happening."

"They had a terrible fight," said Lopez. "Clothing was flying out of the room and into the hallway. They were screaming at the tops of their lungs. I heard Miss LaToya say, 'I can't live here with you, Janet. You're so perfect. Your life is so perfect. Nothing bothers you. You're not even *human*.'

"Then, all of a sudden, Miss Janet bolted out of the room. 'That's it,' she said as she rushed by me. She was furious. 'I'm sorry, but I can't save LaToya. I just can't take it anymore. She's going to have to learn for herself.'"

Janet bounded down the stairs, two at a time. She ran out of the house, leaving the front door open, got into her automobile, and screeched away.

Celia Lopez concluded: "At just that moment Mrs. [Katherine] Jackson came out of one of the rooms. 'What in the world is going on?' she asked me.

"'I don't know, ma'am,' I said. 'I just don't know.'"

LaToya was almost thirty-two when she finally found the strength to move out of the Jacksons' home. She had one of her attorneys send her father a letter—even though she was living in the same house with him—to inform him that he would no longer be her manager when their contract ran out in March 1988. Joseph simply ignored the letter until, finally, LaToya was forced to confront him. According to her, he said, "I will sit on you for five years before I ever let you go." Katherine responded to her daughter's cry for help with a line that might have gone down in history as a classic of parental dysfunction: "I don't want to get in the middle of it."

After that "Dear Joseph" letter from LaToya's

lawyers, Joseph and Jack Gordon practically annihilated each other during a violent battle in the family den. Joseph was extremely bitter about LaToya's leaving home and felt that Gordon had stolen his daughter, much the way John McClain had absconded with Janet and Frank Dileo with Michael.

"I make 'em, they take 'em," Joseph said.

"Gordon threatened my life when I questioned him about some major expenses he and LaToya were running up on Joe's account," said the Jacksons' former family attorney, Jerome Howard. "The man is dangerous. But LaToya feels Joe is the dangerous one. 'Do you know my father?' she once asked me. 'No, you don't,' she answered for me. 'You don't know what he's like. You don't know what I've *been* through.'"

"One day, Miss Janet was in the dining room when Mr. Gordon walked in," Celia Lopez remembered. "I went to be near the door because I was afraid there would be a physical fight between them. I didn't want Miss Janet to get hurt. I overheard her tell Mr. Gordon that if he ever hurt Miss LaToya, she would come looking for him. 'I'll hunt you down,' Miss Janet told him. 'I love my sister very much. She's very delicate. She's the most wonderful person. And if you hurt her, I swear to God, I'll hurt you.'

"Mr. Gordon laughed in her face. I think he thought she was joking. But she wasn't."

The next day, according to the domestic, Janet and LaToya had a loud disagreement.

"You threatened Jack," LaToya accused Janet. "He told me so. He told me you threatened to kill him. How could you?"

"That's not true," Janet said, defending herself. She tried to explain what really happened, but LaToya didn't want to hear it.

"The sooner we get out of here," LaToya said of herself and Jack, "the better. I think you're going to try to kill Jack. I really do. I think you, Joseph, and Katherine are going to hurt both of us."

LaToya moved as far away from Hayvenhurst as made sense to her at the time, first into Helmsley Palace, then the Waldorf-Astoria, and finally the Trump Parc in New York. Though she left Encino with only two suitcases and four pairs of pants, she was obviously not in financial straits, thanks to Jack Gordon.

It was time for LaToya Jackson to begin a new life. But the remnants of the old one lingered on, as she got constant reports from her siblings about what was going on in Encino. One particular conversation was to have a memorable impact.

"I hate Joseph so much," Michael told her on the telephone soon after she moved to New York. "I'll never forgive the times he hit Mother."

LaToya was shocked. She claimed later that this was the first time she ever heard of Joseph's being abusive to Katherine. She telephoned Rebbie for confirmation, then discussed the matter with Jackie. She claims they both insisted it was true. "That man is no good," Jackie told her. "He's never been a father."

Nor, apparently, much of a father-in-law, either.

Enid Jackson, Joseph's former daughter-in-law, has said of Joseph, "He jumped on top of me once and started choking me because I'd said something he didn't like about Jackie. 'Mother' [Katherine] came in and said, 'Joseph, you get off of her. What do you think you're doing?' I was scared to death. Then Katherine told me Joseph had hit her in the past. I think Janet, Rebbie, and LaToya had reason to be scared of Joseph. I really do."

"Oh, that is a bunch of crap," Janet responded when told of the allegations that Joseph had hit Katherine. "I hate this *stupid stuff*. You know what? The 'in' thing right now is Joe bashing. Everyone is doing it, exaggerating what he's done to all of us. I am sick of it. It's just out of control. Okay," she conceded, "he's not the greatest father in the world, but he's also not the worst. And I never saw him hit Mother, and I don't believe he ever did. That's bullshit."

Indeed, it would seem that no human being on God's earth could be quite as evil as Joseph Jackson's family makes him out to be, yet no one could have said he did not care deeply for his children and even Katherine. And it is virtually certain that the Jacksons would never have become *The Jacksons* without Joseph's motivation, harsh and unsentimental though it often was. Sadly, however, most of his offspring—and even their mates—were so traumatized by his temper and manipulations over the years that it was difficult for them to appreciate his genuine contributions to their long-term well-being or to recognize any love he might have felt for them. Or, perhaps most difficult of all, to recognize that even his most terrifying actions may have been the blind thrashing of a man who was, underneath everything, screaming out for help.

In late March 1988, Janet, Katherine, and Rebbie went to see LaToya perform at Trump's Castle in Atlantic

City, New Jersey. A press conference to tout the opening was scheduled in the casino the afternoon of the first performance. In her scathing book, *LaToya— Growing Up in the Jackson Family,* LaToya claims that Janet tried to discourage her from attending the press conference by telling her no one had shown up. But then, according to LaToya, Jack burst into her dressing room and began berating her for keeping the press waiting. Janet, who was standing next to LaToya, screamed at Jack, "Don't do this to my sister!" Then Jack grabbed LaToya and hustled her down to the casino. When they got there, Rebbie was standing at the mike, fielding questions from the press. LaToya felt that her siblings, at Katherine's direction, had purposefully tried to sabotage her press conference. But Janet, in her own defense, later explained that she felt the assembled media would "make a fool out of LaToya." She insisted that she "just couldn't let it happen." Janet felt Jack Gordon had not prepared her sister for the kinds of probing questions she would be asked. She felt that Gordon was hoping to humiliate LaToya in front of the media, and that she was really rescuing LaToya from a bad experience.

Many similar incidents, upsetting to Janet, occurred during the week. Jack was not physically abusive—at least not as far as Janet could tell—but he badgered LaToya, hounding her and making her feel incompetent. LaToya seemed almost as beleaguered now as she had before she left Encino, and Janet simply did not like seeing her sister being harshly treated by any man. Each day they were all in Atlantic City, a rage was building in Janet Jackson as she watched Jack and LaToya interact.

It was obvious that Jack cared about her sister, but

what good was that? Janet probably wondered. Certainly, Joseph cared about his children as well. But that wasn't enough to save them from a great deal of pain.

Janet would tell friends she didn't understand why LaToya was willing to accept mistreatment from Jack. "After she left home, you'd think she'd never allow another man to mistreat her," she said. "But I guess it doesn't work that way."

Another troubling episode occurred later in the week, one that LaToya chose not to write about in her memoirs. Apparently, Janet was waiting to talk to LaToya in her sister's dressing room after a performance. LaToya came off the stage sweaty, hoarse, exhausted, and completely disheveled.

"The two of them were getting ready to talk when in stormed Jack Gordon," remembered a witness to this scene. "And he started screaming at LaToya, 'Hurry the hell up, goddammit. Vanna White is waiting to take a picture with you. What the hell is wrong with you? Are you stupid or what? You hit that last note all wrong, 'Toya. You sounded like shit. . . . Now hurry the fuck up.'

"Janet suddenly just exploded. I mean, you could just see her erupt. She said, 'Don't you dare talk to my sister like that!'

"Jack told Janet that she should just butt out, mind her own goddamn business.

"The next thing I knew, Janet was standing up to Jack, telling him, 'LaToya is my goddamn business, mister, and I can swear as good as you can, *goddammit*! Don't you *ever* talk to my sister like that, you son of a bitch, you. Do you hear me? Do I have to get all up in your face for you to hear me? Am I talking to you in language you can understand?'"

According to the witness, Katherine walked in at that moment to find a wild-eyed Janet swearing like a truck driver, squaring off against Jack Gordon as if she were a fighter in the ring. Aghast, Katherine stood in the doorway with her mouth wide open, unable to move. LaToya, who was acting like the Stepford-wife Jackson, just ignored the scene unfolding between her sister and her manager, and walked out of the room. Jack followed quickly, telling Janet, "I'm gonna deal with you later."

"Oh, yeah? You just try it," Janet shot back. "I'd just like to see you try it. I'm not LaToya, you know. You can't push me around, mister."

After Jack and LaToya left, Janet was shaking with rage. Then she burst into tears.

"I'd never seen her cry before," said the eyewitness. "Janet rarely cries. She is just too in control. But this thing with Jack really rattled her. 'I can't believe she lets him treat her like that,' she said of LaToya. 'I just can't believe it!' Janet rarely raises her voice when other people are in the room who aren't family. I wanted to give her a standing ovation. I was, like, 'Go, girl. Let him have it.'"

"Just because you're not loud doesn't mean that you don't have control over your life," Janet told writer Steve Pond. "It's just like my brother Mike: he's the shyest of us all. I don't think I could ever find anyone with more control over their life than he has, and he's very soft-spoken, very shy. He's quiet. But when it comes time for him to be assertive and put his foot down, he does it. It has to do with being walked over a few times in the past. You let it happen, you let it go by, and then it happens again. And you get madder and madder each time and then you finally say, 'I'm not going to take this anymore.'"

Evidently, however, LaToya didn't feel that Janet was defending her as much as she felt her younger sister was attempting to break up her relationship with Jack, her savior.

After their visit to Atlantic City, Janet, Katherine, and Rebbie all appeared to feel differently about LaToya. In fact, they didn't want much to do with her for a while.

The feeling seemed to be mutual.

**chapter
ELEVEN**

Trying to explain why most pop stars set their sights
on film careers after conquering the music charts is
akin to attempting an explanation of why salmon swim
upstream to lay their eggs, why humanity spends bil-
lions of dollars discovering new planets, or, even more
puzzling, why the creators of the Batman comic books
killed off Robin. Salmon notwithstanding, the answer
in most of these cases usually boils down to that *other*
question: why not?

In the case of the average rock star, the answer
surely has as much to do with ego as it does commerce. Who wouldn't love the idea of seeing their
larger-than-life image up on the so-called silver
screen? Besides, despite the fact that various occupa-
tions such as President of the United States, news-
caster, talk-show host, and, well, rock-and-roll singer
have led to faces and names becoming nationally and

internationally familiar, no line of work has ever embodied the true down-to-it, in-your-face concept of "fame" any more thoroughly than has *Movie Star.*

The fact is, several pop stars actually have made the leap from music to movies while retaining a certain amount of dignity. For instance, David Bowie, at this point in his career, is probably considered as much an actor as a pop star. Sting has appeared in both film and on stage, garnering reviews that range from decent to promising. Phil Collins, leader of the rock group Genesis, has turned in a couple of convincing performances. And Cher has, over the years, built such a strong reputation as a serious actress—with some measure of *commercial* success, no less, an element that seems absent from the films of most pop-stars-turned-actors, no matter how good they are at it—that the public needs to be reminded that she is, indeed, a pop singer who successfully made the transition. Of course, Cher manages to remind us all of her rock-and-roll beginnings by occasionally turning up in one of her music videos wearing almost nothing, just like a pop star.

The advent of music videos has created another category of star, and also spawned its share of would-be matinee idols. Invented primarily as a marketing tool, the medium does require some measure of acting ability on the part of pop singers and groups (as do live performances, for that matter), and many pop stars have found themselves bitten by the acting bug.

However, while some are attracted to film because it is another legitimate form of artistic expression and communication (this handful of pop stars, deservedly called recording *artists,* would probably be prompted to try their hand at oil painting and book writing for the same reasons), most are drawn into "reading scripts" and "taking meetings" with film executives because, well, hey, Frank Sinatra did it, Elvis did it, the Beatles did it. And, besides: who wouldn't like the idea of seeing their thirty-foot-high image projected on a giant white screen in front of hundreds of people in thousands of movie houses all over the world? What's wrong with wanting *that*?

Because of her background, Janet Jackson seemed exempt from most of the aforementioned inclinations to excess. After all, she'd found some success as an actress long before *Control.* She'd earned an income with supporting roles on prime-time television shows such as "Good Times" and "Fame"—not to mention her cute and comical parody of Cher opposite Randy's Sonny during the family's revue-style shows at the MGM Grand in Las Vegas. But, *movie star . . .* It seemed like the obvious career move.

After the success of *Control,* Janet probably could have gone back to television in a big way, could have had a pivotal role in some big-budget mini-series or another, playing the young vixen stealing an older, rich, married (and for the sake of drama, *Caucasian*) man from a Linda Evans type. Thanks to the success of *Control,* Janet no doubt could have gained a foothold in the lucrative, albeit somewhat schlocky Movie-of-the-Week market, like Lisa Hartman or, better yet, Valerie Bertinelli, knocking out a couple of those a year. In a different place and time, Janet could even have gone back to school—via "Beverly Hills 90210," of course—or she could have moved, with a roommate, into a funky little apartment on "Melrose Place."

Any of those scenarios would have been considered

great for Janet because she was one of the Jackson Girls, and no one expected greatness from the Jackson Girls. They were the *girls*. The real money had always been on Michael and, to a lesser extent, Jermaine and the other brothers. Janet on "Good Times," Janet on "Fame"—that was more than what was expected by most, including maybe even her family.

"Janet was the baby, and I mean the *baby*," reasoned a former employee who was close to the Jackson clan in the early eighties. "Everyone figured she'd be hard to handle because she grew up in a famous, rich family. You have to keep in mind that all the brothers and sisters are old enough to remember the tough times in Gary, Indiana. Except Janet. She was a direct recipient of what I call the Dynasty, so no one figured she'd work hard to achieve anything.

"Randy was the youngest of the boys, and he sort of went in the wrong direction—chasing women, hanging out, wrecking cars, that sort of thing. We all half expected Janet to end up, not like that, but definitely wilder than the rest. Or I should say, *openly* wilder. When she got the 'Fame' gig—not so much the 'Good Times' part because she was a little kid then and basically did what she was told—it was like, 'Yeah, Jan has found her niche, something she can do.'"

Perhaps, but *Control* changed all that. It made her a budding pop star, still in the shadows of her older brothers, but a pop star nonetheless. Her brother Michael had forever talked about starring in a movie, something beyond his Scarecrow role in *The Wiz*. However, by the mid-eighties, the closest he had come to moviemaking was starring in the long-form John Landis–directed "Thriller" video. If Janet could simply find herself a film project to star in, that would be something Michael had not done. So, in 1987, by the time *Control* had sold more than a million copies, Janet had decided she wanted to make a movie. She began to think about the possibilities.

Getting twenty-one-year-old Janet Jackson into the movies, like almost everything about her career during the period of *Control,* fell to A&M Records' vice-president of black music, John McClain. McClain figured Janet's first film should be something simple and to the point, pretty much like Prince's *Purple Rain.* That film, about a band in a small town that beat the odds to become a success, elevated Prince to superstar status.

For Janet, McClain came up with a treatment for a film not unlike the classic *A Star Is Born.* The general idea was that Janet would play a young singer from a small town who came to the big city seeking success. Once there, she'd fall in love with another singer, played by Morris Day. Day and the real-life band he fronted, the Time, had also costarred in *Purple Rain,* but the band that appeared in the film didn't include Janet's producers, Jimmy Harris and Terry Lewis, who were the outfit's original keyboardist and bass guitar player, respectively. The romantic subplot of McClain's treatment called for Janet, Day, and Time guitar player Jesse Johnson (generally considered the band's bad-boy sex symbol) to become involved in a nasty love triangle. Ultimately Janet and Day would find happiness rocking out, backed by the Time. Diehard Janet Jackson fans may be interested to know that the long-playing music video for the track "Control"—which features Janet first in spoken dialogue with Harris, Lewis, Time drummer Jellybean Johnson, and *Purple Rain* costar Jerome Benton, and then later onstage performing "Control" live (in reality,

Harris, Lewis, and Janet simply went into the studio and recut a line-sounding version of the song for the video)—is actually a preview of what McClain had in mind for the film.

For McClain, the film would serve a dual purpose. Ideally, it would make Janet a movie star, but it would also reunite the original Time, putting back together one of pop R&B's most potentially successful young bands. (A few years later the original Time did reunite briefly, but it was ill-planned and only produced a dismal comeback album and animosity among some of its members.)

McClain, in fact, approached Warner Brothers about producing the film, and they were interested. He called in a young African-American director/screenwriter named Reginald Huddlin (who, years later, with his producer-brother Warrington, would go on to make the *House Party* comedies and produce and direct Eddie Murphy's comedy *Boomerang*) and paid him a five-figure fee to come up with a script.

There were problems from the very beginning. For one, the brass at A&M, themselves starting a film division, weren't crazy about the idea of their biggest star making a film for Warner's. McClain was having problems convincing all of the members of the Time to do the film. Some of them saw the film as just another feather in the hats of Harris and Lewis. There were also questions about which company would release the film's soundtrack album. Such a soundtrack had the potential to be huge. Warner's would have certainly wanted its record division to have the album—the Time had, in fact recorded their last album for Warner's—but there was no way A&M would have permitted Janet to record for another label.

And then there was the script. McClain and Huddlin didn't see eye to eye on many of its elements. According to insiders, Huddlin saw Janet's character as having more middle-class characteristics, like the young Huxtable that Lisa Bonet played on the early Bill Cosby shows. McClain, however, felt whatever Janet portrayed on-screen should have more of an urban attitude. Huddlin saw blaxploitation film queen Pam Grier in the role of the female vamp who comes after Janet's man, Morris Day, in the film, while McClain wanted Prince's ex-girlfriend, actress/singer Vanity. Apparently, in Hollywood, it's the *little* things in life that can make a deal go bad.

"It was basically chaos," said a film executive who worked for Warner Brothers at the time. "There were some problems all around—half-baked scripts, who was going to direct, stuff like that—but nothing that could not have been worked out. Warner's had just had success with *Purple Rain,* which was exactly the kind of low-budget film Janet's people wanted to do, but we just couldn't get it together."

By early 1988, Janet still hadn't begun work on her follow-up to the *Control* album, much to the consternation of A&M Records. Katherine, who was never one to bite her tongue when it came to telling her children what she was thinking, advised Janet that she'd "better hurry up and get that album going. People forget, you know." But Janet was unconcerned about the public "forgetting" and told her mother that artists often go long periods of time between albums, which often serves to heighten suspense for the forthcoming record.

A&M had an idea for Janet's follow-up to *Control:* that she do an album called *Scandal,* based on aspects of what was happening in her personal life and on the turmoil in the Jackson family. She vetoed it.

"You're kidding me, right?" Janet told the executive who came up with the notion. When he assured her he was not, she laughed. "You must think I'm crazy."

Later she told a reporter, "I said, 'What's the point in that? So people can talk? There's enough stuff going on as it is.'"

But Janet gave in enough to write a song for the proposed album called "You Need Me" (which would go on to be released as the B-side of "Miss You Much"), a song to a distant, neglectful father who's asking for help. "It isn't really about my father," she has observed. "But everyone loved the song and said, 'We've got to do more stuff like this,' and I started thinking, 'Oh, God, no, we *don't.*' So we didn't."

Janet had been busily renegotiating her contract with A&M, with the help of attorney Jerome Howard. "She knew what she wanted," Jerome recalled. "All I had to do was implement it, to follow her directions. I had a lot of suggestions, though, and she took them. You can talk to Janet. She'll listen. Some members of her family won't listen, which is what has gotten them in trouble. But that's not the case with Janet."

Janet's intention was to give her parents three and a half percent of her royalties on the next album, which could translate into hundreds of thousands of dollars. But Katherine told Janet that Marlon was having financial problems, so Janet had Jerome Howard rearrange the deal so her parents got two and a half points and Marlon the other point. (Janet also stipulated that Katherine be paid hers and Joseph's percentage directly. She didn't want the money going to her father's office.)

Janet's problem at this time was that negotiations with producers Jimmy "Jam" Harris and Terry Lewis were not going well. The duo had asked for $1 million to produce the next Janet Jackson album. But A&M executive John McClain did not want to give it to them. Harris and Lewis felt McClain was being cheap—after all, A&M had made about $50 million on *Control*—and acting as if the money was coming out of his own pocket rather than the company's.

Of McClain's involvement in these negotiations, Harris has said, "At the time, he was acting both as Janet's manager—or adviser, if you will, I wouldn't say manager—and also working for A&M. It was kind of a conflict of interest, I think we all eventually realized."

John McClain, a company man at heart and loyal to owners Herb Alpert and Jerry Moss, insisted that he simply felt that the duo was asking for too much. Also, he did not feel it was in Janet's best interest to give them that much money. "As far as my managing Janet, or whatever they thought I was doing, she was like my sister, someone I had nurtured," he explained. "It was a tough situation because I was an officer of the company, but Janet wasn't just a regular artist. And I never managed Janet. We just had a close relationship. But it didn't endear me to Jimmy and Terry, because we had to fight to work the deal out."

This situation was made more complex by the fact that Alpert, Moss, and company president (at that time) Gil Friesen really had no rapport with Janet Jackson. None of them ever had anything to do with her personally. When she was signed to the label by Joseph in the mid-eighties, no one at A&M paid much

attention to her. Her first two albums were not successful and didn't exactly merit the attention of company
honchos. But then, when she became McClain's
protégée, he handled all aspects of her career and
assisted in turning her into a star for the label. As a
result, the company's bigwigs had no relationship with
their most popular recording star.

"The deal was this," says one A&M executive.
"Janet Jackson's success affected everyone, and everyone wanted more money, including Janet. She had
Jerome Howard renegotiate her recording contract, and
he did a great job in getting her a solid deal. Now John
McClain was telling her she didn't need Harris and
Lewis, that she was so big anyone could produce her,
that she'd go straight to the top as long as the music
was good. Janet wasn't sure about this."

Still, she went into the studio, at John's suggestion,
with A&M producer Bryan Loren. Loren produced a
couple of upbeat songs for Janet for an album he was
going to call *Work*. This made everyone in Janet's
camp certain that A&M didn't need to pay Harris and
Lewis all that money.

"Then Janet took the tracks home and listened to
them. She made her decision: she wanted Jimmy
Harris and Terry Lewis, not Bryan Loren. She telephoned Michael to ask him what she should do. He
laid it on the line for her, telling her that if she changed
producers now, she'd be nuts. He said it would be up
to her to work this deal out, that it was time for her to
take charge."

That was all she needed to hear. The woman was
going hunting.

Janet picked up the telephone and made an appointment with Gil Friesen, president of A&M. She had

never been alone in a meeting with the president of A&M, nor with either of the owners, Herb Alpert or Jerry Moss. Rather, she was always surrounded by representatives who spoke for her, and agreed or disagreed for her. But not this time. Feeling that John McClain had somehow botched her relationship with her producers, she was weary with what was happening with negotiations, anxious to get started on the project, and determined that the time had come for her to step in and take charge.

"But Janet got a surprise she didn't count on," said a former A&M executive. "She went in with a tough, businesswoman's attitude, determined to clean up this mess and be tough with A&M to get her producers the money they wanted. But Alpert and Moss had instructed Friesen to get tough with Janet.

"A&M had a check for $1 million due to Janet as a bonus for the exceptional sales of *Control,* but the company wasn't going to give it to her unless she worked out these problems with McClain, Harris, and Lewis. By contract, they were allowed to hold the bonus money up until production of the next record. This was a million dollars, certainly incentive enough for Janet to get to work on Harris and Lewis.

"Then she learned that A&M was actually willing to pay Harris and Lewis the million dollars they had asked for. It was John McClain, not A&M, who was holding things up by not wanting to pay them the money. This really irritated her.

"She called Harris and Lewis up personally."

"Do you guys want to do this or not?" Janet has recalled asking the two producers. "Let me know now so I can start thinking about the future. They said, 'We want to do it, but are you sure you want to work with us again?' I said, '*Yeah.*' And they said, 'Okay, then we've got to straighten this stuff out.'"

"Janet struck a deal with them herself—I don't know what it was, but it was close to the million they asked for," says the A&M executive. "And the next thing everyone knew, they were in and John McClain was out."

In Janet Jackson's mind, John McClain had apparently served his purpose. Romantically, anything she had with him—and it's never been clear to outsiders exactly what that was—was history. Professionally, he had profited from their relationship in many ways. But now it was all coming to an end. Like her brother Michael, who fired his attorney John Branca after eleven years of stellar service, Janet is tough as nails when it comes to business.

"But it really wasn't fair," said the former record-company executive. "All John ever cared about was what was best for Janet. He was practically her manager, but never took any percentage as manager. He trusted Janet, then felt she'd stabbed him in the back."

Had she? If one of the features of striking a business deal in the real world is doing what works without deliberately injuring people but without being crippled by sentiment, either, perhaps Janet had done precisely the correct thing.

At any rate, Janet, Harris, and Lewis left for Minneapolis to begin work on the new album. "With *Control,* we wanted to do an album that would be in every black home in America," Harris has said. "We were going for the black album of all time. Gritty, raw. For the follow-up, we were determined to try something bigger."

Details of the production were kept a secret; the company knew of the record only as "The 1814 Project."

Actually, the production would go on to become *Janet Jackson's Rhythm Nation 1814.*

"I must say that A&M, for a record company, was very understanding, because during the whole process they never heard a thing," Harris said, laughing. "Right at the end, Gil Friesen called and said, 'Look, I'm the president of the record company, and I ain't heard *nothin'*. What's the deal?'"

As Jackson, Harris, and Lewis worked on the album, McClain was left behind in Los Angeles to cool his heels and figure out what had happened. He had lost control of Janet, and this did not bode well for him at the company.

McClain went to Minneapolis, trying to take charge of the recording sessions for *Rhythm Nation*—as he had done so brilliantly with the *Control* album—but Janet was incensed by his presence.

"She refused to sing a single note unless he was removed from the studio," remembered one observer. "It was pretty clear that she was really irritated at McClain. He was saying things like, 'What happened to you? What's wrong with you?' and Janet was just not hearing it. She was incredibly rude to him. It was hard to believe. I felt there was a back story here— something else going on that no one knew about."

Later, in the press, Janet would be less than charitable in assessing McClain's contribution to her career. "It was his idea to put Jimmy Harris, Terry Lewis, and me together," she said curtly. "To be honest with you, that was it. On the second album, he came to Minneapolis and wanted to stay, but we convinced him that we could take care of it, and he should just go back to Los Angeles. He did."

McClain left Minneapolis, completely dismayed by his former protégée's behavior. Janet, on the other hand, was just as disgusted with John, who, to her way of looking at it, was trying to bully everyone in the studio. Suddenly he must have reminded her of her father.

When John McClain lost Janet Jackson's trust, he saw his power base at A&M begin to disintegrate. (In 1990, he resigned from A&M.) "It's a cutthroat business," Jerome Howard observed. "A sad, tough business. But John left a millionaire just due to the bucks he received as executive producer of *Control* and *Rhythm Nation.*"

The strain was taking its toll and would continue to do so on Janet as well.

By May 1988, the album was finished and it was time to begin work on an extended *Rhythm Nation* video featuring several songs from the album, including the first single, "Miss You Much."

Production began on May 16, 1988, Janet's twenty-second birthday. The pace was grueling. Every day she arrived at a Long Beach warehouse—site of the shoot—by 3:00 P.M. She would film until seven the next morning. As a result, she came down with a stomach flu. She had also put herself on a nine-hundred-calorie-a-day diet, which did little to help matters. She woke up one day shaking and vomiting, then later collapsed on the set and couldn't stop crying. She was sent to the hospital, where she spent a couple of days recovering from exhaustion and dehydration. While she was in the hospital Michael called her. "Janet told me he said she needed to slow down," said one of Janet's confidants. "But she said she couldn't.

'It's like a merry-go-round and I can't get off,' she told Michael. 'I want to slow down, but there's so much to do. I'm afraid I won't get it all done.'"

"I'm worried about Janet," René Elizondo said at the time. "She's been on a low-calorie diet, and with all the work she's been doing, that's not enough."

On one occasion, when photos had to be taken of Janet and her band after a rehearsal, René cracked, "Maybe we could put the band behind Janet while she's sleeping and take the group photos that way." He added, sarcastically, "I mean, can't we figure out a way to utilize her twenty-four hours a day, even when she's sleeping?"

"She works hard," Katherine Jackson said of her daughter. "She doesn't always know when to stop. She has that in common with Michael. She has to work hard; she has to communicate to her audience."

"I don't feel I work *that* hard," Janet told writer Steve Pond. "Consider the rest of my family. Take Michael, for instance; he's a workaholic. Compared to him, I don't even come close."

"I feel what I've witnessed is the coming-of-age of an artist," said Richard Frankel, director of creative services at A&M, who first began working with Janet on the *Dream Street* album. "In retrospect, I think she probably has always had good ideas. But what I've been able to see develop is her ability to communicate them and feel confident about expressing them. It's an age function as much as it is an experience function. She's *there* now."

In November 1988, Janet went to visit LaToya in Manhattan. Janet had business in the city and decided to catch up on her sister's activities. What she saw displeased her, as it seemed that LaToya's life was now being completely controlled by Jack Gordon.

"I don't know how you can let any man run your life like that," Janet told LaToya. And thus, the two of them became embroiled in a heated debate about feminism.

Now Janet was more independent in her thinking than ever. For instance, of her own boyfriend, René Elizondo, Janet would go on to tell *Rolling Stone,* "One thing I hate is that everyone thinks he manages me. And he doesn't. He doesn't manage me in any fashion, shape, form, size. . . ." Indeed, Janet was clear that she is her own boss. She would not even allow René to comment on her statement for the reporter.

To another reporter, Janet clarified her relationship with René. "He has helped me a great deal with visuals and things. He wants to direct. He comes from a family that is in the film business, and I know he will direct because he has talent.

"But he doesn't try to stick his nose in my music. If I ask for help, he is there. If I say there is something I want to do by myself, he says, 'Okay, you got it. If you need me, just let me know.' That's the way it is with us. I thank God for René, I really do."

"Actually, I don't think Janet trusted René as much as outsiders thought she did," says Gino Brando, a friend of the Jackson family. "As far as her career was concerned, she believes in his instincts. He's got talent as a video director. But where her heart is concerned, she is just as leery of him as she is of any man in her life. It's second nature to her.

"After seeing what her father did to her mother, it's understandable that Janet would have that kind of distrust," observed Brando. "She once said, 'No man should be so important in your life that he takes over that life. You can't give a man that much power, because he'll only abuse it.' I think she has a fairly cynical viewpoint when it comes to men. Big surprise, huh?"

Janet tried to make similar points to LaToya, who didn't want to hear them. "Jack treats me well," LaToya insisted. "He saved me from a life of hell. You should know what he saved me from. You lived there, too."

LaToya also told Janet she had something she wanted to share with her, a secret. But according to LaToya, Janet didn't act particularly interested and so she decided to keep it to herself.

Three months later, in February 1989, Janet discovered what LaToya was trying to tell her. In fact, the whole Jackson family was given a jolt when renegade LaToya posed nude in *Playboy* magazine, a publication she had once never dared look at because reading it was against her religious convictions.

When Janet saw the layout, she simply could not believe her eyes. She immediately telephoned her mother, who was already hysterical and in tears. Mother and daughter could not fathom how LaToya could pose for *Playboy,* and still can't. "I know she wanted to show her independence, but couldn't she find another way to do it," Janet complained to one reporter. "You can't imagine how those pictures hurt our mother. I think LaToya just didn't know what she was doing, or how it would affect all of us."

Janet, who was seething, telephoned LaToya from Katherine's home. She later said that her anger was not because of LaToya's having posed for the suggestive photos, but because she didn't tell anyone about them or, at least, try to prepare the family for the shock.

"But I had a confidentiality agreement, Jan," LaToya told her.

To Janet, the argument seemed disingenuous, if not an outright, self-serving manipulation of the facts. "Oh, that is such bullshit," she answered. "You're just trying to hurt us. Admit it."

LaToya denied that was the case. Then she hung up on Janet.

"Janet was furious," says Steven Harris, a former associate. "I don't think I have ever seen her like that. From that time on, she felt LaToya was purposely setting out to tarnish the Jackson name—and Janet is big on keeping the name and image intact. Janet doesn't believe most of the 'family harmony' hype she sells, but still she sells it big time. She was very angry at LaToya. To her, what LaToya did was a slap in the face of anyone named Jackson."

The family held one of their "family meetings," which Janet did not attend, and decided that Jack Gordon had poisoned LaToya's mind, turned her against them, and coerced her to have the photos taken as a demonstration of her defiance. LaToya, on the other hand, insisted she made the decision to pose for *Playboy* because she wanted to make a statement that she was her own woman, free of her family—her father, in particular—and her religion. "I am living my life for me now," she said, "not for my family or anyone else."

LaToya, in one of her "exclusive *National Enquirer* interviews," said, "Posing nude for *Playboy* was an opportunity to show the world that women should not be ashamed of their bodies. I'm very proud of what I've done, and I think my fans will be, too."

"What a joke! 'Toya is *not* a feminist," Janet Jackson told Steven Harris. "If anything, she's setting feminism back years because of her relationship with Jack—the guy tells her what to do every minute of the day—and the fact that she wants to be perceived as only a sex object. How can she let someone else dictate her life to her? I know the only reason she posed for those pictures is that he told her to."

"I'm not saying I wouldn't pose nude one day," Janet told another friend. "But if I ever did, I would prepare my mother for the shock, number one. And number two, I would do it because I wanted to, not because some man made me."

That was Janet's private reaction. Publicly, she was mum about any strife the *Playboy* layout may have caused her or her family. "When LaToya did *Playboy*," said Jimmy "Jam" Harris, "Janet was very much: 'So what? That's my sister, I love her, she can do what she wants to do.' She didn't come out in the press like Jermaine, who was on a show saying he thought it was wrong. I think Janet's way of handling family issues is to say, 'Look, I'm doing my own thing here. I'm not involved in what they're doing. If you want to talk to me about what I'm doing, great.'"

Also, Janet had to admit that her sister looked "pretty damn good." She told a reporter, "It caught me by surprise. What has she done to herself? Where'd you get that body, girl?"

LaToya, who seemed painfully desperate to justify her actions, insisted that Michael approved of the photographs and that this was all she needed in terms of sanction. She claimed that he told her, "You are one of the most gorgeous women in the world, and not enough people realize it. I've known it for years."

But actually, it seems that Michael did not approve of the photographs at all. "Let me tell you, Michael Jackson hates pornography," says his former videographer Steve Howell. "He doesn't like to look at it because he thinks it's all demeaning—gay porno and straight porno. It doesn't turn him on at all. He hated Prince, he told me, because Prince was so anxious to take his clothes off. He said, 'I think that's disgusting.' Janet felt the same way. She was just as puritanical, always covering up from head to toe when I worked there. To have LaToya bare herself like that is not something Michael would approve of. No way."

According to well-placed sources, Michael told his sister he certainly could not stop her from stripping for the camera, but he would rather she didn't. For weeks before the pictures were published, he was on edge wondering what they would look like. Remembered one former associate, "His whole concern was, 'I know she'll show her breasts, but do you think she'll show her you-know-what?' That's what he called 'it.' Her 'you-know-what.' He said, 'If she shows her "you-know-what," I'm going to kill her. I swear it.'"

When the photos were published, Michael shrieked, despite LaToya's not having shown her "you-know-what." Nevertheless, the bare-breasted photos were what bare-breasted photos of attractive women in a men's magazine are: alluring, provocative, and immodest.

"This ruins the family image," Michael stormed. "That's it! There's nothing left."

Actually, the death knell, at least for LaToya's relationship with Michael, sounded when she appeared on "The Phil Donahue Show" on February 9, 1988, after the photos were published, and she reported that Michael approved of them and encouraged her in what she had done. Michael was indignant and decided to change his phone number so she could no longer get in touch with him. As of early 1994, LaToya still does not have her brother's phone number.

"I don't want to hear one more word about my sister's breasts," Michael finally announced to some staff members. "Let's just get on with life. I want to forget this ever happened."

"Janet stopped taking LaToya's telephone calls after the *Playboy* layout," says Steven Harris. "In fact, the whole family practically disowned her after the photos were published. Each had their own reasons, but Janet's was not that LaToya had posed. It was that she felt LaToya would stop at nothing to hurt anyone with the name Jackson. This really was the end of LaToya's relationship with her family. They banded together against her from that point on, Janet included. LaToya was now persona non grata."

As if she expected anything else?

By posing for *Playboy* magazine, LaToya Jackson—obviously seeking attention from a family who, she believed in her heart, never really cared about her—had gone to drastic measures to be noticed by her parents and siblings. And notice, they did. But the question is: Was it a heart-wrenching cry from a wounded young woman seeking love and acceptance or was it a rageful and mean-spirited public attack intended to inflict the greatest possible damage on the family's image? If it was the former, it didn't work. If it was the latter, it did, and it also succeeded magnificently in alienating her almost completely from her parents and siblings.

chapter
TWELVE

For any recording artist, following a successful album is not easy. Michael Jackson sweated out the follow-up to *Thriller* for years, not wanting to release the *Bad* album when it was finally completed because he was afraid of the critical reaction. But Janet, in her own subsequent work, harbored no such fears.

She was thrilled with *Control*'s phenomenal success—it would ultimately sell almost ten million copies worldwide. "It was a goal to sell millions of records, and we reached it," she told one writer. "I was so excited. Now everybody was saying, 'Oh, she did it, but can she do it again?' They said, 'She's just going to be a flash in the pan.' But I knew what I felt. I knew what I had inside me. The thing was to get it out and do it again."

"There was an added pressure," Janet noted in another interview. "A lot of people said, 'Ah, she's just running off her brother's success and it's not going to happen again.' That just fueled the fire. It made me try even harder just to prove them wrong."

Janet felt the follow-up to *Control* was even stronger than she hoped it would be. In fact, she couldn't wait for its release, which was scheduled for September 1989. "I knew I was going to have a big, big album," she told a reporter. "There was just no way around it."

"She's grown up," Jimmy "Jam" Harris told *USA Today* of Janet. "She's moved out of her family's house and she's started to experience different things. Her confidence level is way up."

In pop—as in "pop culture," as in "trend," as in "what's happening 'right now'"—timing is everything and, conceptually, the timing of *Rhythm Nation 1814* could not have been better. The 1814 referred to the year the American National Anthem was composed by Francis Scott Key, but the record company asked Janet to keep that to herself, since they hoped to build a mystique about the title. For better or worse, commentary about the state of the nation—homelessness, joblessness, education—was particularly in vogue in 1989.

"I've always loved socially conscious artists like U2 and Tracey Chapman and Bob Dylan," Janet had said. "But it seems like everyone who listens to their music already shares their views. That's not necessarily the case with people who listen to my music, so I'm trying to help them think about issues and ways of tackling them. Hopefully, we'll be able to hold their attention long enough through dance and music to make some sort of progress."

The album's first single, the nondescript funk-groove "Miss You Much" (released in August 1989, and one of the biggest selling singles of the year) never indicated what was to come; the album's rambunctious title track and muscular, hip-hop-based grooves such as "State of the World" and "The Knowledge" were even harder and sounded more definitely urban, or African-American, than anything on *Control.*

Despite the seeming self-righteousness of the album's lyrics, Janet's *Rhythm Nation* valiantly pointed out the woes of the post-Reagan era but never really offered any solutions. "You know, a lot of people have said, 'She's not being realistic with this *Rhythm Nation* stuff,'" Janet observed. "It's like, 'Oh, she thinks the world is going to come together through her dance music.' And that's not the case at all. I know a song or an album can't change the world. But there's nothing wrong with doing what we're doing to help spread the music."

Indeed, *Rhythm Nation* didn't have to offer solutions. Its real mission, which it accomplished beautifully, was once and for all to crystallize the Janet Jackson Sound, highbrow contrary protestations from Janet aside.

There are three aspects or sides to the album.

First and foremost, there's the danceable, edgy, urban funk side, which, along with the album's title track, is also present in coy, innocent songs such as "Escapade" and "Love Will Never Do (Without You)."

Then, there is the sensual side, with lush, sultry chord-colored ballads such as "Come Back to Me" and "Someday Is Tonight." All of this was sexy material that would make a love meister like Barry White blush.

Finally, the sensible side. The rock-oriented "Black Cat"—no doubt included to capture rock-music lovers, the way brother Michael snared rockers with "Beat It" on his *Thriller* album—was thrown in for the sake of savvy marketing and crossover appeal.

Needless to say, the music lent itself eloquently to the medium of video. The clips, though far more expensive to produce than those of *Control,* weren't necessarily any more expressive. The "short film" representing "Rhythm Nation" was decidedly dark and pretentiously artsy. Hands down, the most effective clip belonged to "Alright," the fun, rambling adventure of a production in forties Harlem. The video featured great costumes, delightful dancing, and cameos from old-time entertainers such as Cyd Charisse, the dancing Nicholas Brothers, and Cab Calloway. Even more effective was the clip for "Love Will Never Do," during which Janet showed off a devastatingly sexy, streamlined, blue-jeaned body.

All in all, it was ambitious, wide-ranging, smart.

"I expect a lot of myself," Janet has said. "I push myself with every video, every album, because I think that's the only way you grow.

"The minute I'm relaxed with what I'm doing, I know it's time to stop. But I don't feel I'm a worka-holic—I could actually work a lot harder."

During its life on the music charts, *Janet Jackson's Rhythm Nation 1814,* her second number-one album, not only held its own, but, after all is said and done, may end up being one of the best albums of her career.

"One critic said that *Rhythm Nation* is 'dark,'" she told Robert E. Johnson for *Ebony* magazine, referring to the album's concept and the concept for the "Rhythm Nation" video, in which Janet and her troupe of dancers, dressed in black pseudo-military outfits, execute split-second-timed choreography. "The album, the cover, the video, everything was dark, he said. But I think he might be missing the message we're trying to convey.

"First of all, there was a reason the video was shot in black-and-white and not in color. There are so many races in that video, from black to white and all the shades of gray in between. Black and white photography shows all those shades, and that's why we used it. Our wearing black shows that, for once, it can represent something positive and not negative." Janet said she is miffed that the color black is equated with evil, and that, for instance, the day the stock market crashed is called "Black Monday." "I'm just so tired of that," she said. "I really am."

And as for a critic who thought her black attire was drab, "He's been brainwashed because he can't see what I'm trying to show, and that hurts me. I would hope everyone will understand that, for once, black represents something good. That's why we're all dressed in black. We're united to do something good, not coming out in white uniforms to save the day—with the white-horse mentality. Black is so beautiful to me."

*　　*　　*

Katherine recalled that when she heard Janet's new album, she was nervous about the sound. To her ears, it was all quite a departure from *Control.* In her autobiography, *The Jacksons—My Family,* she remembered a conversation she had with her daughter: "'Jan, the *Control* sound was great,' I said. 'Look at how successful Paula Abdul and Jody Watley have been recording songs in that vein. Why can't you at least put a couple of *Control*-type tunes on the album, just to play it safe?'

"'Mother,' she replied confidently, 'I think the public is going to like my new sound.' Janet's like Michael. When someone else jumps in their wagon, they build another wagon."

Immediately Janet began planning the Rhythm Nation concert tour. It would mark the first time she had toured to promote a record. She had been asked to tour for *Control,* but didn't feel she had the body of work from which to compose a complete show. Such was no longer the case.

And now a few moments for some family business . . .

When Janet was about to embark on the nine-month-long tour, she got a telephone call from Jermaine, asking if he could appear with her as an opening attraction. Jermaine hadn't scored with a hit record for a number of years, and an appearance on Janet's tour would have given a significant boost to his career. But Janet couldn't help but remember that in 1984, she desperately wanted to appear with the Jacksons on their ill-fated Victory tour. Jermaine vetoed the idea, as did the other brothers, Michael included. Now that the "shoe was on the other foot," Janet very nicely told Jermaine to forget it.

The answer was no.

And some more . . .

On September 2, 1989, LaToya telephoned Katherine and they became embroiled in a nasty fight while discussing whether LaToya should go back to Encino for an upcoming family reunion, and why LaToya refused to return Janet's telephone calls regarding the event.

"I don't have a family anymore. I don't have a mother, father, or brothers or sisters," LaToya said, screaming at her mother. She was eight years old, lashing out at her mommy. "I've disowned you all," she screamed.

Katherine hung up and called Janet, crying. Janet was furious with her sister and telephoned her immediately.

"Janet told me she and LaToya really got into it, screaming at each other and swearing," said one of Janet's associates. "Janet told her to stop calling Katherine, to just leave all of them alone.

"Janet began to feel she was Katherine's protector. She is very concerned about Katherine's blood pressure. 'LaToya is going to kill my mother,' she told me. 'If she keeps calling and saying things like that, my mother's going to have a heart attack. I'm not going to let LaToya do this.'"

At issue was more than mere disagreement over sibling behavior or even concern for Katherine's well-being. "I think Janet has always wanted to have the closest relationship with her mother," family friend Joyce McCrae once observed. "And I think it's something LaToya has resented over the years, because LaToya always felt that she [LaToya] was her mother's best friend."

"It's true that LaToya and her mother were absolutely inseparable," Gina Sprague, Joseph Jackson's former secretary, has said. "One would never go anywhere without the other. After LaToya left, I heard that Janet and Katherine became closer."

Janet and her mother do have a strong bond. As Janet wrote in her dedication to Katherine in the liner notes to *Rhythm Nation:* "I have never known a more beautiful, caring, loving, understanding, and intelligent woman than you, Mother. Someday, I hope to be exactly like you. I love you with all my heart."

One family member recalled a conversation he had with Janet in early September. "Janet was livid with LaToya," he remembered. "And she said to me, 'You mark my words, LaToya is going to do something to get back at Mother, to get back at all of us.' I asked her what she meant. 'I know how her mind works,' Janet said. 'She's going off the deep end. She's going to do something that is going to be so *stupid*. And it's going to ruin her life, whatever it is.'"

Three days later Janet's prophesy seemed to come true when Katherine telephoned her to give her the news: LaToya and Jack were married.

"She sure showed *us*," Janet said, disgusted.

There was to be a family meeting about this latest drama, in the house's projection room, Katherine told Janet. Of course, Janet would not attend any such meeting; she rarely attended these conferences.

Apparently, LaToya, thirty-three, and Jack Gordon, fifty, were wed in a five-minute ceremony at the Washoe County Court in Reno, Nevada, on September 5, 1989. LaToya wore black jeans and a fringed, black suede jacket. "It was strange. They showed no affection toward one another," says county clerk Cheryl Phay. "Gordon pulled a guy off the street to be a witness, giving him a wad of hundred-dollar bills."

Recalled Deputy Commissioner Cecilia Kounairs, who performed the ceremony, "I pronounced LaToya and Jack Gordon man and wife. They were not affectionate or emotional, just businesslike. They said their vows and left."

Perhaps in order to draw attention away from the event, LaToya quickly denied it ever happened, declaring, "It had to be an impostor."

Shortly after the ceremony, Jack Gordon and his bride, LaToya, claimed the reason they were married was that they were desperate to protect LaToya from being kidnapped by her own family. Gordon asserted that LaToya was being stalked by a three-hundred-pound man, hired by the Jacksons to stop her from writing her autobiography. "LaToya's sick over what her family is trying to do," said Jack, in an "exclusive interview" with the *Globe*. "She's already staved off three kidnaping attempts. It's time to put an end to the harassment. As her husband, I would have more legal options to keep her away from her family than I would as her manager."

Then, that same week, in "An Exclusive Interview with *The National Enquirer*," Jack Gordon said, "We're supposed to be the happiest people in the world now and instead we walk around with six armed security guards because my wife fears for her life because of her own family."

"Oh, *puh-leeze*!" Janet said to one of her confidants when she heard Jack's tale. "You've got to be kidding. Jack convinced LaToya to marry him using whatever story he could come up with, and she fell for it."

"Jack used to tell me all the time how Joe was trying to kidnap LaToya," said Gary Berwin, a former business associate of Joseph Jackson, "and that LaToya was absolutely scared to death. This was not a happy girl. She was miserable, in fact. Knowing both of them, I feel quite sure that Jack married LaToya to protect her, and because he is in love with her. He told me so himself. I don't know how LaToya feels about Jack, but I believe he is in love with her."

"Janet had stopped being concerned about LaToya," said Jerome Howard. "Mostly, she felt LaToya had lost her mind. She had no patience for her and these wild stories she and Jack were purposefully feeding to the tabloids."

There is also no love lost between Jack Gordon and Jerome Howard. Howard contends that Gordon called him a "very stupid man" for "leaving that house without a Jackson." He claims that Gordon said, "You could have had Janet, you idiot. She was looking for someone to save her. She was up for grabs. It could just as easily have been you who came in and got her out of there. How could you leave there without one of those girls? At least I got me a Jackson."

Janet did track LaToya down, telephoning her to ask her how she could marry Jack Gordon, how she could be, as Janet put it, so "idiotic." Janet told friends that LaToya slammed the phone down when she asked the question.

Publicly, Janet—always in pursuit of supporting that elusive image of Jackson-family solidarity—said of LaToya to *USA Today,* "I really don't like to talk about her. It's such a touchy thing. A lot has happened, but she is my sister."

Privately, however, Janet, never one to mince words,

raged to one family member, "What do I need this for? LaToya's gone off the deep end. I've had it with her. I love her. But what am I supposed to do?"

"Stay out of it," the family member suggested. "It ain't none of your business anymore."

The ongoing feud between Janet's brother Jermaine and LaToya continued into October 1989, while *Janet Jackson's Rhythm Nation* remained the number-one album on the charts. "My beautiful sister has married a cockroach," Jermaine told a British newspaper of LaToya's union with Jack Gordon. "One of the worst things Gordon did for her was make her believe she could be successful as a singer. We knew how awful she'd be because she simply doesn't have what it takes."

Jack responded by appearing on a British television program, "Jameson Tonight," and saying that Jermaine is a "jealous animal," envious of anyone in the family who becomes successful. "Jermaine made comments about Michael, saying that he wanted to be white, that he would not be successful . . . and now he's doing the same with LaToya."

Gordon, who is Jewish and who has charged members of the Jackson family with making anti-Semitic comments, claimed LaToya was about to convert to Judaism. He said she was going to lease her equity in the Jacksons' Hayvenhurst estate to a group of Hasidic Jews so they could set up an educational program there. He concluded, "They're going to use Jermaine's bedroom to hold the Hebrew classes in."

Janet, ever the keeper of the flame and supporter of the family image, was aghast at all of this negative publicity. She telephoned Jermaine in England, telling him he was only fueling the fire by making public statements about LaToya. She reportedly told him,

"How can you be so dumb? Can't you see what you're doing? You're just making it worse, playing into Jack's hands."

According to a family friend, Jermaine told Janet that he simply could not just allow Gordon to smear his name and the family's.

"Who the hell cares what Jack Gordon does?" Janet responded bitterly. "After all these years in the public's eye, you shouldn't care what anyone says, Jermaine. If you're really secure, it won't bother you. Just find something else to do."

Matters were made worse when the family agreed to be interviewed by *People* magazine in the fall of 1988. Katherine, who is fairly shrewd at public relations herself, was against the idea; she felt the article could not possibly do any of them any good. But Joseph insisted that they could put many of the rumors about the family to rest if they cooperated with *People*.

In the end, none of the family members, LaToya included, was exactly thrilled with the feature by Susan Schindehette and Todd Gold, entitled "The Perks May Be Great, but Fame Isn't So Simple for the Fractious Jackson Clan." In fact, when the article was published, all of the Jacksons were incensed about it and angry with its writers. Accurate though it was—none of the family members could really argue with what the article said—they did wish the writers hadn't been quite so observant. The feature portrayed the extreme level of dysfunction in the family in such a way as to make them all seem a rather hopeless bunch, what with all of the attention given to Jermaine and Jackie's soured marriages and Joseph's blatant philandering. Also, the reporters noted that Michael had "become a virtual stranger to the family" and that Joseph had lost "millions of dollars to dry oil wells, bankrupt office buildings, and an accountant who pocketed hundreds of thousands of dollars earmarked for taxes."

As for their youngest child, the article reported, "Joe and Katherine are struggling to maintain good relations with daughter Janet."

"What can I do?" Joseph noted in the article when asked how he felt when Janet refused to renew her management contract. "I can't go after her like I would another artist. She's my baby daughter."

Janet was disturbed by the feature. "It's bad for us to be portrayed this way," she told an associate. "You'll notice that I, for one, would not be interviewed. The best thing we can do as a family is to keep our damn traps shut."

Despite what the article implied, Janet maintains a close relationship with her mother. Katherine likes René Elizondo tremendously; he and Janet often joined Katherine and her nephew Tony at the Encino home for word games such as Pictionary and Scrabble. Whereas Michael and LaToya never wanted to set foot in the Encino home—and many of their siblings also seemed reluctant to maintain family ties—Janet simply never had any trouble from her family once she left Hayvenhurst; or, rather, she wouldn't *allow* anyone in her family to make trouble for her.

chapter

THIRTEEN

Nineteen-ninety would be a hectic year. In February, *Janet Jackson's Rhythm Nation 1814* neared the triple-platinum mark, meaning nearly three million copies had been sold; she rehearsed for her first world tour, which was scheduled to begin on March 1; she shot two more videos; and she appeared on the American Music Awards (winning two of them, losing a third to Paula Abdul). In April, she received her star on the prestigious Hollywood Walk of Fame—the 1,911th celebrity to be so honored.

As her reputation as a solo performer became ever more solid, Janet continued to define herself and to impress even seasoned veterans in the entertainment community.

"I watched Janet's rehearsal for the awards show," recalled television producer John Redmann, "and it was amazing. She was very low-key, almost tired. She just ran through the song 'Black Cat' with little to no enthusiasm, doing the steps by rote. The program's producers were afraid she had lost her touch; people were saying, 'We're in big trouble. She looks exhausted; she's not into this; her performance is going to be bad.' But that night, when she hit the stage during the actual telecast, she was magnificent. It was hard to believe this was the same woman. She was alive, dancing up a storm, really into it. Afterward the crew gave her an ovation."

"It's true," René Elizondo concurred. "In rehearsals, she just loafs through the songs. Sometimes that worries directors. But when she's on, she's *on*."

The Rhythm Nation tour, practically a year long, was a grueling but rewarding experience for Janet. It demonstrated, among other things, that while not all moments are good moments, she had the capacity to look misfortune in the face, stare it down, and get on with business.

She performed on a five-story, $2-million aluminum stage set with six dancers, pyrotechnics, an illusionist, and a two-hundred-pound panther. The opening dates—particularly opening night at the Miami Arena on March 1—were a little raw, and some of the early reviews were not favorable.

"Everything went wrong that night," Janet remembered of the Miami concert. "*Everything*. The cat! He peed on the stage! I slipped in it. The other dancers slipped in it. . . ."

If the show was a disaster, at least one person loved it. Katherine. "Janet didn't have to ask me twice to accompany her on the first week of her tour," Katherine

Jackson remembered. "I met her in Miami, the site of her opening-night performance. Not having seen her rehearsals for the show—Janet put it together in the Pensacola Civic Center, the same venue Michael had used to rehearse his solo show—I wasn't sure what to expect. I just knew Janet would be good. She was more than good. Her dancing and singing were fantastic. Some of her moves reminded me of Michael—they're family, after all—but many of them were distinctly her."

Katherine was on the road with Janet for about a week and has recalled what the schedule was like: after each show, Janet and her crew boarded the luxurious tour bus and headed for the next city on their itinerary. During the bus ride, Janet had a massage (from her personal masseuse) and then a meal (prepared by her personal chef). Usually by no later than 3:00 A.M., the entire tour corps had arrived in the next city, checked into the hotel, then retired for the evening—or, as was more likely to be the case, the very early morning.

At 2:00 P.M the following day they all had lunch, then met in the hotel lobby at 3:30 for the ride to the arena. Once there, Katherine relaxed backstage for the next couple of hours as Janet had her makeup done and tended to last-minute details. Just before going on stage, Janet went to a press room that was set up at each stop, and had her picture taken with celebrities, radio-program directors, disc jockeys, and other notables who bought tickets for the shows.

And then it was showtime.

For two frenetic hours Janet would prove herself to be the consummate entertainer, singing and dancing, setting the pace, carrying it through, sweating and pounding and exhorting the audience to enjoy itself until the time had come when she had given everything she could give. Exhausted, she would flow into the applause as it flowed into her until all were one, and then, finally, the show was over.

After the performance, they were off once again to the next city, and once again, the same events and the same schedule.

The person behind it all, as Katherine could clearly see, was no darling, sweet, little grown-up-now Jackson child. This was a *star,* and one who could work nightly, commanding the wildly enthusiastic, collective attention of thousands of fans as she was dealing simultaneously with the pressures of being constantly on the road, and also confronting the ever-present crises and stresses of being the focus of a major live production. This was, and make no mistake about it, a savvy woman of strength and power.

Within a few weeks, Janet really hit her stride. Wrote the *Boston Globe*'s Steve Morse, "Janet Jackson is getting her wings in a hurry. She floundered . . . a month ago in Miami where she seemed scared, defensive and downright lost. But she was a different person last night. She loosened up, took control early and whipped the capacity crowd into a frenzy."

But mundane concerns were not left behind.

Throughout the tour, Janet was practically obsessed with her weight. "I have to be thinner," she kept complaining. "I'm not eating, I swear. I'm not going to eat a thing." She added a rigorous workout regimen to her already tight schedule in a bid to lose weight. But according to people who worked with her on the tour, Janet never felt she looked her best. "She would get dressed for the show, stand in front of the mirror, and make faces," said one former employee. "She was very unhappy, because she thought she looked fat. But she really didn't. She was exercising so hard and dieting so much, sometimes going on stage and doing all of her exhausting routines was actually a painful experience. But she would not let up."

According to Tina Landan, one of her dancers, "Janet refuses to take advice from any of us about her health, because she's so concerned about not letting down the fans she loves. She just won't slow down, and it is terrifying sometimes to see the pain on her face onstage."

But this entertainer with the tough-minded commitment to her fans wasn't Superwoman. Thus it was that on one leg of the tour—when she was performing in St. Louis—she felt dizzy, walked backstage, and collapsed. Her doctor diagnosed "exhaustion" and made her cancel shows in Lexington, Kentucky, and Ames, Iowa. Then it was back on the road.

"She's probably one of the hardest-working and most determined stars I've ever been around," noted Diana Baron, executive director of publicity for A&M Records. "She has incredible strength and focus. She's willing to put in all the work to achieve her desired end. All this talk about her being a 'pop creation' couldn't be further from the truth."

For Janet Jackson, fame was accompanied by the well-known temptations of show-business excess, most of which she was able to avoid. But while she never experimented with drugs or liquor, romance was hard for her to resist. She had so little experience in that area, it was natural for her to want more, though she is loath to discuss whatever came her way. "I like to keep my private life private," she told writer Steve Pond in March 1990. Having watched her brother Michael being pummeled by the media, she was determined that no such thing would happen to her.

She and René Elizondo had been living together for a number of years, and while Janet had—and, as of this publication, still has—special feelings for René, she has indicated in recent years that he may not be the love of her life. This appears to be music to the ears of her first husband, James DeBarge, who told reporter Jerome George in January 1990, "I want her to kick this René Elizondo out of her life. He's a gold digger who wants to exploit her fame." Apparently, James was still singing the same sad song when he said, "If it hadn't been for Janet's family, I'd still be married to her. But I still love Janet. I say to you, Janet, 'Send Elizondo packing and come back to the man who really loves you—me.'"

Janet's relationship with René did seem to be in transition by the spring of 1990. "Of course, it's not been a fantasy life," she said at that time of her romance with him. "We've had our ups and downs and we've gone through a few things, with other people trying to come between us."

Janet had noticed that René was becoming increasingly jealous of the fact that her fame brought a number of men into her life, all of whom seemed to be interested in her sexually. "I was explaining these things to him, because he hadn't ever dated anyone in show business. I said, 'René, this isn't the first time this ever happened to me. It is just the first time it happened to me when I've been with you. It's not going to be the last time, either, and we will have to learn how to deal with it and control it.' He understands now. It was hard for him at first, especially the persistence some of the suitors had for me," she has said.

And what of the inevitable questions about deeper commitment?

"Of course, I would like to get married in the future, but he knows I want to work on my music and he never tries to put on any kind of pressure or anything. He knows I'm here to do something, that there is something I have to get out of my system. He understands that. He's the one who always says, 'First things first. We've got to do what you've been sent here to do.'"

"By 1990, things had cooled between Janet and René," says Steven Harris. "There were never fights between them. Basically, I think they felt they would always be friends, but they were interested in seeing other people from time to time. I guess you could call it somewhat of an open relationship between two mature, single people. There's really no scandal to it."

In the spring of 1990, Janet did have a brief involvement with another man, singer Bobby Brown. Brown—renowned in the entertainment world as much for his fast-lane show-business excesses, multiple relationships, and illegitimate children as for his successful gold and platinum singles and albums—did not seem to most observers to be the kind of man to whom Janet would be attracted. However, she was fascinated by Bobby when the two met backstage after one of her *Rhythm Nation* concerts. "He's sexy," she told one friend. "He just turns me on. I love his butt."

For Brown, the feeling was mutual. He told members of his crew that he found Janet Jackson to be alluring. He was enthralled by her videos and told pal Tyrone Procter, "One day, she'll be mine."

"Brown is a tough, rather raw kind of gentleman who enjoys wearing a lot of gold chains and flashy clothing. He exudes a great deal of charisma, and immediately upon meeting him, Janet must have thought of her father, Joseph," says writer J. Randy Taraborrelli. "Perhaps she couldn't help but be attracted to Bobby Brown because Brown, like Joe, is really charming, a ladies' man. Janet and Bobby seemed drawn to each other. Observers noted that there were fireworks in the room as they spoke after Janet's concert on the evening they met. And then they disappeared for the night. Word got around quickly that Janet and Bobby had something rather intensely romantic and exciting going on."

Said Jerome Howard, "The next thing you know, René was calling Janet's mother and father from the road and whining to them that Janet was locked up in a hotel room partying with Bobby Brown. René was annoyed because nobody could get in touch with Janet. She refused to answer the phone. She refused to answer the door. 'You have to do something,' René was saying to Katherine and Joseph."

Then Howard laughed. "Like Janet Jackson is going to listen to anything her parents have to say! Look, no one tells her what to do.

"She and Bobby Brown were holed up in that room having the time of their lives, and that was the end of that. More power to them. What they were doing in there is anybody's guess, but knowing Bobby Brown, they probably weren't playing checkers.

"Katherine and Joe were not happy about this little romance," he continued. "They didn't know much about Brown other than what they'd heard in the media. But, of course, they were powerless to do anything about Janet's love life. They lost control of Janet a long time ago."

It is said by their friends that René Elizondo was angry at Janet because of her brief—two weeks, actually—romance with Bobby, even though his relationship with Janet was such that both of them had made room for little indiscretions along the way.

"Bobby Brown knocked himself out to get Janet Jackson, and when he did, he was on cloud nine," says his friend Tyrone Procter. " 'I got me the sexiest girl in the world,' he kept saying. 'She's mine. A classy girl like that, and she's all mine.' Bobby's whole thing was that he always wanted to land a sophisticated black woman, someone who would make his 'homeboys' jealous. Well, everyone who knew Bobby was envious of his new thing with Janet, that's for certain.

"But then Bobby was in for a big shock: Janet dropped him like a hot potato."

Suffice it to say that Janet Jackson is nobody's fool. To understand her, one has only to remember what she observed in her parents' marriage. Her mother suffered through decades of emotional abuse from Joseph, with Janet watching in horror as her father paraded a string of affairs and a child out of wedlock in front of Katherine. Thus, despite the fact that Janet found certain aspects of Bobby Brown's personality interesting, those that reminded her of her father were more than sufficient to put her survival instincts on full alert.

"She didn't think he would be faithful to her," says Procter. "And, worse, she thought he would make her look like a fool in the process. She wasn't sure. But she was fairly certain she didn't want to take the chance.

"She heard that Bobby had fathered a number of

illegitimate children. He has not denied this and has, in fact, confirmed these stories in the media. Janet was affected by this revelation."

"She never really got over what Joe had done to Katherine by fathering Joh' Vonnie," says J. Randy Taraborrelli. "So for Janet, Bobby Brown was certainly exciting—a thrill a minute, you might say—but not for anything long-term."

Her friends say Janet was firm but loving with Bobby, telling him in no uncertain terms that there could never be anything serious between them, but that he was a wonderful, caring person who would make some other girl a terrific husband.

Recalled Tyrone Procter, "I've heard that getting dumped by Janet Jackson is tough, because she does it in a way that only makes you fall more in love with her. 'Damn,' Bobby said after Janet gave him the heave-ho. 'I ain't never been dumped like this.'"

Brown pursued Janet for a few more weeks. But in time, he respected her wishes.

Eventually Bobby Brown would marry Whitney Houston, another vocalist the public perceives as being wholesome and clean-cut, and who, like Janet Jackson, actually has a provocative side that's not evident on first viewing. Some associates of Bobby Brown said that he married Whitney on the rebound, but this does not seem to be the case, since Brown was involved with a number of women between Janet and Whitney.

Still, it would appear that Whitney Houston is uneasy about the fact that her husband once dated Janet Jackson. When Houston and Brown ran into Jackson in an airport in Florida during the summer of 1993, their meeting was chilly, with Whitney standoffish and eager to get on her way.

"Frankly, Whitney Houston doesn't know what to make of Janet," says one of Janet's confidants, "or how to feel about her. If Bobby had dumped Janet, that would be easier for Whitney to live with. But the fact that Janet had Bobby first, used him all up, so to speak, and then practically handed him over to Whitney makes Whitney feel like she got Janet's sloppy seconds. And then to complicate matters, whenever Janet sees Whitney, Janet is as sweet as pie to her because she thinks she's a great talent, which makes Whitney absolutely nuts. One of the interesting things about Janet Jackson is that she has the ability to disarm her enemies with kindness."

It's a fact: Janet Jackson doesn't pay much attention to the so-called competition. But she does have a great admiration for Whitney Houston's tremendous ability as a vocalist. "That girl is a *singer*," she has said. "I mean, I wish to God I could sing like Whitney Houston. I'd probably be singing all the time—around the house, to friends, in the supermarket. I mean, she is a singer's singer. Not like Madonna."

Now, there is a party-stopper among the Jacksons: mention the name Madonna, and you'll likely get a grimace from Janet. Like her brother Michael (who thinks Madonna is overrated and once called her a "heifer"), Janet has no interest whatsoever in Madonna. "What is it people see in her?" she asked one friend. "I mean, she can't sing, she can't dance. What is it? So she's nasty. So what? If I took my clothes off in the middle of a busy highway, people would look at me, too. That's not exactly talent."

In 1992, Michael was considering having Madonna appear with him in a video of "In the Closet" and he held a few meetings with her about the possibility. He told associates he found her to be tremendously self-involved and that she acted condescending toward him. But he was willing to put his personal feelings about her aside for the sake of creating a terrific commercial product.

Madonna agreed to appear in the video on one condition—she and Jackson would have to appear in drag. Him as a woman, her as a man. Michael's instincts were that this would only fuel the long-standing rumor that he is homosexual, which he has denied repeatedly over the years. So Michael asked Janet for advice.

"Janet said, 'Do it, Mike,'" reported one colleague. "She thought he should throw it in their [the public's] faces. 'They'll never expect that from you. It's as if you're making fun of *them*,' Janet told him, 'as if you're telling the public you not only don't care what they say about you, you're *encouraging* it.' And with Madonna? That should make it even bigger."

Michael said he would consider all of this, then asked Janet if she would talk to Madonna about the project. "I think she has something up her sleeve, but I don't know what it is," he said. "Maybe you can find out."

Reluctantly—*extremely* reluctantly, because Janet really did not want to have to speak to Madonna—Janet telephoned the so-called Material Girl.

"After five minutes of the most frigid conversation in the history of the telephone," reported her colleague, "Janet called Michael back and said, 'Don't do it, Mike.' When Michael asked her why the change of heart, she told him that Madonna has one thing on her mind: to make fun of Michael Jackson and to see what he would look like as a girl. 'I don't trust her at all,' Janet said. 'I don't know if I like the way her mind works.'"

"Janet," concluded the colleague, "is very protective of Michael. In the end, he didn't do it."

At a recent awards show, Madonna noticed Janet Jackson standing alone in a corner, waiting for directions from a technician. She walked over to her and said, "Must be nice to have nothing to do, huh?"

Janet just stared her down.

"Oh, lighten up, girl," Madonna said as she sauntered away. "You Jacksons have no sense of humor whatsoever."

As Madonna turned back toward her and winked Janet looked at her as one would look at an insect that had just crawled out of the salad.

To writer Denise Worrell, Janet summarized her feelings about Madonna quite succinctly. "Aside from dance music, I don't think there's anything whatsoever that Madonna and I have in common. And she doesn't really dance, does she?"

Later, using an urban slang phrase, Janet said of Madonna, "She ain't all *that*. She ain't all *that*, at all."

chapter

FOURTEEN

Nineteen-ninety had been an astonishing year for twenty-four-year-old Janet Jackson. Her Rhythm Nation World Tour was a tremendous box-office success; the *Rhythm Nation 1814* album was a huge seller, containing four number-one singles. Together, her two recent A&M albums—*Control* and *Rhythm Nation*—sold more than fourteen million copies in the United States alone.   According to press reports, Janet Jackson was the biggest-selling recording artist in the history of A&M Records.

The release of *Janet Jackson's Rhythm Nation 1814* brought Janet to the end of her relationship with A&M Records when her recording contract expired. By the end of 1990, an intense bidding war for her services was being waged among eight major labels, including Capitol, Atlantic, Virgin, and A&M. Janet Jackson was clearly a hot commodity. In fact, it could be argued that she was the hottest act in the record biz, not only because of her prodigious talent, creativity, ambition, and record sales, but also because of her youthfulness. Explained Joe Smith, president of Capitol, "What was appealing to me [about the possibility of having Janet Jackson sign on as a Capitol artist] was that by the end of the agreement she would still be a very young woman. Often, when you are making a deal with an artist at the top of their game, they are in their late thirties or early forties. For instance, if you wanted to sign Mick Jagger, he'd be sixty by the time the contract is over. You wonder what relevance he'll have at that point."

At the same time Janet Jackson made a significant business decision. For the previous year she had been managed by Roger Davies Management, but after the Rhythm Nation World Tour ended on November 16, she severed her ties with that organization.

"Roger Davies and I made an agreement specifically to put the Rhythm Nation World Tour together," she said in a prepared statement. "After working a short time together, he took on more managerial duties at my request, but it was always the understanding that this would be a yearlong relationship. The termination of our deal was predetermined when we entered the agreement. Seeing the benefits of managerial representation, I decided to find a personal manager. I had a wonderful working relationship with Roger, which was beneficial to both parties." After that announcement, Janet signed with Howard Kaufman's HK Management.

"What was really happening was that Janet was getting her ducks in place for the negotiation of her new deal, now that A&M was out of the picture," said Gino Brando, a family friend (and no relation to Marlon

Brando). "She wanted someone who could put this thing together for her; she was putting together her team.

"Janet was about to set herself up for life," he continued. "She had said that she worked hard to achieve all she accomplished and that the time had come for her to begin planning her future. She has this fear of going broke. I don't know where the fear comes from, since she's never experienced poverty, at least not that she really remembers. But she's heard enough stories—it's part of the family lore—and she's also talked to Mike about it, who has the same fear.

"Even with all of his money, Michael sometimes feels cash-poor, especially if he spends a few million on some project that didn't work out the way he had planned for it to, like the long-form *Moonwalker* video in the late eighties," says Brando. "And, unfortunately, Janet's brothers are always busted and rarely have enough money to get by, even though they've earned millions. Also, money is always an issue with Katherine and Joe. There often doesn't seem to be enough to pay for their rather lavish life-styles.

"Now Janet was about to start looking to the future, getting herself in a position of true financial power. Making some solid investments, that sort of thing. This, as she explained it, was her goal," Brando concluded.

In March 1991, twenty-four-year-old Janet Jackson signed a three-album deal with Virgin Records, valued at $32 million, thus ending the intense bidding war for her services. It was touted as the largest recording contract in history. "I am very excited to be part of the

Virgin family," Janet said in a prepared statement. "I am confident that together we will break new ground."

Six months earlier she met privately with Virgin Records Group Chairman Richard Branson. Branson, a renowned entrepreneur who holds several hot-air balloon records (including a flight from Japan to Alaska), took Janet on a demonstration flight near his country home in England. "She loved it," recalled one of her associates. "Believe it or not, it helped clinch the deal. She thought Branson was a kid at heart. He fascinated her."

"A Rembrandt rarely becomes available," Branson said of Janet. "When it does, there are many people who are determined to get it. I was determined," he concluded. "She wants to be the biggest star in the world."

Virgin, long an international force in the recording industry, did not inaugurate its United States operation until 1987. In the three years from that time until Janet's signing, the company was admired for its excellent recording and promotion of artists such as Paula Abdul, Keith Richards, Lenny Kravitz, and Soul II Soul. Jeff Ayeroff, co–managing director of Virgin records in the United States, told Chuck Phillips of the *Los Angeles Times* that one of the reasons Virgin pursued Janet with such zeal was her enormous international appeal. "We're trying to establish a roster that will make us competitive throughout the world," he said. "We are a European-based company and the bulk of our revenues comes from outside the United States. Janet is a world-class artist, and we expect her growth to be tremendous."

According to parties knowledgeable about Janet Jackson's business affairs, one reason her deal was so lucrative was that she was a "free agent" at the time of negotiations, which meant prospective buyers did not have to pay off prior contractual obligations. Standard recording-industry practice is for record companies to strive to prevent successful artists from ever becoming free agents by luring them to extend their contractual obligations.

For instance, a contract with a new artist frequently gives the record company options for as many as six albums, ordinarily at a relatively low royalty rate of twelve to fourteen percent. But if an album by that fledgling artist becomes successful, the company is usually eager to renegotiate with the artist rather than waiting for the full term of the original contract to expire. The artist is also eager for such a renegotiation, as this is commonly an opportunity for her royalty rates to be increased. Usually, at the time of this rene-gotiation, the royalty rate is escalated to about sixteen percent of retail, but this raise comes with a price attached—the record company ordinarily calls for the artist to add another album, sometimes more, to the original obligation. If the artist's sales continue to climb, there may be subsequent negotiations, all increasing the royalty rate but requiring the artist to deliver still more albums. This practice usually ties an artist to a label for many years, making it impossible for her to be considered a "free agent," or to go to another label clear of obligations.

"It was absolutely essential to the Jackson–Virgin deal that she [Janet Jackson] was a free agent," said attorney John Branca, the man who masterminded Michael Jackson's amazing career for eleven years. (Branca left Jackson in 1991, but has since returned to the Jackson organization.) "The last time there was a free agent of this stature was the Rolling Stones in 1983, and they set the all-time record for the largest guarantee in a record deal at that time.

"So when Paula Abdul walks in or Steve Winwood or some other Virgin artist walks in and asks for a contract like Janet's, the company is just going to say, 'Hey, look, when you're free, we'll sit down and talk about it, but you're not free, so you can't get the deal that Janet got.'"

"Do you think it's happenstance that Janet was a free agent?" one of her advisers asked. "Of course not. Just after the success of *Control*, A&M sought to renegotiate her contract to include further albums for the label. But Joe [Jackson] wouldn't go for it. He understood that renegotiating in this manner, at that time, would tie his kid up for years.

"Then, just after the release of *Rhythm Nation*, A&M approached Janet again with the same offer. Following Joe's shrewd example, Janet rejected it. Because of that sound business decision, Janet was in such a powerful place of negotiation when her contract expired. So if anyone ever says Joe didn't teach his daughter a thing or two about the complexities of the music business, that person would be greatly mistaken. Janet owes a debt of gratitude to her father, and she knows it."

Janet Jackson's deal with Virgin guaranteed her about $30 million for three albums, plus a twenty-two-percent royalty on the retail price of every record she sells. (That translates to about $2.35 per album. In comparison, Madonna's royalty rate is eighteen percent. Most other superstar acts make twelve percent.) Virgin will also subsidize the majority of expenses for Janet's high-priced videos. And surprisingly, according to industry sources, Janet's contract does not tie her to the label for as long a period of time as one might expect. In fact, she retains an unusual option that allows her to exit the label after just two albums, leaving her a free agent again and able to negotiate an even bigger deal with a new record company. "Nobody has ever inked a more artist-oriented deal than Janet," one insider told the *Los Angeles Times*'s Chuck Phillips. "In terms of freedom, Janet still wins the contest, hands down."

It was said that Michael Jackson, who is known to be extremely competitive, was upset about Janet's deal. This is not true according to people who know him well, for Michael is not as competitive with his sister as many might like to believe. In fact, not only does he champion her efforts, but he also gives her counsel whenever she asks for it. He was fired up by her good fortune, impressed with her business savvy, and delighted that she and her colleagues had been able to negotiate such a sweet deal.

He told his attorney John Branca that he found *Rhythm Nation 1814* to be "a genius work." His biggest concern was that it hadn't sold as many copies as he felt it should have. "Why did it only sell five or six million records?" he asked Branca. "And what does this mean for me and *my* next album?"

During this time, early 1991, Michael Jackson and his team of attorneys and managers had just finished negotiating a colossal recording pact with Sony, estimated to be worth $60 million. Sources in the Jackson camp claim that Michael and Janet met in late January 1991 to determine the best way to time any public announcements of these mega-deals.

Said one of Michael's associates, "Michael was concerned that the announcement of his Sony deal would take the wind out of Janet's sails if it was made prior to Janet's news. He telephoned Janet to tell her just that. Janet, always with an eye toward maximum public relations, realized Michael was right. So the two arranged to meet. Janet planned to drive out to Michael's ranch and spend the weekend with him, but she just didn't have the time. So the two of them met at his condominium in Westwood.

"It was said that at the meeting Michael asked his sister when she was planning to make her announcement, because, as he put it, 'Timing is everything in this business.' After they talked, it was Michael's decision to put off the publication of his deal for at least a week. He wanted Janet to have the fame of having the biggest recording contract in history for at least a week before he would have to come in and usurp the honor. It was a gift to her, really."

"Janet and Michael are premiere players," Jerome Howard said. "They got together and they strategized. They're brilliant at this. While it looked like Michael was going to upstage his baby sister, what was really happening is that they made a purposeful decision as to who would come out of the box first. Nothing that ever happens having to do with them is accidental. The two of them know exactly what they're doing, every minute."

Indeed, nine days after Janet's news hit the front pages, Michael Jackson announced that he had signed a huge deal with Sony, Inc. (which bought CBS

Records in 1988) for an estimated $65 million. Michael's deal was structured on solid groundwork laid by John Branca in 1989—including a twenty-five-percent royalty rate, three percent more than Janet's—and Jackson's own Sony-distributed label. "I want more money than anyone else has ever gotten," Michael told Branca when the lawyer began negotiating with Sony. Michael's spokespersons claimed that his contract guaranteed a return of hundreds of millions of dollars. Some press reports even said Michael's deal was "for a billion dollars." In fact, Michael could receive $120 million per album for the next six albums *if* sales match the forty-million-plus level of *Thriller.* So, while he's not bringing in a billion, his deal, including advances and other perks, might actually be worth $50 million, which certainly eclipses Janet's $32-million Virgin deal.

Originally, Branca and Jackson planned to have Janet sign with Michael's custom label. They felt she would be the most obvious first artist to sign and Michael even decided to call his label "Nation Records," presumably in honor of Janet's *Rhythm Nation.* But people in Janet's organization have said that when Michael suggested the idea to her, she was immediately cold to it. As Jerome Howard, her former attorney put it, "Janet has worked years to make it clear that she is her own woman, someone who is not to be in Michael's shadow. Why would she sign with Michael's label and be linked with him as his special pet project? She was clear that this was something she did not want to do. It was absolutely the right decision."

At first, says another Jackson associate, Michael was put off by Janet's decisiveness. "He was a little hurt. He thought she should have been somehow honored. But then, after he had a minute to think about it, he understood her position and he respected it. He never attempted to change her mind."

Ironically, just as Michael and Janet were signing these multimillion-dollar deals, Sony was in the process of dropping the rest of the Jacksons—Jackie, Tito, Marlon, and Randy—from the label, after a commercially unsuccessful but artistically stimulating album entitled *2300 Jackson Street* (which, of course, is the address of the old family homestead in Gary, Indiana). LaToya was also without a recording contract. Marlon, who had signed with Capitol after his Sony deal was lost, then lost his deal at Capitol as well, so the only brother with a record deal was Jermaine, who was under contract to Arista.

"The funny thing is that when word of Michael's own custom label began circulating throughout the family, the brothers thought they should have been asked to sign on the dotted line," said a family friend. "But Michael was clearly not at all interested in them as recording artists. He has never really been enthusiastic about working with his brothers again.

"And then, the inevitable happened. LaToya sent word that *she* wanted to sign on to Michael's label. She said she had some intriguing songs and wanted Michael to produce her. That, of course, was not in the cards at all."

(As of early 1994, Michael still has not launched his own custom label for Sony.)

One woman who was said not to be particularly elated about Janet's signing with Virgin was Paula Abdul. It seems only natural that Paula would be anxious about this turn of events, since she and Janet appeal to the same youthful audience. Actually, not only do many industry observers consider the two women to be in direct competition, but some intimates of the entertainers have indicated that the stars themselves think of each other as competition.

Paula Abdul's associates have indicated privately that Abdul was, at first, uneasy about Janet's huge deal with Virgin. Said one of them, "There were stories that [Paula] was furious and throwing temper tantrums, saying she hated Janet and how could Virgin do this to her. But that's not true. However, she was concerned that, as a result of all the attention Janet was getting, Virgin might not be as responsible to her future recordings as the company should be. So Paula met with Virgin executives and was assured that Janet's signing did not change anything where her own career was concerned.

"Satisfied, Paula sent Janet a huge basket of beautiful flowers with a congratulatory note."

In October 1991, Janet's sister LaToya published her memoirs, *LaToya—Growing Up in the Jackson Family*. To the Jacksons collectively, it must certainly have seemed as if LaToya just would not go away.

Presumably to promote the book, Jack Gordon told *Rolling Stone* magazine that Michael offered his sister $5 million to stop its publication. Though the magazine printed the story, it was simply not true.

What actually happened was that Jack Gordon telephoned Jerome Howard, Katherine and Joseph's savvy business manager and attorney, and suggested that Howard pass an offer on to Katherine: LaToya would not write the book at all if Katherine paid her a cool $5 million. According to Howard, Gordon offered him a percentage of the money if Katherine agreed to pay it. Jerome Howard says he refused to accept any such percentage and that he considered the offer to be "extortion," but that he would relay the offer to Katherine anyway—with instructions to telephone Gordon for further details. Outraged when she learned of it, Katherine refused. (It's not likely that she would have been able to come up with that much money, anyway. Chances are she would have had to go to Michael or Janet for that kind of cash.)

Gordon then presented Michael with the same offer. Michael was stunned that his sister and her husband would have such audacity. His reaction: "Tell LaToya I said to go jump in a lake."

The offer was not presented to Janet. "She most certainly would have gotten on the first plane to New York just to smack LaToya across the face," says one of Janet's associates.

After Michael rejected her proposal, LaToya somehow twisted the whole story around, or perhaps she was just getting wrong information from Jack Gordon. She told writer Mitchel Fink of the *Los Angeles Herald Examiner* (in July 1989) that she wouldn't comment on the amount of money Michael had offered her, "except to say that it's awful, a sign of bribery. Nothing is going to stop me, no matter how much I'm offered."

LaToya then went to the press, claiming that on September 1, 1989, Michael told her, "I'm going to do everything I can to stop your career."

"He said all the publicity was making me notorious and he didn't like it," she claimed. "The problem is, Michael wants to hog the limelight. He's actually jealous of all the exposure I'm getting. He told me, 'I've been doing this since I was five years old, and here you come out of nowhere—what justifies your fame? You're not entitled to this yet.' I ended up slamming the phone down on him. I told him it's over between us, and that I'd never speak to him again, and I mean it."

"Mike should be so lucky," Janet said when that quote was read to her.

Jack Gordon apparently then planted untrue stories in a tabloid about what LaToya's memoirs were going to reveal about Michael—all as a means of promoting the project. According to one tabloid reporter, "Gordon was on the phone touting LaToya's book, telling anyone interested that it would include the shocking revelation that Michael would pay up to $1 million to new parents to allow him to buy their baby sons for playmates." That amazing claim ran as part of a lurid cover story in the July 1991 issue of the *Globe*, a story that also claimed Michael "used to dress up in women's clothes and make-up." The article claimed that, according to LaToya's book, Michael is gay.

But in actuality, none of that information is found in LaToya's book, nor does any of it appear to be factual anyway. Still, the article infuriated the Jackson family when it was published, because, as quoted, it was quite clear that the information had come from an exclusive interview conducted with Jack Gordon by writer Ellen Grehan. Noted Cheryl Lavin of the *Chicago Tribune*, "If LaToya's book contains half the dirt that Gordon has said is in there, it's quite a nasty piece of work." Referring to the *Globe* article, Gordon told the *Chicago Tribune*, "A lot of this is made up." It was not clear, however, whether Gordon was saying it was "made up" by the tabloid . . . or by him.

When asked about Jack Gordon's claim that Michael was buying infants, Katherine reported to the *Chicago Tribune,* "We were all [at Michael's house] for a family day, and there were no babies there. Gordon told a friend of mine, 'I know [the charges in the book] are all lies, but when I put this book out, Michael Jackson will never be able to set his foot on another stage again.'

"I don't know how Gordon gets away with this stuff," Katherine continued. "Why doesn't somebody stop him?"

She also told the *Chicago Tribune* about the offer Gordon had made via Jerome Howard involving Joseph and Katherine paying to stop the book's publication. (In her interview with the *Tribune,* Katherine mistakenly recalled the amount as having been $15 million.)

Once the dreaded book was published, the entire family reeled from LaToya's subsequent charges of emotional and sexual abuse (although the allegations of sexual abuse were not included in the book). Each member was outraged by what LaToya had to say about him or her. The only family member to escape her critical assessment was Michael, who came away from the literary melodrama completely unscathed, though in the early stages of the project, LaToya threatened to write that he had been sexually abused as a child. When Michael learned of LaToya's plans—he read about it in *Newsweek* and then heard about it on CNN—he was angered enough to have his attorney, John Branca, meet with her representatives. Branca threatened a libel suit against LaToya if any such claim about Michael was made in her book. She backed off immediately.

"None of the family ever wants to cross Michael because he's the one with all the money," observed Jerome Howard. "It's part of the family's credo. You do not make Michael mad, because if you do, when you need him for something he'll be gone."

Janet was particularly offended by LaToya's book. "It's all a bunch of crap," she told one confidant. "It makes me sick to think this was written by my sister, someone I love. I'm disgusted about it."

LaToya painted a rather unflattering picture of Janet Jackson, claiming she is anti-Semitic, power hungry, jealous of Michael's fame, and duplicitous in her dealings with the family. As much as she may have wanted to, Janet found that dismissing the book was difficult. "She took it to heart," says a family friend. "She was hurt. She read the book from cover to cover, not believing her eyes. She sobbed at some portions. Mostly, she was sorry that Katherine would have to be subjected to this book. There were also a few things Janet was afraid would be in the book that weren't. 'I'm glad I didn't confide *everything* to LaToya,' declared Janet. 'I'm glad I still have some secrets.'"

"Janet was also furious because of the way LaToya was promoting the book. She was saying that she [LaToya] and Michael were in constant communication, and that he was supportive of her exploits," says Jerome Howard. "It wasn't true."

"Honest to God, I swear, they haven't even seen each other in at least five years," Janet said. "Mike doesn't want anything to do with her. He loves her, but he knows he must stay away from her just to protect himself. All of this she keeps saying about Michael's talking to her and helping her out is bullshit. She's just exploiting the fact that she's Michael Jackson's sister.

"She doesn't even have his phone number, because Mike refuses to give it to her." (For that matter, no one at all in the family except Janet and Katherine have Michael's telephone number. Both have been sworn to secrecy and told that should they reveal the number to other family friends, Michael would have it changed and then not allow them to have the new one.)

"As far as Michael is concerned, LaToya is a huge disappointment and he doesn't want anything to do with her," says Jerome Howard. "LaToya couldn't reach him now in a million years. It's a shame, because Michael is very worried about LaToya, generally speaking, but he feels she has made her own bed and now must sleep in it. Basically, I believe, that's how Janet feels as well. The entire family feels betrayed by this girl. They'll probably never get over it."

"LaToya was obviously crying out for love and attention by writing her book, just as she had done with the *Playboy* layout," observes J. Randy Taraborrelli. "But because she had caused all of the family so much stress, they found it impossible to want to reach out to her. Also it should be noted that if, just if, her claims of sexual abuse are true, then she has lived a difficult life and is a very courageous person for the way she has gotten on with things. I think we have to give this woman the benefit of the doubt."

In September 1991, the family planned a press conference at their Encino home to publicly denounce LaToya's memoirs. Katherine and Joe would be joined by Jackie, Tito, Jermaine, Randy, and Rebbie. Marlon had purposefully distanced himself from the family's controversies and would not attend. Katherine asked Michael to be present, but he quickly turned her down, saying he did not want to validate LaToya's book by even showing up. Janet made the same decision.

"Janet's position was clear," says Steven Harris, a former associate. "She believed her presence at any such press conference would give the book validity. So she was dead set against the idea of a press conference. 'From a public-relations standpoint, the less we say about this, the better,' she decided. She talked to Katherine and tried to convince her that the press conference would backfire. 'I can see so clearly what will happen,' she said. 'Whatever we say, LaToya will quickly refute with her own press conference, which'll promote her book even more.' Or, as Janet has said in the past, 'The best thing we can do as a family is keep our traps shut.'"

When Janet speaks, people listen.

On September 16, 1991, the family issued the following statement: "After careful consideration, the Jackson family has decided not to dignify LaToya's allegations with a response. We know, and we hope all our friends and fans know, that her ongoing statements are a pack of lies and any comment from us would only add fuel to the fire. Our sincerest apologies for inconveniencing everyone who planned to join us today."

In other words, the press conference was canceled.

Still, Katherine could not resist an interview with *Jet* magazine, in which she said, "I don't want our black people to believe these lies she is telling. I don't want them to believe any of LaToya's lies because we are not that way. We haven't done anything to anybody but been nice."

One of the reasons the public often seems ambivalent about the veracity of much of what the Jacksons say is that they frequently make absurd statements, such as Katherine's to *Jet*, in closing: "We're just a plain family. We don't claim to be big shots. We are just down-to-earth people."

Indeed.

Perhaps Janet has a valid point: "The best thing we can do as a family is keep our traps shut."

chapter

FIFTEEN

As far as Janet Jackson was concerned, LaToya's besmirching of the family name by writing a "tell-all" book was unforgivable. But since LaToya was already considered the black sheep of the family, what she had to say in her book—and in the television interviews in which she promoted it—was in keeping with her renegade image and, as a result, not really surprising to most people who knew anything about the Jacksons. However, when Janet's thirty-six-year-old brother Jermaine openly denounced thirty-three-year-old Michael, the public was amazed and even Janet was astonished.

Jermaine's song "Word to the Badd!!" was leaked to radio by unnamed sources in November 1991, perhaps not coincidentally at the precise time of the release of Michael's first single from his forthcoming *Dangerous* album, "Black or White." In the thinly veiled tell-all tune, Jermaine ordered his younger brother to "get a grip" and criticized him for having had so much plastic surgery and also for lightening his skin. He also reprimanded Michael for being ashamed of his race. The version of "Word to the Badd!!" found on Jermaine's 1991 Arista album, *You Said,* is completely different, with lyrics having nothing to do with Michael. Jermaine claimed not to have any knowledge as to how the controversial version was ever leaked to radio. However, a source close to Jermaine told the *New York Post* about that version: "These are his true feelings. He wrote it for himself. Michael comes out with this song 'Black or White,' saying it doesn't matter if you're black or white, you have to get along. But Michael doesn't know if he is black or white. Jermaine is proud to be black."

Naturally, because of the fervor, Arista decided to release the "controversial" version of the song to the public.

It seemed to even the most casual observer that Jermaine Jackson, who hadn't had a hit record in five years, was somehow masterminding an attempted public-relations coup, thus to ride on the coattails of advance publicity surrounding the release of Michael's long-awaited *Dangerous,* his first album in four years. However, Jermaine steadfastly denied that this was the case, saying, "The point is that Michael lost touch with reality and he left the family. My song is an attempt to heal our relationship."

Because Michael would allow only Janet and Katherine to have his personal telephone number, Jermaine was not able to reach him when he wanted to, which, he said, agitated and frustrated him enough to write the song. "If I can't tell him on the phone," he said to *USA Today,* "I'm going to put it in a song. I needed to do it for myself. He's my brother. I love him."

As for whether or not he was exploiting the publicity surrounding his brother's new album, Jermaine declared, "If there's any competition, it's not done intentionally. Our timing is perfect, that Michael has a record coming and I have one out. We're all family and we have to fight the world."

"When Michael heard the song, he was hurt at first, then angry," says Gino Brando. "He telephoned his sister Janet, to ask her what she thought. They always call Janet to see how she feels about things. She's known in the family—by the family—as someone who can look at a situation and see it clearly for what it is.

"Janet said that the worst thing Michael could do would be to respond to Jermaine in the media," said Brando. "When Mike indicated that he was considering an interview with *USA Today* to put the matter into perspective, Janet urged him not to do it. She is extremely suspicious of the press and believed that anything Mike said would be misquoted.

"In the end, he didn't do the interview."

Katherine was planning a family picnic at just about the time of the release of Jermaine's record, and even though Michael had no intention of attending, he asked Janet to be there and to "find out what you can about what's going on."

Janet did go, since she enjoys seeing her more than twenty nieces and nephews. And, as she told *Ebony* magazine, "What makes me happy is being with my family, all of us together. Family is number-one, and we know that."

At the event, Janet took the opportunity to have words with Jermaine about the controversial song. Remembered one observer, "Janet stayed away from Jermaine for some time, until finally he went over to her to find out why she was acting so coldly toward him.

"'Because of what you did to Michael,'" Janet said.

"'Oh, come on, Janet, he deserved it. You know he deserved it.'

"'First of all,' Janet said, getting ready to level Jermaine, 'he did *not* deserve it. What did he do? Not give you his phone number? What are you, a baby? You're all upset about something stupid just because you can't talk to Mike when you want to?'

"'But . . . ' Jermaine stammered.

"'There's no excuse for what you did, Jermaine,' Janet continued, without missing a beat. 'We weren't raised like this. It's not the public's business. Not only that, I hate the record, Jermaine. I really do.'

"Then, Janet turned and walked away."

"I think now, he regrets that he did it," Janet has said about Jermaine's record in a recent interview. Of her having confronted Jermaine, she declares, "Mother always said if you have a problem with someone, you don't hold it inside; you go to that person and work it out, especially if it's a family member. We have to stick together as a family. I know Jermaine loves Michael. Whatever disagreement he was having with Mike, he should have worked out in another way."

Michael Jackson apparently did not need his little sister, Janet, to stand up for him. According to his former sister-in-law Enid Jackson, he took matters into his own hands when he went to the family's Encino home, where Jermaine was living, to confront his brother. Said Enid, "Michael will only go to the house on rare occasions, to pick up mail or deliver something. When he does go there, often he'll pull into the driveway in his white GMC four-wheel-drive Jeep, see whose car is parked there, and then do a quick U-turn and leave if he sees someone's car he doesn't want to deal with—like Joseph's. On this day, though, he probably wouldn't have turned and left regardless of whose car was there, because he came to talk to Jermaine about 'Word to the Badd!!'

"The angry confrontation between Michael and Jermaine took place in the driveway, between the guard's gate and the recording studio.

"Michael asked Jermaine, 'Why do you want to say stuff like that? What's wrong with you? How can you do that to me?'

"Jermaine's reaction was, 'Because it's what's going down, man. You don't call me. You don't want to even know me anymore. You treat us all bad. You act like you don't want to know us anymore.'

"This infuriated Michael, and they had more angry words. Finally, Michael was ready to beat Jermaine up.

"Jermaine taunted him, saying, 'What's wrong, Michael? You want to kick my ass? C'mon, then. Show me what you got. Kick my ass, then.'

"And Michael just lunged at him. 'Okay, man,' he said. "I'll kick your ass. I'll be glad to kick your ass!'

"Just then, one of Katherine's friends jumped in the middle of the two of them, and the security guard was trying to pull Jermaine away. All the while, Jermaine was saying, 'C'mon, hit me. Hit me!' and Michael was trying to get at him, saying, 'Lemme at him, lemme at him.' It was a real mess. It was also a side of Michael you don't see too often, but a side that's there. He doesn't let people mess with him. People don't know that about Michael."

When Janet heard about the wrathful confrontation between her two brothers, she was delighted. She told a family member, "Way to go. That was great. Mike should do that more often. He really put Jermaine in his place. Jermaine needed that."

"Well, that's the way they were raised," Enid says. "They were kept locked up in that house as prisoners and then they were pitted against one another by Joseph, saying things like 'LaToya, Janet's gonna have a hit record before you. Makes you look plenty bad,' or 'Janet, what are you gonna do about Michael's *Thriller* album? You gonna try to beat him? Put him in his place?'"

Janet has acknowledged that a competitive atmosphere existed among the siblings. In an interview with *Ebony* magazine, she noted, "That's how we were raised, really. It comes from my father as well as my mother."

"Joe was fostering competition he thought was friendly, but I think the kids were affected by it," says Enid Jackson. "They were always trying to prove they had guts, nerve, all the things you don't really associate with the Jacksons—but traits that are there.

"Like when Joe found out I slapped Jackie in the face in court, he laughed and said, 'That boy don't have no backbone.' And that comment just made Jackie more determined to be belligerent.

"They all grew up trying to outdo one another, especially Jermaine, who is very competitive with both Janet and Michael. It's a shame, because Jermaine is a great talent in his own right. He doesn't need to compete, but still, he does. It's just part of who he is, who they all are."

Once Michael's slick fourteen-song *Dangerous* album—the first of six under his new Sony contract—was released and his eleven-minute, $4-million "Black or White" video debuted on Fox, MTV, and Black Entertainment Television on November 14, 1991, everyone seemed to forget all about Jermaine's song.

Michael's video, directed by John Landis, who also directed the "Thriller" video, culminated in a four-minute segment that ignited an international furor. It found the frail star alone on a soundstage streetscape, snarling in a rage while he smashed a car to pieces with a crowbar, hurled a garbage can through a car window, and repeatedly grabbed his crotch and simulated masturbation, all in a violent fury.

His rebellious and risqué video seemed to communicate the rage of long-repressed emotion, which alarmed his younger fans and some of his sponsors, and had everyone talking about Michael Jackson again (which is, no doubt, what he intended). On November 15, Washington, D.C., radio talk-show host Mark Davis of WRC-AM lost no time announcing his topic: "Michael Jackson—has he lost his mind, *or what*?"

"He needs to get married, quick," quipped Davis's first caller.

The video only aired once before Jackson snipped the violent ending, apologizing to his public and saying he was concerned by negative parental reaction. The ruckus left many wondering whether he staged a massive publicity stunt or had just naively blundered. Perhaps the question can be answered by the fact that one Jackson associate claims to have seen a draft of the Jackson apology on a desk at the office of Jackson's manager—three days before the video aired.

*   *   *

The controversial year ended with a bang—with another nude pictorial spread of LaToya in *Playboy* magazine. In the accompanying feature, LaToya said Janet had called her in 1988 to tell her that she—LaToya—had been the subject of a number of family meetings, "about the way you're dressed on your new album cover." Said LaToya, "I listened, my heart pounding, as I thought: 'Wait until she sees what's coming next.'"

LaToya says she tried to tell Janet she was planning to strip again for *Playboy,* but Janet was not interested in hearing about it.

Perhaps Janet's interest was diminishing because she was, in a fundamental way, changing her attitude toward her sister. "The person who is there today is not the person I knew when we lived at home," Janet told *Ebony* magazine about LaToya.

According to LaToya, Jermaine telephoned her after the second layout was published. "I want you to know," he said, "that you're a piece of shit. And I'm saying this because I know you're mad at me for cursing. But I want you to know that's what you are. You've degraded our family and made us all look bad."

LaToya said she found his criticism "interesting, coming from the father of an out-of-wedlock child."

"This had to be so hurtful to LaToya," said J. Randy Taraborrelli. "It's clear, though, that this whole family was in terrific pain and turmoil. But since Jermaine had always looked out for LaToya, was always protective of her, for him to be so critical of her now just demonstrated the degree of disappointment in her that he was feeling."

"Whether or not my parents agree with everything I do, I am still their daughter," LaToya said, echoing her sister Janet's comments of just a few years before. "But, now, *I am* in control."

What might one conclude from all this? That LaToya was engaged in a pitiful and unsuccessful emulation of her sister's successful move to independence? Or that LaToya had actually made the transition from rebellious child/adolescent to self-responsible adult and had, in the process, discovered the vocabulary of maturity?

Perhaps the only thing to be said for sure was, as one observer noted, "Indeed, maybe LaToya Jackson had learned a thing or two from Janet's example."

chapter SIXTEEN

In early 1992, the announcement was made that Janet Jackson would star in a new film by John Singleton, the young African-American director whose first feature, the 1991 urban drama *Boyz N the Hood*, had become an instant hit. Ultimately, that movie earned Singleton, then twenty-four, the dual distinction of being both the first African-American nominated for a Best Director Oscar and the youngest person ever to be so nominated by the Academy.

Singleton was gifted, no doubt. And expectations were high for his forthcoming film, *Poetic Justice,* which he had written after *Boyz N the Hood* and intended to direct. A contemporary love story, it involved a young African-American man and woman from the inner city who find themselves dealing with interpersonal relationships and blossoming romance during a road trip up the scenic California coast from Los Angeles to Oakland.

It didn't exactly sound like something Janet Jackson could handle. First, the role called for her to portray "Justice," a young black poet from the gritty streets of South Central Los Angeles. What, asked critics, did Janet Jackson, a product of a rich family in the affluent Los Angeles suburb of Encino, know about the inner city? How authentic could her portrayal be?

But Janet insisted she'd had many of the same experiences and challenges any so-called homegirl might have had, as well as those that were a result of her skin color.

"I was in a store recently in Beverly Hills," she said in a recent interview. "And there were these salespersons, three of them lined up on each side. I walked in wearing my jeans, carrying my bag. I had sunglasses on. Rather than helping me, they just stood there staring dead ahead, as if I did not belong there.

"I'm just standing there thinking, 'Okay, one of them *has* to come up to me.' And you know, none of them did.

"And so, finally, one lady came to me and said [here, Janet assumes an offhand, rich-bitch voice], 'Yes, may I help you?' And suddenly it must have clicked in her mind that I am who I am, because she stopped for a minute, checked herself, and started saying [whispers and gushes], 'Okay, right here, right here, honey. I know I can help you find just exactly what you need. I'm so glad you're here with us today.'

"'Sure,' I thought. 'You're treating me this way because I'm Janet Jackson. But I know you treat my people the other way. I know you treat blacks like second-class citizens around here.'"

Said Gino Brando, "Not only has she experienced that superficial racism, but Janet also spent time in the ghetto when she was married. She was out there in the middle of the night looking for her husband's drug dealers. She saw a lot of shit out there. She got an education about the 'hood then. I know it. She's told me that's when she got her eyes opened."

As J. Randy Taraborrelli concluded, "This question always comes up for actors. 'Do you have to have killed anyone to play a murderer?' For Janet, this issue should not have been whether she spent a certain number of weeks or months in the ghetto or had endured certain specific racial taunts or any other litmus test. It should have been, 'Does this woman have the talent, the presence, and the emotional range to play Justice?' Those who saw her, Singleton included, decided yes."

Janet Jackson's relationship with John Singleton didn't begin with *Poetic Justice*. While in high school, Singleton had actually been bused to Jackson's junior high school. While they weren't exactly locker mates—they were a couple of years apart in age—they were aware of each other. "He was kind of a nerd who used to wear these Coke-bottle glasses," Janet likes to tell the press.

"She was one of those girls trying to look like a woman," Singleton says of Janet, laughing.

After Singleton became a successful writer and director, he and Janet began communicating again following a chance meeting in a Hollywood film studio. When Janet and René Elizondo invited John over for dinner one night, the director had already come up with the idea of *Poetic Justice*. However, he had not considered the film as a potential vehicle for Janet Jackson.

René Elizondo remembered, "Over dinner, Janet was telling a story about how these four girls approached her one time. Three of them were really nice, saying they liked her music. But one of them—there's always one—was saying how 'she ain't all that, she ain't all that,' meaning Janet wasn't such a big deal.

"John was surprised to hear Janet slip into street slang and imitate the girl's voice. He realized there's a side to her that most people don't see, and he began writing the role with her in mind."

As Singleton commented later, "Janet's in this movie because, as a person, she has a quiet intensity to her."

Nevertheless, the mob gathered against both Janet and Singleton early on. Nay sayers insisted that Janet had decided to essay this obviously "ethnic" part in order to boost her popularity among African-Americans, and that this was a continuation of her *Rhythm Nation* phase. With the inner city setting international musical, cultural, and fashion trends, critics suggested that Janet, even as her brother Michael is known to do, was merely jumping on the bandwagon.

Singleton, on the other hand, was accused of casting Janet in the starring role as the introspective young hairdresser for the marquee value of her name. That might have been partly true—and what would have been wrong with it?—but the fact is that Janet Jackson had to audition for the part just like every other African-American actress in Hollywood who was fighting for whatever good parts, and there were but few of them, became available.

For her screen test with Singleton, Janet showed up dressed as Justice: black baseball shirt, baggy pants, and long braids flowing out from under a big, floppy cap. "You could feel the tension on the set when she walked out there," a member of the skeleton film crew recalled of that day, March 25, 1992.

"We all knew she acted in videos and TV, but film is something else altogether. To be honest, while some folks wanted her to make it, some were rooting against her. You know, she's already rich and a star. Why should she take this role from someone else who could really use it? But more important than that, some of us were wondering, If she's *not* good, is John still going to cast her? That was the real question."

As it turned out, Janet *was* good during the screen test. She walked through her lines with a fine sense of timing and with ease. The next day, as Singleton and his team looked at the footage of the test, they were even more impressed. There was no question about it: Janet Jackson was the actress for the role.

Once cast, Janet began her homework for the part. At Singleton's suggestion, she visited a beauty parlor in the predominately African-American Crenshaw district of Los Angeles in order to get the feel of working in such a place. She also had lengthy conversations with young African-American women who told her what it's like to be a real 'round-the-way girl (slang for "your average, young, no-frills, black teenager").

To further understand the style and language of the 'hood, Janet invited four young women—two from South Central Los Angeles and two from Harlem—to live with her for a couple of months. She says she got along famously with all four.

"When people see me on TV, for some reason they

think I'm snooty or bitchy or something, and then when they meet me, they realize how down-to-earth I truly am.

"The day I met these girls, we hit it off really well. We slept in the same room, went dancing together, got into some really deep conversations."

Singleton thought Janet might be a little too thin for the role, so he requested that she put on a few pounds—which she did gladly. "That was one of the best perks," Janet said, joking. "Gaining weight *purposely*. A dream come true."

Principal shooting for *Poetic Justice* commenced in South Central Los Angeles on April 14, 1992. Singleton's first film, *Boyz N the Hood*, had been made on a budget of about $6 million, paltry by Hollywood's standards of opulence and excess. The budget for *Justice* was more than twice that, although, as Singleton has pointed out in interviews, still not equal to the funds a studio would have allowed a hot young white director. The differences between movie budgets for black productions and white productions are just another one of Hollywood's double standards.

When the time came for Janet to report to work, she did so eagerly. "From what I saw, she was on time and always ready when John needed her," recalled someone who worked with the caterers on the set. "I expected her to be stuck-up and have this big entourage, but it was usually just her, her boyfriend, René [who had a small part in the film as "E.J."], and a couple of bodyguards."

But could the woman *act*? When push came to shove, was she going to be able to produce?

In one crucial scene, Justice, while in her apartment, happens upon her reflection in a mirror. At first she admires herself. But then she begins to look disconcerted, as if unhappy, not with what she sees, but with what she feels inside. Frustrated, she takes her braids, wraps them around her neck as if she wishes to strangle herself, then quietly breaks into tears. According to that caterer, Janet's character wasn't the only one crying. "People watching were upset," he said. "Some had tears in their eyes. I know I did. *Janet moved us to tears.* I think a lot of them were surprised that she could turn on those kinds of emotions."

Indeed. But as Janet Jackson said in an interview after the film was released, "I don't know why people think that just because I grew up in the family I did, I didn't have sad times. I've gone through my share of pain and frustration like anyone else. When you're acting, you just pull from those feelings."

Back on the set, Janet wouldn't need to pull from painful emotional memories to conjure up disturbing feelings. The city of Los Angeles itself did that when, on April 29, 1992, riots broke out in protest over a not-guilty verdict handed down to a group of police officers charged with the beating of Rodney King, in what was perhaps the most widely seen episode of police violence in contemporary history.

Singleton was on his way to the set of *Poetic Justice*—which that day, ironically, happened to be at a drive-in theater location in Simi Valley, the Los Angeles suburb where the controversial trial was held—when he and his assistant heard reports of the verdict on the radio and abruptly headed to the courthouse, the scene of the trial. There, among the protesters and police, Singleton expressed feelings of outrage to the news cameras.

Meanwhile, on the set, Janet was having her own problems. The role of the male lead in the film belonged to Tupac Shakur, a young Oakland, California–based rapper. After finding success in the hip-hop group Digital Underground, he stretched with a starring role in the dramatic urban film *Juice* and a successful solo recording career. Shakur, who was from the streets, didn't have to play at being a thug; he proudly stated in interviews that he prides himself on actually being one.

In the beginning of their working relationship, Janet and Tupac seemed to get along fine. But soon the rapper reportedly began making advances toward her, which caused her to feel uneasy.

Actually, Tupac unsettled several people on the set with his attitude. Increasingly, he showed up for shoots hours late, while the other actors, including Janet, waited around in full makeup. He made no secret of his drug use either, often smoking pot on the set along with his posse of fellow hip-hoppers, rappers, and assorted homeboys. One crew member joked that you could get a contact high just walking by Tupac's dressing-room trailer.

"Janet mostly ignored all of that," said Gino Brando. "She wasn't happy about the drugs, that's for sure. 'That's his thing,' she said. ''Long as he doesn't offer 'em to me.'"

Visitors on the set were well aware that Janet wasn't looking forward to her kissing scenes with Tupac, but she was willing to do them—*if* he took an AIDS test.

Tupac's head reportedly went through the roof of his

mobile dressing room when that request was relayed to him. "I'm from the ghetto, and I ain't gonna take no AIDS test," the rapper/actor was quoted as replying. "Maybe if I was gonna be sleeping with Janet, I'd take the test. But I don't think I'd really want to know if I was HIV-positive."

Despite his hard stance, those close to Tupac later insisted that in reality, he was hurt by Janet's attitude. "I'd heard that the boy fell in love with the stuck-up bitch," said a source back in the actor's Oakland stomping grounds, laughing. "All that shit Tupac gets himself into—beating up on folks, pulling guns and shit—it's all for attention, just like a little baby does when he throws his cup full of milk off the high chair. The man needs attention. That thing with Miss Jackson should have really let y'all know somethin' about hard ol' Tupac. Inside, he's just a softy who wants to be loved, just like the rest of us."

Indeed, in speaking about Janet Jackson as his leading lady, Tupac confessed, "I wanted to show her that I love her. I'm not good at showing my feelings, so it was hard being romantic. The hardest thing was to kiss her as Lucky [his character]. It might have been a little movie kiss to her, but I really felt it. Everything I didn't have, she had—money, family, attention."

"Janet was simply not attracted to him," said an observer. "But she didn't want to tell him that, because she was afraid of what it would do to their on-screen chemistry. So there was some stress over that. She was professional, but *very* cool—chilly even, at times—toward him. It was determined, I believe, that there was no way they could do any serious love scenes together."

Indeed, love scenes between Janet and Tupac had

been written, but were cut from the script. Janet explained, "Justice is real to me. I feel her pain. But she's not ready for sex yet, not in the time frame of the movie. She's lost too much, and trusts too little.

"John had originally written in some lovemaking scenes between me and Tupac, and I was willing to get under the sheets with him. But I was not willing to show my short-and-curlies." Not that Janet actually said she would *not* do a discreet love scene with Shakur; rather, her attitude about such a scene was clear. She didn't want to do it. In the end, she didn't have to.

"The story is really about two people, both wounded by tragedy, learning to touch and be touched all over again," she rationalized. "John could have heated up the thing with some steamy bumping, but he was more interested in incorporating the poetry of Maya Angelou. Rather than sensationalizing, he wanted to give the work substance."

As soon as the film was finished, Janet cut off all communication with Tupac Shakur. "She clicked with me the whole movie," he said. "But as soon as it was over, her phone number changed. I thought I knew Janet. I guess not."

"She was being careful," said one of her friends. "How could she trust this guy?"

After *Poetic Justice* had come and gone, Tupac would be arrested three times—first in Los Angeles for allegedly beating up a limousine driver; later in Atlanta for allegedly shooting two off-duty police officers; and again, while out on bail, for allegedly participating in the rape of a young woman.

* * *

Janet's problems with her costar were small compared with rumors that began popping up about the film itself. Word had circulated around Hollywood that executives at Columbia were getting nervous about the production. Company snoops visiting the set said they weren't being bitten by any cinematic vibe or excitement. The shooting was going fairly well, they said, but there was no spark of anything happening on the set that would have indicated the studio had a hit on its hands.

As it turned out, the snoops were right: there was reason to be concerned.

When the film was finally finished, it was screened by the studio before an audience composed of the general public, mostly youngsters and young adults, in the Northern California city of Sacramento. On the scene with Singleton were Columbia brass—Michael Nathanson, president of worldwide production; Mark Gill, senior vice-president of publicity and promotion; Sid Ganis, president of marketing and promotion; and several other studio executives—or, as they are commonly called, "suits." They discreetly took the back row of the theater and gave close attention to both the film and the audience.

At first, everything seemed fine. The audience responded positively to the opening scenes of Justice and her first boyfriend in the film, Markell (played by rapper Q-Tip), kissing, and loved anything that was comical, attitude-laden, or (sadly) violent. But they *hated* the poetry readings interspersed throughout the film and sneered at the artsy scene of Justice's walk among zebras that she and the other characters encountered during their cinematic journey.

When the film was over, the audience was asked to

fill out information cards, which were tallied just after the theater emptied. The news wasn't good. The audience, while saying they enjoyed Janet's acting, generally felt the film was too long—and was boring. Bad, *bad* news.

Singleton's mission was clear—go back and edit the film, make it shorter . . . and get rid of the hokey zebra scene.

"I think we've got a problem on our hands," one of the studio executives was overheard to say. "Just pray that Janet Jackson can pull 'em into the theater before they know how bad the movie is—because, otherwise, we're in big trouble."

chapter
SEVENTEEN

In November 1992, art imitated life when ABC-TV aired a two-part, five-hour mini-series about the Jackson family entitled "The Jacksons—An American Dream" (screenplay by Joyce Eliason). The $12-million production presented the story of how Joseph and Katherine Jackson—played brilliantly by Lawrence Hilton-Jacobs and Angela Bassett (who went on to portray Tina Turner in the critically acclaimed film *What's Love Got to Do with It?*)—and the five brothers and three sisters scraped their way to the top despite emotional and physical abuse that, at least as it was depicted in the mini-series, would have scarred any person for life.

"No more beatings, Joseph," Katherine begs her husband in one scene when he is about to beat his boys for leaving a towel in the pool. "No more. You can*not* do it anymore."

In another scene from this drama that was broadcast to the entire nation, Katherine discovers that Joseph has not only been having an affair, but has also made love with the "other woman" in the household's master bedroom. Seething and sobbing, she leaps at him and pummels him with her fists. "You're a liar and you're a cheat," she sobs uncontrollably. "And I don't want you no more." With that, Katherine grabs a framed wedding photograph of herself and Joseph from a wall and hurls it to the floor, breaking the glass to bits.

Yes, indeed, in this mini-series—which, surprisingly enough, was produced by Jermaine Jackson and his wife, Margaret Maldonado Jackson—Joseph Jackson is depicted as a thoroughly unlikable, even loathsome character. The Jacksons, who were hoping to "set the record straight," in fact exacerbated negative public opinion about the family patriarch by depicting his treatment of his sons—and everyone else around him—as particularly insensitive and mean-minded.

"He never speaks to me," Dee Dee (Tito's wife-to-be) sobs in one scene. "He never even acknowledges my presence."

"But that's just the way Joseph is," Tito explains.

Later, Joseph threatens Tito: "You marry that girl and it's the end of the Jackson 5." But, as Tito explains to Jackie in a subsequent scene, "Getting married is the only way out of here."

"If this is what they as a family authorized, one can only imagine where they drew the line," one TV critic observed. It does cause one to wonder: with this kind of toxicity being shown publicly *with* their consent, in regard to what events did they *withhold* their consent?

The frank mini-series—filled with many of the Jacksons' Motown and post-Motown hits (with the actors lip synching to the songs)—picked up the chronicle of the family with Katherine and Joe's courtship and ended with the Jacksons' 1984 Victory concert tour, which was depicted as a family triumph rather than the continuously troubled event it actually was.

Some of the more interesting castings included the three child actors—Alex Burrell, Jason Weaver, and Wylie Draper—who adeptly portrayed Michael at different ages (Michael Jackson had, and exercised, a script-approval option and participated in some facets of the production), and Holly Robinson in one of the silliest, most ill-conceived Diana Ross impressions ever to be seen in any medium.

Scripted ironies abounded. Among the many: "You cannot live your life trying to fit into other people's fantasies," Katherine tells a teenage Michael with a straight face. "You just be who you are." Great advice, Mom. Which parallel universe did *that* line come from?

Janet was, as might have been expected, very much against the idea of a mini-series because, as she put it privately, "We can't tell the whole story and expect people to understand it. Anything we do, will make it look worse than it was. You'd think they [meaning, presumably, her family] would know that by now."

When it aired, according to one confidant, Janet was upset and brimming with rhetorical questions. "Are they crazy? What are they thinking? How can they do this? How will this help anything?"

"But most of it was true," she was told by the confidant.

"So?" Janet said, annoyed. "That is *not* the point."

*   *   *

Jermaine had hoped his sister LaToya, who had nothing to do with the mini-series but was reportedly paid a significant amount of money by the network for the use of her name and likeness, would not bad-mouth the family when the mini-series aired. "She had no part in building the Jackson 5, and she has no right to tear it down," he said. "She should just keep her mouth shut."

No such luck.

No mention of sexual abuse was made or even hinted at in the mini-series' script. Explained Suzanne DePasse, executive producer of the film and the woman who groomed the Jackson 5 for Motown stardom decades before, "Since no one else in the family seems to agree with LaToya's charges, we decided to go with the majority version." In fact, in the end, Janet, LaToya, and Rebbie were barely mentioned in the script.

According to the Neilsen ratings service, the mini-series was the number-three program of the week the first week it aired in November and number one the second week, a runaway commercial success that proved beyond a shadow of a doubt that the public is eternally fascinated by this taiented, albeit often perplexing, family from Gary, Indiana.

The week the Jacksons' mini-series aired, Janet had other more pressing matters on her mind.

Like sex.

"Sex isn't just fire and heat," Janet Jackson told writer David Ritz in an interview for *Rolling Stone*.

"It's natural beauty. Doing what comes naturally. It's letting go, giving and getting what you need. In the age of AIDS, it certainly requires being responsible. On a psychological level, though, good satisfying sex is also linked with losing yourself, releasing, using your body to get out of your body. Well, for the first time, I'm feeling free. I love feeling deeply sexual, and don't mind letting the world know. For me, sex has become a celebration, a joyful part of the creative process."

Without doubt, by the end of 1992, Janet Jackson had become much more open about her personal feelings. The press was reporting that she and René Elizondo were still friends, but no longer an "item." Janet was now dating a number of men; she was a sexual being—she'd certainly made that point clear in interviews—and proud of it. It was as if she had, perhaps, taken a page from LaToya's life book of erotica and begun to apply it to her own experiences.

In the winter of 1992, Janet had a romantic encounter with handsome film actor Robert De Niro. De Niro, forty-six at the time and single, was introduced to Janet, twenty-six, by an acquaintance of his at a cocktail party.

De Niro had wanted to meet Janet for some time; he told friends that when he had watched her perform on television's American Music Awards show, he was astonished. He remembered Janet as being an annoyingly precocious little kid, Michael's baby sister. But after seeing her performance, he exclaimed to one confidant, "Christ! Look at what's happened to Michael Jackson's kid sister! I can't believe it! She's turned into the most beautiful black woman on the planet."

"Bob simply loves women of African-American

descent," says Janet's former attorney, Jerome Howard. "He finds them very attractive and exciting. He's had love affairs with a long list of beautiful black women. So it's easy to see how he could fall for someone as beautiful as Janet. And he did fall for her, big time."

When Robert asked Janet to have dinner with him, she said yes. She wanted to discuss *Poetic Justice* with him and perhaps even solicit a few acting tips. Afterward, she told one friend, "He's the most sexy, handsome man. He seems like such a gentleman, so devoted to satisfying a woman, and I don't mean sexually. You just always have his attention. I don't see how anyone could resist this guy."

One evening in November 1992, Robert and Janet were seen dining at the ritzy St. James's Club & Hotel on West Hollywood's Sunset Strip. According to witnesses, Robert was dressed in a natty black tuxedo; Janet wore a low-cut black bugle-beaded dress. The couple was seated in a dark, intimate corner of the restaurant.

"Every man in the room had his eyes on Janet Jackson," says Thomas Dillon, a witness to the sparks that seemed to be flying between Miss Jackson and Mr. De Niro. "She absolutely glowed; her skin actually had an iridescent quality to it. Her hair fell softly at her shoulders. She was the most beautiful woman in the club that night. I kept saying to myself, 'Man, Janet Jackson has grown up! She's turned out to be a real doll.'

"They had a sumptuous meal," says Dillon. "Janet was under De Niro's spell and he was sort of hypnotized by her. After dinner, they left the table arm in arm. They walked out into the marble lobby, stopped in front of the elevator, shared a soft kiss, and then went into the elevator.

"I understand that Bob always has a room at the St. James's where he takes his dates," says one of his associates. "And no one knows what happened in that room between Janet and Bob. Guess it has to be left up to the imagination."

Says J. Randy Taraborrelli, "Many of his friends have indicated that De Niro was quite infatuated with Janet Jackson. She'd remarked that she found De Niro hard to resist. In fact, Janet said in early interviews I conducted with her that she sometimes fantasized about being swept off her feet by a leading man, a movie star. Perhaps De Niro fit the bill perfectly.

"She no doubt wanted to live the experience first-hand—and she did. But then, apparently, when it was over, it was over."

"It didn't last long at all," said Jackson-family friend Gino Brando. "In the end, they had nothing in common. He was too old for her, and they didn't know what to talk about. It would appear that the two of them had a hot, very intense, one-night stand. After that, they seemed satisfied. I've never heard of the two of them ever being seen in public again."

According to friends of the two, it wasn't that Janet rejected De Niro, or that he spurned her. Rather, they just never telephoned each other again after that night at the St. James's. Perhaps they instinctively knew that after one night of candlelight romance, there was nothing for them as a couple in the future.

While the old year for Janet may have ended bliss-fully in the arms of a movie star, the new one began on a sour note—in a recording studio with LaToya.

In January 1993, Janet had an in-person confrontation with her estranged sister in Minneapolis, where Janet was finishing recording her first album for Virgin Records. LaToya had telephoned to tell her she was in town and said she wanted to speak to her about "some urgent family matters." Reluctantly, Janet agreed to meet with her older sister; the two hadn't seen each other or spoken in years. The day of the meeting, according to Janet, Katherine warned her to "be careful. There's no telling what LaToya has up her sleeve."

LaToya showed up at the Flyte Tyme Studios in Minneapolis at the appointed hour. At first, according to witnesses, relations between the two sisters were pleasant, if not a bit superficial, as they recounted old times and discussed the recent television mini-series about the family. But then things took a turn toward the ugly when Janet suddenly demanded to know why LaToya had said she was sexually abused as a youngster. Janet also insisted upon knowing how LaToya could hurt their mother by some of the anecdotes she told in her book and on talk shows. When LaToya began to defend herself loudly, the two ended up in a loud, acrimonious argument during which LaToya accused Janet of having once drugged her.

The incident to which LaToya was apparently referring allegedly occurred years earlier when she was scheduled to be a presenter at the American Music Awards show. According to LaToya, on the day of the performance, she became ill. Joseph, who was determined that she not cancel the appearance, insisted she take tranquilizer pills. He instructed Janet to administer one tranquilizer every two hours to her sister—who claims never to have taken any drugs of any kind.

Once she was at the awards show, every time LaToya said she wasn't feeling well, Janet took the plastic vial from her purse and gave her a tranquilizer. LaToya says she was eventually so drugged she couldn't even stand up, and at that point Janet forced her to open her mouth so she could shove in even more tranquilizers. By the time LaToya was called up to the stage to present an award, she could barely walk.

"Where am I?" LaToya recalls having asked Janet, totally bewildered and incoherent.

"You're at the American Music Awards, now get out there on that stage." LaToya says Janet shook her by the shoulders and said, "Go!"

LaToya managed to get through the presentation, but could never bring herself to forgive Janet.

"How could you be so cruel?" she demanded to know.

Janet said she didn't have the vaguest idea of what her sister was talking about, claiming LaToya made up the whole story.

And that was only the beginning.

LaToya wanted to know: Why hadn't Janet seen fit to give her any gifts? Janet had recently bought Katherine a $200,000 top-of-the-line 600 SEL Mercedes-Benz. She also purchased a fifty-five-foot boat for her father and various gifts for her siblings. But nothing for LaToya.

"It actually got physical," said one witness. "They started pulling each other's hair, shoving one another, screaming at each other, swearing. All you heard was, 'You bitch, how dare you!' and, 'Goddammit, LaToya, you're nuts.' It was nasty. A real cat fight."

Janet declared that she never wanted to see LaToya again, then banished her from the recording studio. LaToya left in tears. Afterward, Janet was so upset she could not finish work. She left for the day. Again, LaToya—one of the only people with the ability to do so—had gotten to Janet.

Janet said that after the incident she couldn't stop sobbing. She telephoned Katherine, to whom she recalls saying, "You were right, Mother. You were right about her.

"Please, don't ever try to reach LaToya. Let her come to you if she wants, but be careful," Janet continued. "Because I don't ever want you to go through what I just went through."

"I just couldn't stop crying on the phone. Yes, she's my sister, but," Janet added, as if determined to break her ties with LaToya, "I did *not* give birth to her.

"The whole experience was one big, huge mess," she has recalled. "I felt like she wanted something more to write about and thrive upon, so she came to Minneapolis and caused this big commotion, hoping something would happen.

"And it just so happens that two weeks later she was on 'The Howard Stern Show,' talking about how we saw each other in Minneapolis, yet she said *I* was the one yelling and raving and cursing and screaming.

"It's all an attention thing, and I think the guy who is with her [Jack Gordon] has made her like this. He keeps her away from the family, and now he's brainwashed her so much she keeps herself away from her own family."

What motivates LaToya Jackson to do what she does is anybody's guess. It is an inscrutable aspect of her personality that she certainly has in common with her brother Michael Jackson.

To wit:

On February 10, 1993, the enigmatic Michael tried to explain himself by giving an extremely rare, much-publicized, and ballyhooed television interview to Oprah Winfrey. Janet said later that she was proud of her brother, since he spoke openly—or, at least, as openly as he possibly could—about an array of subjects, including a denial that he ever slept in an oxygen chamber or wanted to own the Elephant Man's bones. (However, that was really old news, as both rumors had been set to rest previously, in the 1990 J. Randy Taraborrelli biography, *Michael Jackson—The Magic and the Madness.*)

Michael also spoke about his tortured upbringing and acrimonious relationship with his father, Joseph. (Michael, sensitive to the core, felt so guilt-ridden after the program due to having confessed on national television that he sometimes threw up at the sight of Joseph, he had a Range Rover Jeep delivered to the Encino house as a gift to his father a few days after the broadcast.)

Occasionally, the mysterious superstar slipped something unbelievable into the interview, thereby damaging his credibility. For instance, he insisted that he has had "very, very little" plastic surgery. "You can count them on two fingers," he claimed. He also said that he and Brooke Shields were dating, which raised more than a few eyebrows. (In a subsequent statement, Shields clarified Michael's statement by characterizing her relationship with Michael as "platonic.")

Oprah Winfrey threw only few difficult questions in Michael's direction. When she asked about LaToya's book and her subsequent allegations, Michael cagily answered that he hadn't read the book. Oprah decided to change the subject rather than simply inform Jackson as to the book's contents and then solicit a reaction from him. Still, she said, beaming, after the interview, "We weren't prepared for his candor." Perhaps candor is in the eye of the beholder.

The interview was a huge success for Jackson, a man who always appeared to be guarded about revealing anything that might make him seem approachable. Though he wasn't as revealing as Oprah likes to think he was, he did establish a new pseudo-candid relationship with much of his public—sixty-two million viewers—which is what he intended. It was the first time Michael allowed his audience the *illusion* of familiarity.

Janet was thrilled with the interview and sent a message to her brother via the wire services: "Go, Mike."

"I thought he was wonderful," she said later to *Sky International* magazine. "I was proud that he opened his heart and everyone could see he's not this crazy guy living in some fantasy. And even if he *did* live in his own fantasy world, he has the right to. People say he doesn't know what's going on outside his own little world . . . and he does. Michael is so incredibly brilliant. And you know, sometimes you need to get away," she concluded.

Though the world heard for the first time that Michael suffered from the skin disease vitiligo when he made the announcement on Oprah's broadcast, Janet apparently knew about his problem for years. Vitiligo affects one to three percent of the population, but dark-skinned people often feel disfigured by it, as it lightens their skin in patches. Michael says his disease started to affect him in late 1982. He first told Janet about it in 1990. In 1991, he placed a frantic phone call to his sister to tell her it was getting worse. Janet said the two cried about it together.

"But don't tell," he warned Janet. "I don't want the press to know about this. Promise me."

"Janet was extremely distraught about the skin disease," says one confidant. "She didn't want to see Michael suffer. She asked what she could do to help. But there was nothing she could do, except keep Michael's secret. She never even discussed it with her mother."

"It was hard for me because, in interviews, people would talk about bleaching and all of this shit they say about Michael," Janet said recently. "I felt sometimes that I wanted to get into a fistfight. But what can you do? I wanted to say it so badly, that he had this disease, but I couldn't because I had promised not to tell. When he announced it on Oprah's show, it lifted a ton of bricks off my shoulders."

Jerome Howard says, "Michael would never have confided in LaToya about the disease, because he knows she would not have been able to keep the secret. But you can trust Janet with anything; that's just the kind of woman she is. She has a great deal of integrity. And she is very loyal."

In April 1993, four months after Janet's confrontation with LaToya in Minnesota, Michael telephoned her with the news that LaToya had been beaten up by her husband, Jack Gordon. "I begged and begged him to stop until I couldn't talk any more," LaToya said in another of her exclusive interviews with *The National Enquirer.* "I was choking on my own blood. But Jack just kept kicking me and hitting me with a chair. I thought, 'Oh my God, he's going to kill me.'"

LaToya says she lost consciousness in a pool of blood, which so upset her husband that he frantically telephoned a friend and said, "I've killed LaToya." Gordon was horrified by what he'd done and called the police himself.

LaToya explained that Jack beat her because he is suffering from lung cancer and, apparently, the medication he takes causes violent mood swings. LaToya, whose injuries required twelve stitches, also claims that the fact that she and Jack have never consummated their four-year marriage has also served to make her husband a bit testy.

"Michael wanted to go to LaToya to console her, but felt he couldn't," said one of his associates. "He felt that Jack would use his presence and assistance for lurid publicity purposes. So he called Janet and tried to get her to go, not knowing the two sisters had that big falling-out in Minneapolis. 'I think I'm the last person in the world she'd want to see,' Janet said. Michael agreed.

"So Michael telephoned Katherine, who certainly has ambivalent feelings about LaToya. He convinced her that she must go to be at her daughter's side, and so she went."

"Katherine and a friend bought first-class tickets and went to New York," says Jerome Howard. "Then they spent a frustrating week trying to get LaToya to take their calls. Finally, Katherine went to LaToya's apartment building and was met at the door by a doorman who had instructions to send her away."

"The message was obviously inspired by Jack, not LaToya, who may never even have gotten any of the communications her mother was leaving for her," said another source. "I honestly believe that if LaToya knew her mother was in New York, she would have seen her."

Janet doesn't look at it that way. She told Robert Hilburn, "My mother flew to New York to see her [LaToya] after we heard about some problems she was having, and she wouldn't see Mother. Then, she goes on TV and says no one reached out. That's what upsets me."

Janet was disturbed by what had happened to her sister—it was exactly what she had feared when she tried to convince LaToya not to leave the Encino estate with Gordon. But she also felt there was little she could do about it.

"She has chosen this life for herself," Janet said. "And I don't think any of us can do anything for her. She has to begin to help herself now."

Janet and LaToya had one thing in common, however: Hugh Hefner's interest in their bodies.

In the winter of 1993, after Janet had put the finishing touches on the *janet.* album, Hefner telephoned her at her Malibu home with a surprising offer: $500,000 in cash to star in a nude *Playboy* pictorial layout with her sister LaToya. At first, say Janet's associates, she was angry. She called Michael, a friend of Hefner's, who had actually given him her telephone number, to express her anger. But Michael told her she was taking the offer the wrong way, that she should be flattered, not angry.

"You've become a very sexy woman, you know?" he reportedly told her.

Janet has a great deal of respect for Michael's opinion, and so she seriously considered Hefner's offer.

But according to her associates, she made it clear that she would never do the layout with LaToya. She explained that LaToya had hurt her and her family and that she would never consider working with her, let alone appearing nude with her. But, Janet offered, "I may consider doing the layout without her."

Hefner thought that would be fine and offered her $250,000. But Janet insisted that the deal still be for half a million. According to her intimates, she then telephoned Michael to tell him she was considering Hefner's proposal. At this, Michael became frantic, claiming that Katherine would be devastated if another of her daughters were to pose nude in *Playboy*.

"I thought you said I should be flattered," Janet shot back.

"Yeah, be flattered," Michael said. "But don't *do* it, for goodness' sake."

Janet immediately telephoned Hefner and apologized, telling him she would not pose for the pictures. But she also told friends that she was still excited about the prospect of a nude layout, "and maybe in a couple of years this is something I would like to do. If LaToya could do it, I know I could," she boasted. "And, probably, even better."

It was a fascinating turn of events, a mind-boggling revelation of possibilities—that Janet could be involved in *or would even consider being involved in* the same display of public immodesty for which LaToya had been so thoroughly vilified by the family. It pointed to something that armchair psychologists often contemplate with a wry guffaw and astute Jackson watchers might well have foreseen if they'd really been paying attention: criticism and judgment of others' behavior are often projections of one's own disowned and despised wishes. Or, in simpler terms: it takes one to know one.

A shrewd observer might well have anticipated that a few of Janet Jackson's heretofore unrevealed aspects were ready to make an appearance, and that she was, in a simple phrase, about to blow the roof off. Such an observer would not have been disappointed.

chapter
EIGHTEEN

The summer of '93 saw not only Janet Jackson's film debut, but also the release of her first album for Virgin Records.

janet. (which translates into "Janet, period"—obviously meant as another declaration of independence from her odder siblings) was released on May 18, 1993. With this album, it was clear that the Harris/Lewis/Jackson collaboration had lost some of its vitality. Detractors blamed the mediocre album on the pressure of Janet's having to create a record worthy of her new multimillion-dollar Virgin Records deal, but the consensus is that—whatever else may be so—the partnership, at least creatively, might have seen its best days.

Vocally on *janet.*, Janet sounds paper-thin. On the

songs, Harris and Lewis seem more interested in *sounds* and audio concepts than in strong melodies and hooks. The production is often cluttered and noisy.

Thus, by comparison, the few good things on *janet.* sound like mini-masterpieces. The wistful, midtempo "Where Are You Now?" is typical Harris and Lewis at their melodic best, while the sparse "That's the Way Love Goes," the album's first single, emerges as delightfully rhythmic and moody. The lovely ballad "The Body That Loves You" mirrors Harris's growing affection for the romantic chords of Brazilian jazz and bossa nova, and it is followed by the dark, teasing, "Anytime, Anyplace."

Elsewhere on the album, Harris and Lewis seem obligated to make the proverbial artistic stretch that ultimately permeates the pop-music-making process at one time or another. Thus, opera star Kathleen Battle sat in during the monotonous "The Time," and a loud mess entitled "Funky Big Band" emerged as a poor man's version of "Alright" from the *Rhythm Nation* album. Meanwhile, Janet's ode to rock and roll, the barroom-rock-sounding "What'll I Do" sounds contrived, but not as much as the album's ultimate gimmick, Janet's proposed "new sexuality," which she touts via little vignettes, spoken (or sighed) between many of the album's tracks.

In one song, "Throb"—a blatant rip-off of Madonna's club-beat *Erotica* style—Janet's orgasmic sounds culminate in her moaning in ecstasy, "Shit, baby."

How to distinguish the vibrant, convention-shattering explorations of genuine art from random productions of people just splashing paint, stacking rocks, and making noise? How to tell when an artist is speaking to her age and not just presenting naive self-involvement and undisciplined self-disclosure? People wonder about these things, in their hearts even if they don't put them into words. Some of them wondered: What in the world is Janet Jackson doing?

"You don't think of a Jackson cussing," observed disc jockey Tom Joyner, "but I thought it was sexy. And the way she says it—not like when someone cusses at you in traffic—the way she rolls it, almost makes the word sound acceptable."

Yeah, but this is different stuff, Janet. Something's happened. Something new is going on. . . .

"The changes in me have to do with making the film," Janet explained in an interview, speaking of *Poetic Justice.* "It opened me up even more. You can't hang around those people without getting something out of it, without it making you freer. All of that swearing, I mean, shit, that's me. Really." It also seemed to some observers that Janet had somehow been influenced by the sexuality of her sister LaToya's controversial image as much as by the gritty earthiness of *Poetic Justice.* Or maybe "influenced" isn't the right word with regard to LaToya. Maybe it was that LaToya just *did it first,* but didn't have the presence she needed to pull it off without alienating people.

Photographs taken of Janet to promote the album were unusually provocative in terms of her earlier public image. She was shown on the cover of *Rolling Stone*'s September 16, 1993, issue topless, with a man's hands (said to be René Elizondo's, standing behind her in the shot) cupped around each of her perfectly rounded breasts. She boasted a taut midsection, bare above low-slung jeans. According to the cover's photographer, Patrick Demarchelier, "Janet had a pretty strong idea of what she wanted—namely, to duplicate her sexy look in the video for 'That's the Way Love Goes.' She wanted to look sexy and glamorous; she's in good shape." It was all obviously calculated for maximum effect. None of it was accidental. Anyone imagining it *was* accidental, that it was merely Janet's whimsy, would have been well advised to recall her having once said, "Every aspect of my recording or performance is vital. Nothing happens without my approval."

"We came in with no previous thoughts of what the record was going to be," Terry Lewis told *USA Today*. "We just sat down with pieces of paper and started writing down ideas. We came up with the same thing. We thought it should be a more sensual album than *Rhythm Nation,* which was very hard and rough sounding. We wanted an album that was more warm and inviting.

Earlier in the year, when Janet presented Michael with a special award at the Grammys, Michael coyly denied the rumor that he and Janet, who beamed radiantly next to him, were the same person. "You can say that again," quipped one deejay after looking at these photos of *janet.*

"*janet.* is so hot, it should have come with a condom," Elizondo told writer David Ritz. Indeed, some of Janet's videos for the album were racy, to put it mildly. The one for the song "If," which deals with fantasies about sex and seduction, is filled with choreographed images of mock cunnilingus. While grabbing dancer Omar Lopez's crotch in the video, Janet sings: "I'll hold you in my hand and, baby, your smooth and shiny feels good against my lips, sugar. . . ." ("The girl is out LaToya-ing LaToya," said one critic. Indeed, perhaps because she is conscious of the safety and well-being of her younger fans, Janet opens one song by whispering, "Be a good boy and put this on.")

"That's the most personal song on the album for me," she has said of "If." "They are feelings every girl has had, even guys. At one point, I thought, I wonder if this is going to be too much for people to take from me. But I said screw it, this is me. I felt this way, exactly this way. I don't think the album is crass because I don't think sex is crass. To me, it's an expression of love."

"I know there will be people who will look at me and think, 'God, what has she done?'" Janet told Robert Hilburn of the *Los Angeles Times*. "'She used to be this innocent little girl.' Well, I'm still the same person, but there is a point where you grow up and this is the time in my life.'"

Janet had to admit that she was concerned about how her mother would react to the new, sexy image. She recounted this mother-daughter exchange for one reporter: "She wanted to come down and see me shoot 'If' and I said, 'Are you sure you want to go, Mother?' And she said, 'Well, do I make you uncomfortable?' I said, 'No, not at all.' She said, 'What is it, baby? Are you doing something bad? There's enough bad in the world today as it is.' And I said, 'No, Mother, it's nothing bad.' She said, 'Are you being dirty?' I said, 'No, I'm not being dirty, Mother.'

"It was so hard for me to say this to her, but I told her, 'Some of my movements are very sexy. They're not dirty, they're very sexy. And just by you being my mother, I'd be embarrassed.'

"She said, 'Well, if I make you shy in any way or pull back, then I shouldn't be there.' I said, 'No, you can come down if you like.'"

In the end, Katherine didn't go.

Despite her well-known and obvious propensity for keeping one eye on art and the other on commerce, Janet denied that anything was at all calculated about her new product and image. When writer David Ritz asked if it was all some kind of gimmick, Janet became irate. "No, no, no," she protested. "I can't fake it. I can't do it if I don't feel it. It's genuine. You could say I've entered a happy phase of sexuality."

Janet went on to explain that part of the reason for the free expression found on her new album was her being bored by the recent heavy-handed approach to her career. "When the movie was complete, I suppose I did want to shed some of Justice's physical frustration," she allowed. "*Rhythm Nation* was a heavy record and *Poetic Justice* was a heavy movie. I wanted to do something lighter, but also daring. Mostly, though, I wanted to do something that corresponded to my life.

"My concepts are never ones I think will sell or be trendy or attract new fans. I don't think that way. All I can do is sing from my life. When I wrote the album [all of the lyrics and half the melodies], I was still in a poetic frame of mind, inspired by Maya [Angelou]'s beautiful language. You can hear that inspiration on the interludes . . . I felt much freer expressing myself."

"I can't tell you how often I tell her that I am impressed with how much she's grown up in the time I've known her," René Elizondo—who met Janet when she was sixteen and is now directing some of her videos—told Steve Pond of *Us* magazine. And he added, "A lot of it isn't just growing up, but letting people *see* she's grown up. It seemed to come all at once because suddenly she became more extroverted. But I think the friends she has now are just so uninhibited that it's really made Janet say, 'You know what? I could care less what people say.'

"She's always had it inside her, the lyrics she's written on this album. But before, it was always, 'Well, gosh, I can't write that. What would Mom think? What would Mike think? What would the fans think? This time, she just said, 'Listen, this is how I feel, and I'm gonna write it down.'"

John Singleton has added, "It's hard, growing up in the limelight most of your life. And I think she's more adjusted than a lot of people would be. I mean, the girl knows how to cook, you know what I'm sayin'? She can do a lot of normal things. The way I look at it, she just has a really good job."

"We grew up with her," Tom Joyner concluded of the "new" Janet. "She was 'Penny' in 'Good Times,' then she broke away from Daddy with *Control*. We went through her concern for the world. Now we see her sensual side. She's all woman now. That's what she's trying to tell you. It's going to be a nice, hot summer," he predicted, "and Janet's going to be sizzling right along with it."

Indeed, during its first week, *janet.* sold an estimated 350,000 copies, outdistancing even the first-week sales of Michael Jackson's 1991 *Dangerous* album. Janet's album went on to debut at number one on the Billboard chart and has spawned a number of million-selling singles.

Meanwhile, her film *Poetic Justice* opened in July 1993.

Janet was said to be profoundly unhappy with the movie. "It wasn't the film she'd hoped it would be," said a friend. "She wanted a big movie, and she sensed that this was not it. It just didn't work."

Initially, she seemed to distance herself from the film. Though she'd recorded her *janet.* album around the same time the film was made, there was no talk of its featuring any songs from the film, or any plans for her to participate in any album soundtrack.

When it came time to promote the film, Janet seemed caught between the marketing styles of the pop-music and film industries. Columbia, of course, wanted Janet to hit the morning and late-night talk-show circuit, but her own rock-and-roll instincts didn't incline her toward making herself *too* accessible to the press. After all, like brother Michael, Prince, and a handful of other pop stars, she'd managed to build a career with a minimum of personal appearances and interviews.

Poetic Justice finally opened to the public on July 23, 1993, and it shot to number one at the box office. "I can't believe it," Janet exclaimed. "Maybe this thing is going to be a hit after all."

In its first week, the movie did gross $12.1 million, topping Clint Eastwood's eagerly awaited *In the Line of Fire.* Things looked good for *Justice,* except for two things: reviews and "word of mouth."

Generally, both were awful. *USA Today* deemed it unbalanced and compared it to Prince's *Under the Cherry Moon,* his horrid follow-up to the successful *Purple Rain.*

"Jackson, shorter and rounder than most female leads, is a refreshing presence," said the review. "But it's tough to tell if she can act."

Variety said the film had "an obvious appeal to a core ethnic audience, but faces a considerable challenge in tapping into the mainstream." (They were right.)

Entertainment Weekly insisted that Justice "has ambition to spare but no rhyme or reason."

New York's *Newsday* was even harsher, saying, "If this is poetic, there ain't no justice."

It didn't help that some movie theaters, fearing the kind of violence that had marred the run of other urban-oriented films—including Singleton's *Boyz N the Hood*—waited before putting the film in their venues. Los Angeles's eighteen-theater Universal City Complex of the Cineplex Odeon chain said it was trying to program "with an upscale demographic" to ensure that Universal Studios' adjoining City Walk mall was "kept safe with a family atmosphere." (Reacting to having been called racist by community groups, the chain began playing *Justice* a week after its national release.)

*　　*　　*

Janet did begin to do a spate of interviews with national publications, but her interviews were often laced with profanity, which she blamed on having to "learn how to curse" for her role in the film. "Yeah, right," said a friend, chuckling. "Look, she was cursing long before that movie."

In the end, Janet's film debut was all over in a couple of weeks, just about the amount of time *Poetic Justice* played in some theaters. After the reviews were in and the public started thinking of the film as a "turkey," box-office receipts dropped to practically nothing.

And with the film now dead and gone, the entertainment industry at large, as well as members of Janet's public, were still wondering just why she chose to do such a film in the first place.

"There wasn't a single good reason for it," said a Hollywood screenwriter who didn't want his name mentioned ("I've got a script I want her to read"). "Pop stars usually make films for one of two reasons—either they want to reach as many people as possible, or they really want to prove themselves as actors. This film did neither. It was a sad beginning."

Why did Janet Jackson's camp not use more savvy in engineering her foray into film? It's a puzzling question. Madonna, after appearing in her share of duds, was savvy enough to surround herself with stars—Warren Beatty in *Dick Tracy* and the all-star ensemble that included Tom Hanks and Geena Davis for the box-office hit *A League of their Own*. After general agreement was reached that Whitney Houston's teaming with a box-office draw like Kevin Costner for *The Bodyguard* virtually ensured her a hit film, one wonders why a newcomer would want to do it any other way?

(As it turns out, *The Bodyguard* was a bonanza for all parties: it was an international hit for the studio, and Houston's *The Bodyguard* soundtrack, anchored by the film, and vice versa, sold more than 220 million copies worldwide. Moreover, Houston—at least among the film studios, producers, directors, and theater exhibitors—has established herself as a viable player in Hollywood.)

Janet has said, "I was warned by powerful forces in Hollywood that an all-black movie was the wrong move. Conventional wisdom said I should make a musical. Go for the mainstream white market. Play it safe. John [Singleton] had the same feelings I did. Do something different."

The way Janet views it, to do anything simply for the sake of doing it is a waste of time. "The way I feel about it," she told *Us* magazine in 1993, "I *know* I can do a musical. Videos, they're mini-musicals. I can always go back to that, but I don't want to typecast myself so when it's time to become dramatic, they won't take it seriously."

Whether Janet will be so easily embraced with the right project is questionable. Hollywood is a town bent on winning; where everyone loves a winner. In the eyes of many film studios, Janet Jackson is now considered, as one film executive put it, a "mere mortal. Because of the poor box-office performance of *Poetic Justice,* both the studios and the public are going to be just a little suspect of whatever she does."

Regardless, Janet is already pushing ahead with her next project: the story of Dorothy Dandridge—the beautiful Oscar-nominated African-American actress of the 1950s, who starred in such memorable films as

Carmen Jones and *Porgy and Bess*—and it has become to Janet what the story of blues singer Billie Holiday was to Diana Ross. (Janet even looks a little like some of Dandridge's old publicity stills.)

Indeed, Janet is captivated by the story of Dandridge, who died of a sleeping-pill overdose in 1965, and she wants to portray the actress in a major motion picture. She was talking up the idea of the film long before *Poetic Justice* was even written.

"Just like Marilyn Monroe is the idol of a lot of girls, that's how I feel about Dorothy Dandridge," Janet said in 1988. "And she and Marilyn were very close friends. She went through a lot, and people told her she couldn't do certain things. But she didn't let that bother her. She said, in her mind, that she was going to do what she wanted to do, and that nothing was impossible, and she did it. That's my kind of woman."

But can Janet pull it off? According to that film executive, "She doesn't really *have* to. It's not like she's Diana Ross, someone who'd better make her mark in films now or it'll be too late. Janet is still young enough to be allowed some mistakes. The important thing is that she's willing to work at it. Pretty soon, she'll get it right."

John Singleton agrees that Janet Jackson has only just begun to make her mark in the movies. "She has great heart," he told writer Veronica Chambers. "The emotion she feels inside, when you put a camera on her, comes out. Something resonates from her. It's just there. She put high and low moments in her performance.

"In this movie [Poetic Justice], she defined herself as a talent to be reckoned with—an actress. It would be different if people saw the movie and were distracted by her other job as a singer. But you look up on the screen and you don't see the Janet Jackson you know on stage. You see Justice, the character."

chapter

NINETEEN

The disappointment of the *Poetic Justice* box-office
receipts was nothing compared with what confronted
Janet Jackson and the entire Jackson family at the end
of the summer of 1993.

While it still seems impossible for Michael
Jackson's fans and much of his public to fully compre-
hend, Janet's thirty-four-year-old brother was, in early
August 1993, accused of child molestation. Janet
became aware of this allegation the same way much of
the rest of the world did.

"She was sitting at home in Malibu watching television," says a friend, "when this special report came on
that police were looking into a very sensitive matter
regarding her brother. She told me later that she
couldn't imagine what it could be, but she knew it
would be ludicrous, whatever it was. When she found
out, she was thunderstruck."

Michael was accused of fondling and having oral sex with a boy he befriended, the thirteen-year-old son of a Beverly Hills dentist. Michael's spokesperson, private investigator Anthony Pelicano, claimed that Michael was the victim of "an extortion attempt gone awry," one that Michael's camp had been investigating for the previous four months. In court documents, the dentist—who is divorced from the boy's mother and engaged in a custody fight with her over their son—sought a court order preventing Michael from seeing or communicating with the boy.

"A demand for $20 million was made," Pelicano told Associated Press. "It was flatly and consistently refused. The refusals have, in our opinion, caused what has transpired." Pelicano claimed that Michael is plagued by twenty-five to thirty extortion attempts a year. The sensational accusations, and the explosion of media attention that resulted, even rocked jaded Hollywood and startled the most casual observer, what with rumors, innuendo, and fiction all being reported by the media as gospel truth. The investigation and reports surrounding it all very quickly turned into a three-ring circus, and remains so as this book went to press.

"I am confident the department will conduct a fair and thorough investigation and that its results will demonstrate that there was no wrongdoing on my part," Michael said in a statement read by his attorney Howard Weitzman in mid-August. "I intend to continue with my world tour."

The criminal investigation by the Los Angeles Police Department's Sexually Exploited Child Unit began on August 17, 1993, after a complaint against the superstar was made to Children's Protection

Services officials. In the ensuing months, police raided Michael's homes—his condominium on Galaxy Way in Century City, his Santa Barbara County ranch in Los Olivos, and the family estate in Encino—all while Michael was abroad on a tour that had begun in Southeast Asia.

Michael had long associated himself with children, most recently at President Clinton's inaugural gala in January 1993 and at an MTV taping at his personal amusement park at the ranch where he was like a mother hen to a flock of children.

In the past, he regularly invited underprivileged and ill children to tour his ranch. He had often been seen in the company of young celebrities such as Emmanuel Lewis and McCauley Culkin, as well as with many youngsters who are not famous. His philanthropic activities in regard to children, including those undertaken by his Heal the World Foundation, are well-known.

"The accusations hit him right where it hurts most," said one observer, "at the core of who he is, what he is known for, and what he loves most."

In a statement issued by the entire family (they even attached LaToya's name to it), the Jackson family banded together "in unity and harmony to convey our love and unfailing support for Michael." They said it is their "unequivocal belief that Michael has been made a victim of a cruel and obvious attempt to take advantage of his fame and success. We know, as does the whole world, that he has dedicated his life to providing happiness for young people everywhere. . . . We are confident that his dignity and humanity will prevail."

Katherine, Joseph, and some of the siblings held a press conference to demonstrate their support, and also to discuss their Jackson Family Honors television special, which was being planned prior to the scandal (and which has since been indefinitely postponed). Then they made plans to go abroad in order to "be with Michael."

One might imagine, however, that the last person Michael wants to see at this time is his father. Michael's admission of child abuse in his memoirs and in his interview with Oprah Winfrey locate the source of his pain. According to Michael, he is a victim of one person—a person from whom he would never be able to accept comfort during such a stressful time. "Michael will not even do a concert, he will cancel, if my father is in the stadium," LaToya has asserted.

When Michael canceled a performance in Bangkok, the first of many cancelations over the next couple of months (for reasons reported to range from dehydration and migraine headaches to the necessity for dental work), Janet realized he was not well. She wanted to be by his side.

Janet made plans to meet Michael in Singapore, his next stop. But she was first scheduled to appear on the MTV Music Awards at the end of August. She was "torn between her commitment to MTV and her desire to be with her brother," reported KNBC reporter David Sheehan.

In the end, Janet didn't go.

"What really happened was that she found out 'they'—her family—were going," J. Randy Taraborrelli revealed. "When she learned of this, she decided she would stay home. It's clear to anyone who knows her that the last thing Janet ever wants to do is associate herself publicly with her family during high-profile moments. It's my opinion that she realizes many people are skeptical of anything the Jacksons have to say. And because Michael has not hidden the fact that he is not close to some members of his family, she probably felt that being photographed with them while racing through airports in Southeast Asia would only serve to make her look insincere."

"She was extremely upset about what was going on and had long conversations with Elizabeth Taylor," says one of her associates. "When Liz left to join Michael in Singapore, [Janet] asked Elizabeth to keep an eye on things, and to try to keep Michael away from certain members of his family she felt would, maybe even unintentionally, upset him.

"In the end, Michael spent little time with any of his family overseas. I actually believe the trip was done as much in support of Michael as in an effort to show a solid family front for public-relations purposes. The way it was orchestrated, it was almost as if the trip was a prepromotion for their Jackson Family Honors special, which was being planned for national broadcast."

Janet issued a statement that said, "It's truly awful that someone would try to get twenty million dollars by saying Michael did something to their child. He loves children, and he would never do anything like that, ever. I was so angry when I heard that. For someone to say that about my brother, it hurt." She was also quoted as saying that Michael was "very hurt, very tired, and very drained" but that she was sure he "would make it through."

Janet was enraged when LaToya—who claimed she saw "about fifty boys" sleep over in Michael's Encino bedroom when they lived there together—appeared on the "Today Show" in August. In her interview with Katie Couric via satellite from

London, she wouldn't say she thought Michael was innocent of any wrongdoing. Rather, she conceded that she is "not a judge," and so really doesn't know what to think. She does, however, "support" her brother, she hastened to add.

About a week later, on "The Larry King Show," LaToya admitted that she couldn't get in touch with Michael because his handlers wouldn't let her anywhere near him (which, some would argue, was a prudent decision. If LaToya did manage to have a meeting with her brother, there is no telling how she and her husband might have used it for publicity.).

LaToya also took her younger sister to task for not being at Michael's side in his time of need. "Janet didn't go," LaToya observed. "Everybody says Janet went. But Janet stayed here, because she was doing the MTV Awards. She felt that was much more important than being with her own brother, who was under a lot of stress and strain at that time."

"Said like an angry sister," Larry King observed.

"Oh, I'm not angry," LaToya responded, not too convincingly. "It's just that it's being reported that she flew to him immediately, which is totally untrue."

To some observers, it certainly seemed that Michael Jackson had been tried and convicted before any charges had even been filed against him. Over the next three months, the international media coverage of the allegations continued, unrelentingly, with every lurid detail of the "confidential" investigation being enthusiastically reported by both legitimate and tabloid news outlets. *Time* magazine put it best when it characterized the case as "a tangle of maybes, omigods and say-it-ain't-so's." Even more details of the supposed sexual activities between Jackson and the thirteen-year-old were made public when the youngster filed a civil suit against Jackson.

Janet refused to discuss the matter with the media. In fact, she had previously scheduled a series of meetings with members of the press at her home in Malibu. Reporters were to meet with her over dinner to ask questions about her world tour, which was scheduled to begin in December 1993, and also about the *janet.* album. There were to be a number of these dinners with different members of the media. But after the allegations broke about her brother, Janet realized there was no possible way *that* subject would not be brought up over dinner.

"I don't want them to be turned into press conferences about my brother," she told one Virgin Records executive. So the dinners were canceled.

On November 12, 1993, the situation with Michael became more unbelievable when he canceled the remainder of his world tour, admitting he was addicted to painkillers. In an audiotape released by his publicist, Michael—in a quivering little voice that sounded more peculiar than ever—said he began using the painkillers seven months previously, when he underwent reconstructive surgery for a scalp burn suffered during the filming of a Pepsi-Cola commercial in 1984.

"The medications were used sparingly at first," Jackson said, but he added that the frequency with which he used them increased after child-molestation allegations were leveled against him. "As I left on this tour, I had been the target of an extortion attempt, and shortly thereafter was accused of horrifying and outrageous conduct. I was humiliated, embarrassed, hurt, and suffering great pain in my heart. The pressure resulting from these false allegations coupled with the incredible energy necessary for me to perform caused me so much distress that it left me physically and emotionally exhausted. I became increasingly dependent on the painkillers to get me through the days of the tour."

Michael, now not only accused of being a pedophile but a drug addict as well, then disappeared into a rehabilitation center in Europe while much of the world waited to see what would happen next.

Michael's attorney, Howard Weitzman, fielded questions from skeptical members of the press in an effort to end unrestrained speculation that Michael was actually dodging the police by canceling his world tour just prior to its Puerto Rico date. (Puerto Rico is a United States territory, the first such place Michael was scheduled to perform on his tour, and soil where Jackson could have been arrested if any such warrant had been issued.) Asked about reports that the thirteen-year-old accuser had described Michael's genitals in detail, and that authorities now wanted to strip-search him in order to inspect his person for hidden evidence, Weitzman echoed the thoughts of millions of Michael's admirers: *"You've got to be kidding."*

For anyone who has followed Michael Jackson's life and career over the last twenty-five years—anyone who has grown up with him; pitied his lonely, solitary existence; gossiped about his erratic, bizarre behavior; danced to his infectious, unique sound; or been awed by his prodigious talent—the developments of the fall and winter of 1993 seemed surreal and impossible to believe. It's difficult to accept that something like this could happen to "our" Michael.

Because his career has inspired such veneration and commitment from his fans, support from Jackson's public never really wavered. But over the months, as the horrific charges sank in, it was clear that, guilty or not, nothing would ever again be the same for the so-called King of Pop. If anything, these allegations signified an end to a special innocence, one that many people thought would last forever. And while escape from reality has always been the special promise of show business, it would seem that no one could flee this kind of nightmare . . . not even Michael Jackson.

"I don't know *how* he will survive this, but I know he will," Janet said privately, to one of her close friends. "I know his faith will pull him through it. I believe in him, and nothing can change that. Nothing can alter my love for my brother.

"I just refuse to accept this," she concluded, tears streaming down her face. "It can't end this way for Michael. It just can*not* end this way."

EPILOGUE

While her brother Michael Jackson's future seems to be hanging in the balance, Janet's seems guaranteed. Today, at twenty-seven years of age, Miss Jackson seems just to have begun to live her life. Her future lies ahead of her as an endless, luminous vista of hit records, sold-out concerts, and perhaps—if she decides it's what she desires—even film stardom. More important, in a show-business world fueled by ego and ambition, Janet Jackson manages, mostly anyway, to stay out of the fracas.

People expect artists to be strange and that fame will make them stranger. But that, apparently, hasn't happened to Janet Jackson. She knows how to manage her life and career with great heart and considerable intelligence.

As for her personal life, it would seem that Janet and René Elizondo, now thirty, are still not serious about each other. When asked in May 1993 whether she and René were romantically involved, Janet responded, "Right now, kinda sorta. Let's put it this way: I think I'm going to wind up dating some new people."

Is marriage on the horizon, *Ebony* asked her? "Nope. No time soon."

"She is free to be whoever she wants to be," says one of her friends. "She's not ready to settle down. This is the best time of her life. She is young, rich, famous, and smart enough to make the best of all of it. It's also a time of reflection, as she approaches thirty."

"To be honest, I don't know how Janet will ever trust a man enough to give herself to him completely," said her former sister-in-law Enid Jackson. "She was deeply affected by the way her father treated her mother. She saw the way her brother Jackie treated me. And the way her other brothers have treated their wives. I'm sure she's even wondered how [her half sister] Joh' Vonnie's mother feels about the way Joseph treated her as the 'other woman.' And look at how Jack [Gordon] treats LaToya.

"Janet is determined, I think, not to allow a man to ever even *try* to take advantage of her. If anyone tried, I believe she would cut him off at the knees.

"I also think she feels that James DeBarge's drug problem was somehow a betrayal of her trust in him," Enid added. "And that hurt her, too. So, to put it plainly, Janet Jackson does not trust men. It may take her years to work through this mistrust, if she's even interested in doing so. But I think she believes, as all of us Jackson women do, that it's best to keep your guard up when it comes to men."

Or as Janet told one relative, "A woman has to watch out for herself. You can't be blinded by love.

Love can be a wonderful thing, but I've seen the flip side—how it can be used as a weapon *against* a woman—over and over again, and in my family. I'd be a fool to not have learned something from that."

Looking back on her life, Janet told *Ebony,* "I have experienced a great deal of pain in my life. . . . It's made me a much stronger person. That was God's way of doing it. Yes, I am a much stronger person today than I was even a few years ago. As I go along, I become much stronger."

One of the issues Janet seems determined to reconcile concerns her relationship with her sister LaToya, one of the only people still able to rattle her. To writer David Ritz, Janet said in September 1993, "I've thought long and hard about what happened. LaToya was closer to my mother than anyone in the world, yet my mother is the one she's hurt the most. When LaToya left the family, she was unhappy with her career. She was at a terribly vulnerable point in her life. She was taken advantage of. I'm convinced that she was brainwashed," Janet concluded. "She was turned against her family and made to see us as enemies, when, in fact, we love her more than words can say. Right now, there's no contact. But I believe my sister will be back."

"She can't just write LaToya off, as much as she wants to," observed J. Randy Taraborrelli. "The reason LaToya makes Janet furious is obviously because Janet still cares, and cares deeply."

Of her relationship with her father, Janet seems to be taking a more realistic view as well. Recently, she has said, "You understand that we never called our father

'Father' or 'Daddy.' We called him Joseph, and we feared him. We'd be in bed with our mother, playing games, having fun, and when we saw the reflection of the lights of Joseph's car pulling up in the driveway, we'd scatter to our rooms—and not because of the kind of things LaToya has claimed. That's nonsense. There was never molestation or physical abuse beyond normal spankings. But there was a coldness, a detachment from our father, that was chilling. We all learned from his discipline, but I believe we also suffered because he wasn't there for us emotionally."

"Again, she can't cut Joseph out of her life, as Michael has attempted to do," observes Taraborrelli. "It's just not in her character. She'll always be his little girl."

Indeed, Janet Jackson is a caring person. Last summer, a young girl with AIDS sent her a heart-wrenching fan letter. Upon reading it, Janet was struck by the girl's mettle. In order to surprise her, she flew to the girl's home in Las Vegas for her birthday party.

"The thing that impressed me most," recalled Janet, "was her writing. She made up songs on the spot. She sang them to me with incredible spirit and spontaneity." Janet's eyes dampened with compassion. "She was brilliant and made me think that children's intelligence—their artistic intelligence—is the most valuable and purest human resource. That's the intelligence I look for in myself. I don't always find it, but I know it's there. I'm talking about responding to the world emotionally, directly. Art that comes from the heart, not the head."

"I don't believe in luck," Janet has observed pragmatically. "It's persistence, hard work, and not forgetting your dream—and going after it. It's about still having hunger in your heart."

They say that whoever has the gold makes the rules. In the highly competitive entertainment industry, those who possess the vision and know-how will be around long enough to *rewrite* their own rules. If all of that is, indeed, true, then Janet sits with golden pen in hand. If she plays her cards right, the future belongs to her.

And Lord knows, Janet Jackson knows the game.

Bart Andrews is the author of *The Official TV Trivia Quiz Book, Lucy & Ricky & Fred & Ethel: The Story of I Love Lucy,* and several other non-fiction titles. He is also a literary agent and lives in Los Angeles, California. This is his first book for HarperPaperbacks in association with RoseBooks.